T0278757

MARKLESS

MARKLESS

C. G.
Malbúri

LQ

LEVINE QUERIDO

Montclair | Amsterdam | Hoboken

This is an Arthur A. Levine book
Published by Levine Querido

LQ
LEVINE QUERIDO

Levine Querido
www.levinequerido.com · info@levinequerido.com

Levine Querido is distributed by Chronicle Books

Text copyright © 2024 by CG Malburi

Library of Congress Control Number:
2023938686

ISBN 978-1-64614-377-1

Printed in China

Published June 2024
First Printing

The text type was set in Legitima.

for swen
long live all the magic we made

1

R uti saw her first soulbinding when she was six. She was stealing a few coins from the coat pockets of Ayra, whose blacksmith shop sat in the slums of Somanchi. Ayra was prone to little cruelties toward the Markless–a kick or a shove here and there–and he deserved to lose a few pennies so that Ruti and Kita could eat that night. Ruti slipped into Ayra's shop and crept over to the table where he'd laid his roughspun brown coat, made from the cheap fibers of the slums.

A wealthy woman stood in the shop, fine azure cloak held to her round midsection as though she was afraid of touching anything. Her daughter tucked in beside her, huddled into her own smooth cloak and peering around at the clanking-loud, dusty shop. The woman peered at Ayra's intricately wrought metalwork, then began to haggle.

Then Ayra's dusty-faced apprentice tumbled into the room. Not a true apprentice—he hadn't been bonded, then, and he had no skill over metal. Instead, fire followed him from room to room, little bursts of flame whenever he was angry, such as when he kicked Markless away from Ayra's hot stoves in winter. The woman and the girl eyed him with suspicion and lifted their hands in greeting.

Ruti saw the marks on each of their palms—the completed circle on the woman's, an etched pattern made half majimm and half endhi—and the unfinished circle of majimm on the girl's hand. She allowed herself a moment of envy, a weakness no Markless will ever admit, and she watched from the shadows as the apprentice pressed his own palm with its ashto half circle to the woman's and then the girl's.

When his palm touched the girl's, a glow erupted between them, emanating from their hands and joining them, and Ruti felt as much as saw the way that the girl's eyes lit up in quiet ecstasy. Her mother looked on in horror. An apprentice in the slums was no match for a noblewoman, but when their hands separated, they'd each had a full circle on their right palms.

The apprentice left the slums soon after. Majimm and ashto combined means mind, a formidable power but one with no use in a blacksmith's shop, and he had a rich soulbond now, anyway. Ayra had replaced him with another fire-prone apprentice with ashto in the half circle in his palm, and they'd moved soon after to a bigger shop far from the slums.

Ruti had never left the slums. She'd brought back the food for Kita, but he'd still been so sick that he couldn't move. She rubbed the underside of his jaw until he opened his mouth to eat, spooning in mashed corn while he shivered helplessly, skin the pale grey of old snow. In the morning, she felt the cold block of him curled up against her, the breath gone from his body. She was alone again.

There had been others in the twelve years after Kita, more Markless who found her and stayed with her for a time. At first, it was only because Ruti was quick and resourceful, skilled at finding food where others could not. Later, they came to her for her more unique abilities.

"I want a paint," a Markless boy tells her today. He's young, maybe only nine or ten, and he looks around furtively in Ruti's tiny shop. There isn't much to see, only shelves with unmarked jars and dusty books. Ruti keeps anything that matters in the back room where she sleeps. "I know you gave Eidan one. I need one, too."

"Eidan is twice your age," Ruti reminds the boy. "I don't give paints to little ones."

The boy raises his pointed chin. "I'm not afraid. I can take the pain." He pulls down his tunic past his necklace, showing her a scrawny copper chest covered in scarring. "A Bonded guard with lightning once found me in the Royal Square," he says, not without some pride in his voice. "But I survived."

But I survived, the rallying cry of the Markless. It's dangerous to be a Markless in Somanchi, and even more so in the Inner Circle. In the slums, there are few who can afford to do more than harass the Markless. Being Markless in the Inner Circle is a death warrant.

Ruti narrows her eyes at the boy, seeing what he isn't telling her. "And why were you in the Royal Square?"

The boy's jaw clenches. "I was just . . . I was *looking*," he says finally, defiantly. "My parents were nobles. I know it. I have a locket from them." He shows her the necklace again, opening it to show her letters etched inside. "This is *gold*. They left it for me because they knew that I would find them with it. But I can't find them without a mark. I need a paint." He slams his hand down on the table between them, palm up, beseeching. "They want me. I know they do. I know–"

"You know nothing, little one," Ruti says sharply. The dreamers are the ones who get killed first. "Your parents threw you away because you were Markless. They won't want you even if you do find them. Even if you have a false mark on your palm. They will never accept you."

The boy stares at her, his fists clenched, and Ruti waits, staring back with uncompromising eyes. He is the first to fold, sagging as he shatters into tears, and Ruti slips around the table and wraps her arms around him.

He's just a little one, a child who wants to pretend. Ruti had been a dreamer too, when she'd been a babe, and she holds him tightly now, sways with him, and sings a few words in a whisper to summon a spirit to soothe him. Still, the boy quakes in her arms, and only after a long time can he look up to face her.

But there is no acceptance in his eyes now. "You're wrong," he says, eyes like fire, and he twists around and walks to the door of Ruti's shop. He stops in the doorway, turning back. "I'm going to find them. And they're going to love me." He runs from the shop, and Ruti glimpses him through a dusty window as he races off in the direction of the Inner Circle.

"No one loves the Markless," Ruti murmurs, and she knows that she'll never see the boy again. She closes her eyes, hums a quiet chant for his protection, but it won't be enough. Not for a Markless child who hasn't learned his place. Not for a Markless child who still longs to be marked.

There are precious few Markless adults. Children are too quick to dream.

Ruti sighs, closing the door to her shop for the day. After sunset, the older Markless will raid shops and attack strangers on the streets, desperate for something to eat or use. They give her shop a wide berth, fearful of her chants, but it's better not to tempt them.

She tidies up with an eye out the window, watching for little ones who might be out alone. Most of the Markless children are in the orphanages that the late King Adiel opened in the slums. It had been an immensely unpopular decision among the Bonded, but a necessary one as disease from the slums had threatened to spread into the Inner Circle. The Bonded might not see the Markless as worthy of the treasury's coin, but they'd shuddered at the thought of Markless children passing on their sicknesses to the children of the Inner Circle.

The orphanages are grimy, unpleasant places, but still the safest place for the smaller children at night.

She catches sight of a grubby little girl through the window, peering out from behind a pile of old garbage across the road. Ruti hurries to the door and pulls it open. The girl stares at her, matted brown hair plastered against dark, rough skin, quick hands forming into trembling fists. Her fingers are narrow and long, bare of any hint of fat. "In," Ruti orders.

The girl scampers away. Her foot treads on an uneven end of the coarse brown rag that she wears, tearing it free, then she hesitates and peers back. Ruti purses her lips. She hears a raucous shout from down the road, Markless boys who've gotten into the drink, and the girl freezes, clutching her slender fingers around something in her hand.

Aha. The girl has stolen something, something she's fearful of having to share, and Ruti says again, urgently, "In. I don't want it."

The girl only stares.

Down the road, the Markless boys appear, brandishing a green bottle that they take turns drinking from. There are three of them, and they look–not well-fed, but not malnourished, either, an unusual sight in the slums. "Look," one of them slurs to the others. He points at the girl. "What's she got?"

The girl quakes, squeezing her prize more tightly in her grubby brown hand. "Hand it over," the second boy says, sneering down at the girl. The girl squeaks and turns, making a mad dash for an alleyway, but the boys are too quick.

In a moment, one of them is upon her, and he lifts her in the air by the foot as she flails, peering at her critically. "She's not going to survive the night, anyway. Why waste food on this little thing?"

The second pries open her fingers, and the girl's eyes widen, her mouth opening as if she's trying to shriek, but unable. "Well, well," the boy says gleefully. "*Chocolate.*"

Chocolate is next to impossible to find in the slums, and Ruti feels her own mouth watering from her doorway at the thought of it. The girl still doesn't speak, but she reaches for the chocolate, heartbroken, and Ruti heaves a sigh.

It's the little ones. She tells herself that she's hardened, that she is made cynical and harsh by the slums, but she can never stop herself when they're concerned. "Give that back," she says, stepping out from her shop.

The boy holding the girl gives her a scornful look, but the others recoil, their eyes wide and fearful when they catch sight of her. "It's the witch," says the boy with the chocolate, flinching back. "We shouldn't anger her." Ruti tilts her head, waiting.

The first boy scoffs. "I'm not afraid of any witch. Especially not a *Markless* who claims to have the spirits' favor." As though he isn't Markless as well. No one looks down on the Markless like other Markless do. "Give me the chocolate. You can choose to run."

"Put the girl down." Ruti's voice is calm, but she takes a step forward, feeling quiet rage bubbling through her. "Now."

The boy smirks at her. "Or what? You'll sing a spell at me?" He looks speculatively at the shop. "I wonder what I might find inside that little house of yours." He doesn't notice the other two boys creeping back, their eyes on Ruti.

Ruti watches only the first boy. "You leave me no choice," she says, and she begins to sing.

Her voice rises and falls in a glissando, rhythmic and musical, and she feels the bubbling sensation of magic as it emerges with her song. Her music has no words, no definable tune to follow, but she knows instinctively where it will carry her regardless. When Ruti sings, magic comes, the spirits drawn to her voice as though she has the powers of a Bonded.

The spirits gift the worthy men. To the Bonded, blessings ten. That's how the old rhyme goes. The world is alive with magic, drifting through the skies and thick in the earth around them. The hungry spirits seize it all for themselves but they spare some–a gift–for each of the Bonded.

But Ruti is stronger than a Bonded. A Bonded only has mastery over one element, over whatever their joined marks give them. Ruti's magic has no limits, as long as she has the favor of the spirits she beseeches. She collects offerings, prepares sufficient ones to appease the spirits when her song is not enough, and then she sings out her request.

She'd learned her first song on the streets from a wizened old man with no mark on his palm. The rest she had taught herself by watching how the spirits came to him and learning what sounds together might make magic. She is careful never to offend the spirits, to treat them with respect and bring them gifts when she asks for too much, and she can feel their affection for her in return. They have kept her alive until eighteen, and they can stop any Markless bully in his tracks.

She sings and sings until stone creeps up the Markless boy's pale, red-pocked arm, immobilizing him, and the little girl can scramble out of his grasp. The boy stares at her in terror, unable to move his arm from its raised position, and Ruti stops singing and directs her glare to the second boy. "I think you have something that isn't yours," she says.

The second boy, his eyes wide, hands the girl back her chocolate. The girl scurries away to safety, and Ruti says, "I don't want to see you attacking little ones again." She hums a tune, a solemn chant that lets life return to the Markless boy's arm, and the boys scatter and run, stumbling down the road away from her.

Ruti lets out a breath, leaning against her doorpost and casting an eye down the road. "You should go back to the orphanage," she says. The little girl is somewhere nearby, she knows, lurking and watching her from the shadows. "The streets aren't safe at night."

There is no answer, but Ruti sees a flicker of movement in the alleyway beside her shop. "I know it's bad in there, but it isn't forever," Ruti promises. "Stay in there. Get bigger and smarter. It's the only way to survive."

The girl emerges from the shadows and watches Ruti with dark brown eyes. Ruti stares back at her, nonplussed, and the girl takes another step forward, then another, walking toward Ruti with spindly, cautious movements.

When she's standing in front of Ruti, she thrusts out a hand, and Ruti half expects her to ask for a paint, also. But no, her fingers open, and resting on her unmarked palm is the piece of chocolate. She looks up at Ruti, her chapped lips curved into a smile, and waits for Ruti to accept her offering.

Ruti blinks at her, uncertain of what the girl wants from her. Most of the other Markless fear her, or see only how she might help them. The little ones scamper away unless they're in danger. "I'm not taking your chocolate," she says. "I have corn bread inside. Would you like some?"

The little girl's eyes shine. Ruti says, "Do you have a name, little one?"

The girl shakes her head. She touches her lips, eyes trusting as she looks up at Ruti. Ruti rethinks her question. "Can you speak?"

The girl shakes her head again. Ruti twitches, uncertain of what to do now with this girl who won't run from her. "There's no use in saving you if you're just going to get yourself killed anyway," Ruti decides reluctantly. "Come inside. You can eat your chocolate in peace."

The girl follows her inside, and Ruti bolts the door behind them.

It's been twelve years since Kita, and she's still picking up Markless children who will inevitably be gone soon enough, lost to Bonded guards or to other Markless children who see no other way to survive than to destroy their own.

This is the fate of the Markless, the children who never should have existed at all.

The girl stays. It's through no particular effort on Ruti's part. The little ones who take shelter in her shop tend to scamper off in the morning before she awakens, wary of her even as they look to her for protection. But the girl is still there in the morning, curled up at the foot of Ruti's bed in a ball of ragged cloth and tangled black hair, and Ruti doesn't quite know how to ask her to leave.

She tries at first. "This is no place for you," she says on the first afternoon. But then an Unbonded man appears in the shop, demanding that Ruti sing an empty satchel into riches.

It isn't the first time that an Unbonded has tried to throw his weight around Ruti's shop, demanding her magic with a meager payment that would never satisfy a Marked witch. "This is too much to ask of the spirits," Ruti says tersely, but the man insists that she try, his eyes narrowing as they flicker to the little girl huddled in the corner.

He has the ugly look of a man who would push too far, who would force Ruti to sing a defense that might not work, and Ruti is not so desperate and foolish that she picks fights with every Unbonded man who swaggers into her shop. Instead, she sings in a high, thin voice to the Scaled One, master of transmutation, asking a gift so bold that she expects punishment at once.

She feels the outrage at her boldness as she sings, the magic that soars through her veins turning jagged and angry and cruel. The air darkens around her, and she can see–for a single moment–the pale glare of the Scaled One, the fury at a witch who dares to ask more than she offers. The hissing bellow fills the shop, and the Unbonded man flees as Ruti cries out, pain shooting through the side of her abdomen as though teeth had snapped into her.

The spirits leave no marks when they are displeased, only an agony that lingers for longer than any salve can abate, and Ruti has to close her doors and lie down on her bed for the rest of the day. And still the little girl remains, hovering near the bed as though she hasn't heard Ruti's warnings. "This is not a safe place for a Markless who can't sing," Ruti repeats.

The girl ignores her, and Ruti says, "Are you listening to me?"

The girl twists around, her eyes flashing with fierce determination, and she gestures suddenly, a graceful motion that Ruti doesn't understand. Her hand dips, then curves upward to cup the air around her mouth. Ruti shakes her head. "I will not play games with you," she says tiredly. "I have more to do today than negotiate with a little one."

But the girl makes the same motion again, the dip of her hand like a wave rippling through the River Somanchi, her hand moving to her mouth once more. Cupping the air, as though she's drinking. "Water," Ruti guesses. "You want water?" The girl beams at her.

If it will get the girl to leave, then Ruti will give her water. "There is a sealed jug beneath my table in the front of the shop," she says, curling back around her nonexistent wound. The spirits chastise her from time to time, and it hurts enough that it makes her use of casual magic frugal. She only has to wait it out and give the Scaled One some time. For now, she burns a waxen candle of incense in regret, an apology for her nerve.

She listens for the sound of the door closing, of the little one running away and leaving Ruti to her pain. Instead, the girl reappears a moment later with a wet cloth clasped in her hands, and she presses it to Ruti's side. Ruti blinks at her, startled. The girl makes a motion that Ruti can't understand, and another that Ruti does. A hand pressed to her chest, then her palm outstretched over the floor, spread out in a simple and unmistakable message. *I will stay.*

And so Ruti gives her a name. *Khumeía*, she calls her, after the ancient word for mixing offerings, but it becomes Kimya soon enough.

Kimya makes herself useful from the start, cleaning up after Ruti puts together offerings to the spirits and getting them food from the market. The first time Ruti sends Kimya out with a few coins and instructions, she expects Kimya to take the coins and run. Markless can't afford to trust others, not when there's food involved. But Kimya returns with bread and nuts and fruit, and she eats a banana with gusto and vomits up the entire fruit later.

She is too small for her appetite, so Ruti rations out her food after that, a small piece of bread first and a spoonful or two of mashed banana later. Kimya eats everything happily and enthusiastically, and as the weeks pass, her concave stomach begins to fill out. Ruti replaces her rags with a new payment from an Unbonded, a simple grey dress with only a few holes in it, made from scratchy but solid fabric.

"Don't go telling your friends about this," Ruti warns her. "I can't take care of more than the two of us." A joke. Kimya is alone, just like every Markless out there. It's an old, self-deprecating joke that even the Markless don't want to be around the Markless. If someone had taught her the language that she signs, that person is long gone now.

Ruti has managed to make just enough coin to survive until now. Her stomach is never full, but she eats sparingly and is healthy because of it. With Kimya comes less food and more hunger.

Kimya touches Ruti's stomach one day, her little hands pressed to the sunken skin of Ruti's abdomen, and she makes a *tch* sound through a gap in her teeth. Carefully, reluctantly, she offers Ruti her half of their banana.

Ruti blinks at her. "Kimya, no. Eat your food. I'm fine." With time comes a reluctant care for the child, a little Markless girl who can't speak but still manages to survive. "We just need . . . a little more coin."

She looks around the shop, contemplating her options. There are chants that might bring them more customers, a protection chant that she's been working on but couldn't finish. The best protection chants require an offering–to the Maned One, to the Horned One, to the Spotted One, to an animal spirit that must be appeased. Not every song needs an offering, of course. To sing to the spirits is to beg them for their powers, and Ruti has made bold requests before and been granted their largesse. But she is acutely aware that the spirits' favor will only go so far if she offers them paltry gifts or nothing in return, and their wrath will be uncompromising.

But the offerings she needs require far too much coin, specialized items in the Merchants' Circle that she has never dared to haggle for. One glimpse of her unmarked palm and the merchants would chase her from their shops.

Kimya scoffs when Ruti points that out and scampers over to the table to find the black ink that Ruti uses for paints. Ruti shakes her head. "I won't paint us," she says. "It's just a pretty lie." The paints last for a few weeks with a chant, long enough for Markless to experience life with a mark and crave it for eternity. There are Markless who come to her once a month, begging her for a new paint, and she obliges with reluctance.

They will always be Markless. A little bit of paint can't simulate the energies that follow the Unbonded or the powers of the Bonded, and the people they find while painted will come to despise them when they discover the truth. Ruti will never paint herself again, will never let herself taste any other life, not when she's seen so many times how it destroys others.

But Kimya claps a hand to her mouth and then signs in the direction of the ink, patient until Ruti figures out what it is that Kimya is trying to say. "Just ink without the chants," Ruti guesses, and Kimya bobs her head. Ruti tries another argument. "I won't bring you with me. You're too small, and–"

Kimya moves in a blur, barely brushing past Ruti, and she opens her fist when she's on the other side of the room. There's an amulet in her palm, an amulet that had been in Ruti's pocket a moment before. "Little thief," Ruti says, alternately frustrated and fond. "What happens if a merchant catches you?"

Kimya gives her an incredulous look, a *no-one-will-catch-me* look, and Ruti sighs. "Fine. Sit."

She paints Kimya first, carefully moving the ink along her palm in firm, gentle strokes. She gives Kimya the half circle of majimm, the flowing waves that symbolize the water that follows majimm Unbonded wherever they go. Unbonded have half their marks, but they have no control over them. Instead, the energy escapes when they speak, when they move, at the most inopportune of times. It's only once they're Bonded that they have true command over their complete marks.

Her own mark she makes rough and earthy, the sign of endhi. She hasn't seen an Unbonded with endhi in a long time, but she remembers the last, a farmer who'd been so furious with the Markless stealing his crops that the ground had split beneath them and nearly swallowed them up. Ruti hadn't learned how to chant yet, and she'd barely managed to climb out of the farmer's inadvertent pit.

"These won't last," she warns Kimya. "Hold your hand still while it dries or it'll smear. We can't take any chances." The Merchants' Circle isn't as dangerous for Markless as the Inner Circle, but they are equally unwelcome there. Markless are bad for business.

The markets in the slums are the only place where Markless are tolerated, far from the nobles and any Bonded. The markets in the Merchants' Circle are large and busy, clustered near the river that runs through Somanchi and brings traders in from all over Zidesh and beyond. Somanchi is the capital city of Zidesh, the largest of its cities and the home of the royal palace, and the Merchants' Circle does its best to show no sign of the Markless slums to visitors.

When Kimya first sees the Merchants' Circle, she gasps and clutches Ruti's sleeve. Ruti has to stifle her own gasp as well. She hasn't been to the Merchants' Circle in years, and she'd been left with only vague remembrances that were more imagination than truth. But her imagination pales in comparison with what stands before them.

Food. Stands with clusters and clusters of bananas, more bananas than Ruti's eaten in her life. Piles of orange carrots. Cucumbers that are green without a sign of rotting. An entire stand that is only melons, the kind that would feed the two of them for weeks, their sweet scent filling the air. Shopkeepers shout out their wares and crowds of people come to them, haggling over their sales in a cacophony of alternating noise.

"Much too much! I'll give you eight!"

"Do you take me for a Markless fool? I will give you my best for twelve coins!"

"Absurd!" Louder and louder, items clunking onto counters and rustling into bags, an occasional fruit landing on the ground instead to provide a burst of freshness to the odors that suffuse the crowd. Back and forth the customers and sellers fight, the rise and fall almost like a chant of their own. Ruti wonders if she could compose a chant like that, with battling cadences in the highs and lows.

There are winding paths that lead from the road to temples etched with images of the Horned One and the Fanged One, of the Spotted One who is the symbol of Zidesh. Men and women with thick, glossy clothing carry jewels and baskets full of food toward the temples as offerings to the spirits so that their journeys might be blessed.

Brightly colored clothes hang from the closest stand to them, dresses and gowns for the wealthiest of customers. There are hats and shoes and scarves in an array of colors, and Ruti has never seen so much wealth in her life. Little shops sit behind each stand, even *more* inside of them, and Ruti and Kimya wander together, Kimya pointing frantically at different stands with excitement. Her hand flashes out for a moment from beneath her grubby clothes as they walk past the carrots, and Ruti steers them away from the stand before Kimya is seen.

But there are too many people around to be caught, she thinks. The people in the Merchants' Circle vary from wealthy traders to locals. Ruti makes sure to find excuses to raise her hand to her thin lips, to her dark hair, to flash the painted mark on her olive-skinned palm at passersby who eye her suspiciously. They might not like her as a poor Unbonded, but they won't start a fuss over it.

Ruti waits until they're out of the main rows of the markets, where there are fewer stands and more quiet shops, before she says to Kimya, "Give it."

Kimya pulls a carrot from her pocket obligingly, cracking it in half and offering Ruti the smaller piece. Ruti bites into it. It tastes fresh and juicy, better than anything in the slum markets. "What else did you get?" she asks. There must be more. Kimya is too fast and too young to resist the markets.

Kimya bites her lip and then grins, reaching into her pocket and pulling out a silver ring with a jeweled stone on it. Ruti looks at it, openmouthed. "What is that? Where did you–I didn't see any stands selling something like *that*."

Kimya mimics slipping a hand over Ruti's and sliding something off her finger. Ruti lowers her voice. "You stole it off of someone?" Kimya bobs her head proudly. Ruti stares at her. It's a bad idea, stealing from nobles. The merchants might not notice a few missing fruits, but a ring from a visitor will be missed. "Do *not* do that again," Ruti hisses, glancing around. "We can't be noticed. My paints won't last long."

She spots a shop a few feet away, the stand in front of it displaying cheap beaded jewelry, and Ruti moves to it, peering inside. There is little on the walls inside the shop, only a table and shelves behind it with more expensive jewelry. *Perfect.*

The jeweler sneers at them, holding out his palm for each of them to press with their own. "Out, urchins," he says. "This is no place for you."

Ruti holds up the ring. "How much will you give me for this?"

The jeweler pauses, his eyes gleaming with suspicion as he takes in the ring. "Where did you get that?"

Ruti drops her head, crumpling her face. "It was our mother's last possession before she . . ." She swallows, pulling her shoulders together in an attempt to look younger than she is.

The jeweler considers her for a long moment. "I'll give you fifty coin for it," he says finally. "Not a coin more. It's the best deal you'll get."

They're being fleeced. Ruti can see the greed in the jeweler's eye, and Kimya stamps her foot in outrage. But they can't afford to keep the ring any longer, and Ruti pretends to ponder and then nods. "We'll take it."

Fifty coin is more than they'd had before, and Ruti hurries Kimya from the shop, glancing worriedly over her shoulder. With fifty coin, they can collect some of the material that she needs for her chants without stealing it.

"Here," she says, stopping outside one stand. There is no shop, only the stand and a row of shelves jammed into the ground behind the seller. On the shelves are the items Ruti needs: powdered antler, animal skins that have been dried into strips, and herbs and roots from deep in the wet woods.

The seller is a woman who holds out her hand for them to press their palms to hers. Ruti glances at her own palm when she pulls away, relieved that her mark has held intact. "What can I help you with?" the woman says, and her voice lilts, flowers growing in the vase beside her as she speaks. She's a Bonded, her mark made of endhi and majimm combined into a mastery over plants.

Ruti points out the items she wants, and the woman loads them into a bag made of animal skin that they purchase from her as well. Fifty coin buys them more than Ruti had thought it would, and she finally begins to relax. Kimya's foolishness has saved their trip, and they'll be back home soon, safe in the Markless slums.

The woman chats with them as she gathers the last of the skins. "These will tide you over for the Spotted One," she says. "But don't give the Toothed One these roots or you risk offending him. Water spirits require fish offerings." She gestures toward the distance, where the River Somanchi flows through the city.

It's nowhere near the slums, and not Ruti's concern. "Thank you," she says politely, taking a few last wet roots and counting out the coin for the woman. "This is all I need."

"Are you apprenticing with a witch?" the woman asks curiously. "I wasn't aware that Saha took them so young. . . ." Her voice trails off, her eyes on Ruti's hand as it counts out the coin. Ruti follows her gaze and sees, with mounting horror, exactly what it is that the woman sees.

The coin are smeared with ink, and the mark of endhi that Ruti painted onto her palm has been smudged by the wet root. It's nothing more than a blur of black against her calloused skin, and the woman recoils. "Markless!" she hisses, rearing back. The flowers in her vase grow thorns, spiky and long.

Ruti looks around frantically, afraid that someone else might have heard. Instead, she sees the jeweler down the road with two royal guards, gesturing at Ruti. *Royal guards.* Whom had Kimya stolen that ring from?

The woman shrieks, "Markless!" again, and this time people hear. The volume of the crowd rises, people around them scampering back in fear as though Ruti might pass on her condition to them all. The guards twist around, lunging through the crowd, and Ruti shoves the bag into Kimya's hands.

"Go," she hisses. "Run home." Kimya's dark lips form into a scowl. "I'm a witch, remember?" Ruti says urgently. "I'll be fine. *Go.*" Kimya runs at last, and Ruti faces the crowd.

"Markless!" someone else shouts, and a beaded necklace is flung at her, then a ripe tomato. Ruti turns and flees, racing in the opposite direction than the one Kimya had taken, hurtling through the market and leaving chaos behind.

She dodges through malodorous crowds of people, head down and unmarked hand squeezed into a fist. People snap curses at her, shove her back and almost unbalance her, but she's nearly at the edge of the Merchants' Circle, nearly at the stables where she might be able to hide in a wagon and make her way back safely to the slums. It's just a few more turns.

She careens around a corner, toppling over a stand of colorful shirts, and she tangles in soft fabric as the shopkeeper howls at her. On the ground, she rolls over, kicking away a shirt, and she breaks into a run again just as a bolt of lightning crackles from the sky in front of her.

She gapes at it, rearing back, and the energy spreads toward her, consuming her with its acrid scent. At once, she's shaking, seized by the lightning until it feels as though she's being burned alive, her skin crackling. *Lightning. Ashto and sewa.* This isn't an accident. A Bonded has found her.

She can't move, can't escape the lightning. Through the flashing lights surrounding her, she spots a sour-eyed royal guard moving toward her, another two behind him. They flank a beautiful girl who watches the affair with unreadable brown eyes, her face all but concealed beneath a golden scarf and cloak. *Her ring*, Ruti thinks faintly, and then she thinks nothing at all.

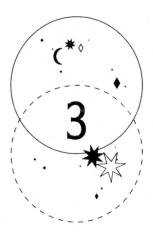

3

She awakens in a pitch-black dungeon, her entire body still burning and the noxious smell of scorched flesh trapped in her nostrils. Beneath her is a hard dirt floor, and the air is cool and wet as it rarely is aboveground. She chants, almost in a whisper, calling on the spirits to heal her. Slowly, slowly, her skin grows soft and warm olive again, the burns fading and her voice rising.

"Hey!" Someone bangs against the wall near her. "Keep it down!" Ruti jumps, banging against something hard.

Upon further examination, she discovers that it's a piece of the stone wall that had never been filed down. Jagged rock pokes out all across the wall of her cell, and she feels her way along it, nauseated with dread.

Markless thieves are often thrown into the dungeons and never emerge. There are no public trials, no grand executions. The rumor in the slums is that Markless aren't fed in the royal dungeons, only locked in and abandoned until they starve to death.

She can't sing her way out of a dungeon, not when she can't even see where she is. The spirits might give her a little help, but they won't transport her to a whole new place. Even requesting it of them is asking for a reprimand that will leave her incapacitated for days. If she could feel her way to the bars of the cell, perhaps she might be able to make them bend open, but she can hardly move.

With a sigh, she stretches out on the uneven dirt floor again and begins to chant, ignoring the banging noises from the cell beside her. Her body still aches once the burns are gone, but her skin no longer feels as though it's aflame, every movement searing her anew. The spirit of the Fanged One is strong in the darkness, and she can feel his healing venom with every word from her mouth.

She's hungry and she's tired and she has no idea if Kimya made it home, and that last one niggles most. She chides herself for getting too attached. She hasn't made it this far by hinging her contentment on the survival of other Markless. She *can't*.

But she does.

After what must be hours, there's a movement from one side of her black cage. A flicker of light, and Ruti follows it hungrily, desperate for any chance to illuminate this dungeon. But it's distant, only a gleam far away, and she curls up again and whispers her chants as she waits for the light to approach.

It comes, and Ruti sees that it's a flame held in the palm of a Bonded guard. *Ashto and ashto. Fire.* Now she can see the dungeon around her. There is nothing but a stone wall across from her cell, corrugated with years of water that slides down it. Her cell itself is a cramped space with little to see inside.

The guard kicks the metal bars at the front of the cell. "Up, Markless," he orders. A second guard moves forward, a woman with ashto and endhi bonded on her palm. Under her command, the metal moves, bending outward to form a diamond doorway for Ruti.

"Up," the first guard growls again, and Ruti stands unsteadily. Her knees pop, her chest aching still from the lightning attack, but she manages to stagger through the doorway to stand in front of the guards.

The woman guard says, "Hands out together." Ruti holds out her hands, and the woman carefully places a long metal rod across Ruti's wrists. With a motion of her hands, the rod bends, twisting to hold Ruti's wrists together.

That's fine. Ruti doesn't need anything but her voice to escape.

A second metal rod is turned into a cuff for her ankle and a chain to hold it by, and the woman scowls. "I hate leading Markless slum brats," she mutters to the man. "They always leave my metal smelling foul."

The man grunts in acknowledgement. "A public trial for a Markless is a waste of a sword," he says, and Ruti stiffens as she stumbles forward behind them. A public trial means she's almost sure to be executed, but it isn't the death warrant she'd expected. The guard echoes her thoughts. "Why bother with this for a Markless?"

"She stole a ring from the Heir," the woman says dryly, and Ruti freezes. The woman shakes her chain, yanking her forward. "*Move*, Markless. I don't have all day."

From the *Heir*? Ruti remembers the girl she'd seen, dark eyes and smooth skin beneath her coverings, and feels sick. She doesn't look much like King Adiel's face does on Zidesh's coin, but it must have been her. The Heir to Zidesh's throne is never seen outside of the Inner Circle, and Ruti had never thought. . . .

She's in *so* much trouble.

"How did anyone allow a Markless so close to the Heir?" the man mutters. "That idiot Orrin. He'll do anything the Heir asks. If I were the Regent, I'd make him–"

"If you were the Regent, we wouldn't be traipsing through a dungeon with some Markless dog," the woman shoots back. She yanks the chain again, impatient. "Keep up."

Ruti follows, quiet dread suffusing her limbs. Maybe she *can* call on the spirits to carry her from the dungeons. Once her trial begins, there will be no escape.

There is a door ahead of them. The woman presses her hand to it, manipulating the metal lock until it clicks open. The man extinguishes his flame and pushes the door open.

The sun beats down on them from the top of a long staircase, the light blinding. Ruti's eyes burn and she trips, crawling up the stairs as the woman yanks her chain, squeezing her eyes shut as they adjust again to the light. "Up, dog," the woman barks. "The Regent awaits."

Ruti blinks, her eyes wet with tears from the light, and she scrambles behind them up the stairs. They're in an area of Somanchi where Ruti has never been foolish enough to venture before: the Royal Square, a walled compound that houses the Heir, the Regent, and his wife.

The Royal Square is enormous and fortified on all sides with buildings meant for soldiers and guards and servants. At the center is the massive, boxy royal castle, and Ruti sees it towering above her now. The staircase emerges beyond the castle, in the courtyard where the Regent, Kornanu, judges the people.

King Adiel died when Ruti was a child, just a few days after the queen. Ruti remembers the wails and the sorrow that spread even to the slums. King Adiel had been kind, and he had opened the orphanages for the Markless. He left behind a single daughter, a girl only a few years older than Ruti. So Adiel's brother had been named Regent.

Dekala. Ruti can see her, a figure up ahead who sits on the second throne in the courtyard. In the Royal Square, she is no longer wrapped in a cloak. She sits tall, her hair coiled in long locks and wound into a silvery headpiece. Her gown is white, intricately designed with gold along a wrapped opening across the front, and she sits straight, watching Ruti's approach with cold eyes.

She's just as beautiful as she'd been at first glimpse, and Ruti looks away from her, staring up at the Regent instead. Kornanu is a Bonded who has command over water, and his eyes glitter like the sea as he takes Ruti in. "This is the Markless who dared lay a hand on the Heir," he says, sneering down at her.

Princess Dekala shudders delicately. There is a distant rumble of thunder, an uncontrolled reaction of sewa, and Ruti realizes, startled, that the Heir is Unbonded.

The guards drag Ruti closer, past a throng of royal subjects who have come to the courtyard today to watch the Regent rule. They claw at Ruti from either side of the long aisle to the Regent, throwing rocks and shouting curses at her. Ruti keeps her head down, whispering a chant so the rocks glance off of her head before they ever touch her. No one can hear her over the shouting, not even the guard who pulls her.

She is finally yanked to the space before the thrones, and Ruti peers up at the Regent in his own robes of white and gold. He wears the skin of a Spotted One on his shoulders, a sign of his spirit-gifted right to rule, and he looks down at Ruti as though she is unworthy of his gaze. "You stole from the Heir," he hisses, wide nose flaring. "You *defiled* the Heir with your touch."

Ruti looks at the Heir again. Princess Dekala is watching her, her face sculpted as though from stone. She doesn't speak, but her eyes burn into Ruti, and Ruti feels a wind whip past her.

Beside her is a pasty-pale guard who glowers at Ruti, his eyes glowing with righteous rage. "She must be killed!" he bursts out. "She dares to–"

"Silence, Orrin!" the Regent barks. "You do not speak while I judge!" He gestures to his own guards, who take threatening steps toward the third guard. Ruti recognizes Orrin. He'd been the one to blast her with lightning. He looks at her now with pure loathing.

The Heir puts up a hand and the guards hesitate, looking from the Regent to the Heir. "Orrin is only concerned for my honor," the Heir says. Her voice is deep, sharp, and she speaks with the same authority as the Regent. "I wish to know . . ." Her eyes burn into Ruti again. ". . . was the Markless healed before being brought here?"

Ruti feels it as all eyes turn to her, the distant sound of thunder rumbling again. No one else had noticed that her burns were gone, but the Heir has eyes that miss nothing, that look down on Ruti with the cool authority of royalty.

The guard who holds Ruti's chain shakes her head. "No, Your Highness. She was locked away in the dungeons until her trial. No one had access to her. No one healed her." She looks at Ruti in bewilderment.

They all watch her keenly now, eyes taking in her unblemished skin beneath the rags that had been her best clothing before she'd been burned. Ruti swallows, standing tall, and the Regent growls, "Then *how* has she been healed unless Orrin failed at–"

"She's a witch!" Orrin snarls furiously, jabbing a finger at Ruti. "A filthy Markless witch!"

The guard holding Ruti's chain takes a step back. The crowd bursts into shouts and jeers. Ruti clenches her bound fists, dirty and ragged. Afraid for her life, she feels the whisper of wind around her, the reminder that the Heir is still watching her. But the heat of the sun overhead bolsters her, carrying with its warmth the whisper of the Winged One, watching. "And what if I am?" she says boldly. She has little to lose now. "The spirits protect me. You can't hold me here."

"Enough!" the Regent shouts. His eyes look as though they might pop from his head in fury. "You dare to speak before me, Markless? Put her to death! Now!"

The guards snap into action, but they circle her warily, afraid of what she might do. The Bonded may have their special gifts, but witches are unpredictable. The Bonded fear the unpredictable more than they do even their Regent, and the Regent barks out again, "What are you waiting for? Kill her!"

The Heir watches as the guards drag themselves forward. Ruti looks up at her and sees something new in her eyes. It's a glitter of interest, and Ruti shivers beneath it and in the wind that she still feels on her neck.

She is waiting to see what Ruti does next. Ruti knows it, just as she knows that there's nothing she *can* do. She can't chant herself out of this or chant herself an army to overpower the guards. The Regent is shouting for the guards to come closer, to "Kill the Markless girl, she's only a girl!"

Ruti is *not* only a girl, so she clears her throat and sings.

The guards step back again, frightened by the melody of her chant, and Ruti blends two protection chants together, finding the threads of the melody in her new feeling of urgency. Her voice is throaty, her voice is light, her voice rises and falls in a plea to the spirits who have made her their protected child. The bonds that keep her wrists locked together become soft and stringy. Ruti pulls and they come apart.

The Regent is shouting, the crowd is roaring, and Princess Dekala is watching Ruti with hunger in her eyes. Ruti keeps her eyes fixed only on the princess, on the thin smile that curves the Heir's fine mahogany cheekbones as she watches. She reminds Ruti of a Spotted One, of their lithe bodies and the muscle that lets them move fluidly through Somanchi's forests. A Spotted One's face means instant death, and the Heir's face has the same cold doom written across it.

Ruti sings to the Spotted One, calls for protection with a higher, lilting chant that she's never sung before. The guards are massing again, and one raises a sharp knife as Ruti sings more desperately. She may be asking for too much, but she has more to lose right now.

And then, chaos. Even the Heir looks away from Ruti, the thunder booming in the sky behind them, and the Regent shouts, "Kill her! *Kill her!*" but no one is listening. Ruti follows the Heir's gaze to the wall of the courtyard, and she sings ever more urgently, gaining new strength with a sudden arrival.

A Spotted One has leaped over the wall of the courtyard, prowling toward Ruti.

The crowd erupts in screams, royal subjects falling over each other to escape. The guards hurtle toward the Regent and the Heir, abandoning Ruti as they array themselves around their rulers. The Regent summons water from the moisture of the air to turn into arrows made of ice, which he aims at the Spotted One. But the Spotted One doesn't seem to notice them as it runs gracefully to Ruti.

Ruti chants and chants, her heart pounding with terror and exhilaration. She's rarely seen Spotted Ones in Somanchi proper. The slums have little shelter from wild beasts, and the Markless have nothing to offer the spirits for protection, but Spotted Ones have plenty to eat in the woods and the grassland just outside the city. They have little interest in people, and she's never seen one wander this deep into Somanchi.

The Spotted One approaches, and Ruti holds out a hand, singing the song she's composed for it. The song goes low now, Ruti chanting in calming tones as the Spotted One circles her and growls at any brave guards who dare come close. Ruti feels the Spotted One nuzzle her fingers.

Her heart is pounding. "I take my leave," she says finally, her voice shaky, and she feels, again, the whisper of wind against her skin. Her eyes lock with the Heir's gaze, the Heir unmoving as guards cluster around her. Orrin, the loud lightning guard, crouches beside her as though to comfort her, but the Heir doesn't look at him once. Ruti feels a chill deep in her skin.

The Spotted One nuzzles Ruti again, and Ruti sings and sings and walks, unscathed, from the courtyard of the Royal Square.

4

The Spotted One leaves her when she stops singing, after she's reached the slums and it's nearly evening. "Thank you," she whispers with a hoarse voice, touching its short, soft fur once more. It lets out a low hum that vibrates through its body to her palm, then runs off into the night. A few Markless are crouched in a corner, watching her with fearful eyes, and she turns to face them. "What's the word from the palace?"

Only one speaks, a girl nearly her age. "They say a Markless witch got the better of the Regent," she says boldly, eyes flickering over Ruti's torn clothes and the chain still attached to her ankle. "The Regent has issued a call for her death."

"I see." Ruti should have expected it. "Are his guards in the slums?"

The girl snorts. "No one comes to the slums," she says, running a finger over her close-cropped hair. "And everyone knows that the only thing worse than having a death warrant is living as a Markless."

Ruti grins, humorless, and the girl grins back. "Thank you," Ruti says, and she chants a quiet call to the spirits as she leaves, a request that this girl will find food tonight.

Kimya is home in their little shop when she arrives, gesticulating wildly as Ruti enters. She mimics the claws of a Spotted One and wraps her arms around Ruti, and Ruti says, "I guess you heard what happened."

Kimya bobs her head. She ducks into a cabinet behind the table in the shop and returns with a sharpened knife in hand. Ruti blinks at her. "Were you going to come after me?" she asks, touched and aghast. "Kimya, *no*. When I'm in trouble, you stay here, understood?"

Kimya scoffs silently and kneels down beside Ruti. A few movements of the knife and the chain is cut from her ankle. "Oh," Ruti says, feeling very foolish. "So you weren't planning on a rescue mission." Kimya raises her eyebrows and says nothing. Ruti squints at her suspiciously.

They sit on the bed and eat a simple meal of flattened corn cakes and a few juicy tomatoes that Kimya managed to steal on her way out of the Merchants' Circle. Ruti devours it all, hungrier than she's been since she first settled in the shop, and she sleeps that night with Kimya draped over her, arms around Ruti as though Ruti might run away while she sleeps. Ruti runs her fingers through Kimya's thick hair, pulling dirt from within it. It still carries the scents of the marketplace, body sweat and cloves and coriander.

She's home safely, but she wonders how long it will last. The Regent's honor has been besmirched with her escape. She won't be allowed to live.

She has to leave. But she can't leave Kimya behind. A girl with no voice won't survive long without a witch to protect her.

That decided, she finally sleeps.

In the morning, she tells Kimya to pack. "We can sneak onto one of the merchant boats leaving for Kaguruk. The farther away, the better." Kimya nods without argument. "We'll have to sell the bed and the table for coin before we go. We'll take my ingredients with us. Who knows who might have use for us in Kaguruk?"

Kimya's face is bright with excitement, and Ruti does her best to look confident. She has no idea what Kaguruk does to Markless, if they're as cruel as the people of Rurana are rumored to be. Kaguruk might be just another stop as they search for a place to settle, but at least there they'll be safe from the Regent.

Kimya gathers ingredients from the shelves as Ruti heads outside to find a buyer for their table and cot. They are old and rotting, and Ruti had traded for them with a few chants, but they're still better than what a lot of shopkeepers in the slums have. She can get ten, maybe twenty coin for both, and that can serve as bribes if they're found on the merchant ship.

After a few minutes of hurrying from shop to shop, she realizes she's being followed.

Her first thought is Kimya, who is rarely contained, but these footfalls are the heavy steps of someone who is bigger than Ruti and wears sandals instead of going barefoot. The movements are abrupt behind her, stopping and starting as she stops and starts, and Ruti tests them without looking back. Gingerly, she walks to the next shop and stops just before it. The heavy steps cease again with her, and she ducks into an alley and breaks into a run.

Her stalker follows. Ruti races down another road, weaving through Markless beggars and peddlers and the rare Unbonded who have come to the slums for cheap prices. She can hear her follower in hot pursuit, so she turns sharply into another alley, running swiftly through it and making another quick turn to her shop.

She bursts inside, hissing to Kimya, "Hide under the bed. Someone's here." Carefully, she snatches the knife from the cabinet and emerges from her shop.

Her pursuer emerges, and Ruti's eyes narrow. It's Orrin, the big, hulking lightning guard from the palace, and he raises his hands in threat. "You will come with me if you want to live," he orders.

Ruti doesn't budge. "Your lightning can't kill me," she snaps, bristling. "Do you want me to call another protector? A Maned One would eat you for lunch."

Orrin's eyes flash in fury. "I will kill you before you begin to sing," he snarls.

Ruti feels intense dislike building for the lumbering fool who'd blasted her, whether or not it might be foolhardy to taunt a Bonded royal guard. "Or you could hide like a coward, as you did the last time I chanted," she says, smirking.

"How *dare* you." Orrin's hands crackle with energy. The street empties swiftly, Markless fleeing from a Bonded guard and the confrontation sure to follow. "I am no coward."

"You've come down to the slums to attack a defenseless Markless girl," Ruti shoots back, the tips of her fingers playing against the hilt of her knife. "Am I the best you can do, you cowering dotard?"

Orrin roars, reaching back to hurl a sparking ball of pure energy at Ruti. Ruti tilts her head, readying a song, and then, abruptly–

A low rumble of thunder. "Enough."

She knows that commanding voice even though she's only heard it once. Orrin freezes, the lightning fading back into his hand, and a girl glides from the shadows, wearing the same silken cloak and translucent scarf she'd worn at the Merchants' Circle. Her brown eyes are piercing as they take Ruti in, and Ruti's bravado fades under Princess Dekala's stare.

The Heir puts a hand on Orrin's arm, her brown skin and red nails vivid on his pale skin, and Orrin deflates, scowling at Ruti but waiting, obedient, for the Heir to speak again.

"Bring us inside," the Heir says. It's an order from someone accustomed to being obeyed, and Ruti turns without thinking, walking unsteadily into her shop.

She doesn't put the knife down.

Kimya has listened for once, and she's nowhere to be found. Ruti stands behind the table, watching as the Heir glides into the shop. Her golden cloak outshines the entire room, more luxurious and expensive than every item around her. Ruti gulps and says, "If you've come to have me executed, it will go the same way as it did before. I won't be killed by that oaf," she says, jerking a thumb at Orrin. He glowers at her.

The Heir says, "What magic can you sing?"

Ruti blinks, startled. The Heir meets her gaze. She is made to look delicate by her clothes and the elaborate styling of her hair and jewelry, but there is iron in her eyes, something fierce and dangerous that forces respect and accepts nothing less. "I . . ." Ruti stumbles over her words, unable to tear her eyes from the Heir's. "I can sing anything," she says finally. It's a bold statement, but it's true. "I taught myself to sing. If I have the right offerings for the spirits, I can teach myself whatever magic I need."

The Heir regards her for another moment, then speaks her next words carefully. "My uncle demands—my uncle *requests*," she amends, and there's a flicker of resentment in her voice, a note that makes her seem, for the first time, as young as she truly is. "My uncle wishes that I be Bonded before I take the throne," she says. "He has employed scholars who have studied the patterns of soulbonds for months before suggesting my most likely match. Princes and nobles will be flocking in soon, each hoping to be my Bonded."

Ruti snorts, unable to hold back her amusement. "And he's so sure that your Bonded will be a noble?"

The Heir gives her a cool look. "Never in the history of Zidesh has a princess bonded with anyone less," she says, and sweeps her eyes around the room again, settling on Ruti as though she finds her wanting. "You will use your magic to ensure that I bond with none of these princes."

It isn't a request. Ruti bristles. "Why not bond with your soulbond?" she says, wrinkling her nose. She can't imagine what it might mean to have a soulbond. Men hold little interest for her, but perhaps if she did find one matched to her, she might. . . . "Isn't that what you people live for?" She says it disdainfully, earning a sharp look from the Heir and a glower from Orrin.

It's Orrin who responds, placing a hand on the Heir's back. "We're in love," he says, and his eyes glow with adulation as he looks at the Heir.

Ruti dislikes him even more. "With each other?" she says dubiously. His palm is open at his side, and she can see that he is already Bonded from that as much as from the lightning he uses so carelessly.

There's a flicker of something that might be amusement in the Heir's eyes. She turns, placing a hand on Orrin's cheek, and he leans against it and gazes at her as though awestruck. When she turns back to Ruti, there is no humor in her eyes. "Spare me the judgment, Markless scum," she says coldly. "You will help me, or you will suffer."

Ruti can feel her hackles rising. "You forget who you're talking to," she says, smiling thinly. "I'm a Markless. I have nothing to lose."

"Oh?" The Heir looks down at her, lip curled. It isn't Orrin's sneer, but it's as cold as the icy wind that whips through the shop. "I watched you at the marketplace before we knew you were a thief," she says. "I saw the girl you brought with you." Ruti stiffens. The Heir smiles, victory written across her face, and Ruti hates her as much as she does her lightning guard. "Everyone has a weakness."

There's a movement in the next room, a bang as Kimya's head hits the underside of the bed. The Heir doesn't turn to look, though Orrin glares suspiciously at the doorway. "I am not some hapless noblewoman from the Inner Circle," she says, enunciating every word as though to give it more power. "I will take everything from you if you try to test me." She prowls the room like a Spotted One, eyes fixed on Ruti. "And you will see far worse than the inside of my dungeons if you dare speak of this to anyone outside of this shop."

"I can sing my way out of–" Ruti begins scornfully, and the Heir is in front of her at once, dangerously close, closer than any self-respecting noble would come to a Markless. She smells of scented oils, her hands bathed in soaps like none

Ruti has ever touched, and her eyes are like pools of molten gold when she's this close. Ruti falters, forgetting her gibe, and then the Heir's hands are on her face.

She doesn't caress Ruti's cheek as she had Orrin's. Instead, her hand moves to Ruti's throat, stroking the line of her neck with a smooth, soft finger. "Remember," she says, her voice a ruthless purr. Ruti's mouth is dry, her heart pounding. "Your voice can be taken from you, too."

The wind whips around Ruti, pulling her hair from her face. "Do we have a deal?" the Heir asks, stepping back, her voice still deadly soft. "Will you come work for me?"

Ruti swallows, her neck still burning where the Heir had touched it. "I'll need some ingredients," she says. The Heir tilts her head in lazy acknowledgement. "An assistant," she says, thinking of Kimya beneath the bed. "One I'll bring myself."

"No royal servant would work for a Markless, anyway," Orrin says haughtily.

Ruti ignores him. "Food and drink," she says, and she wonders if they might still escape, if this is better or worse than slipping onto a ship and fleeing Zidesh. "Shelter."

"I swear on the spirits themselves that I will give you it all for eternity if I take the throne without a soulbond," the Heir says, gathering her cloak and turning away from Ruti, effectively dismissing her. Orrin moves to stand beside her, smug as he looks down on Ruti. As though he has *anything* to do with her capitulation.

And it's sheer irritation at both of them–a royal and her guard, who can enter Ruti's life and restructure it without a single thought for the Markless girls they've selected–that has Ruti ask boldly, "Why were you watching me at the marketplace before you knew I took your ring?"

The Heir's back stiffens, but she doesn't turn. "Orrin will return after nightfall to escort you to my palace," she says. "If you flee, I will find you." It's a simple statement that Ruti doesn't doubt for an instant.

She reaches into her cloak and tosses something at Ruti. Ruti catches it without thinking. It's a pair of gold silken gloves, bound together, the material thick enough to conceal a mark–or lack thereof–on one's palm. The Heir smiles, her eyes cold, and throws Ruti a second, smaller pair.

She had known that Ruti would ask to bring Kimya, had read her easily from two interactions, and a shiver passes through Ruti that has little to do with the wind that the Heir brings with her. "I will always be one step ahead of you, Markless witch," the Heir says, and she whirls around. "Do not forget that."

She steps from the shop, the wind racing wild through the room for another moment, and then, finally, the air is still.

5

"We could still run," Ruti mutters to Kimya. Night has fallen, and their possessions are all packed up. The table and cot had gotten Ruti fewer coin than she'd wanted, but she hadn't had time to haggle, not when they had to leave tonight.

But to where, she hadn't decided. The Heir's eyes follow Ruti when she thinks of hurrying to the harbor and finding a ship to smuggle herself out of Somanchi. *If you flee, I will find you.* Ruti knew too much now to be forgotten, and running away is no longer so simple.

She loathed the Heir for casting her into this position in the first place. For sauntering into Ruti's shop and taking away all of her choices, for bringing Kimya into this. For having the temerity to be *handed* a soulbond and reject it when Markless have nothing at all.

And for *Orrin*, no less, a hulking brute of a fool who was going to arrive any minute. "We could just . . . climb onto a boat and run far away," Ruti says wistfully. "The Heir would give up eventually. How hard is it to disappear?"

Kimya's hands sign a familiar motion that she has taught Ruti, a question: *How would we eat?* The Markless aren't prideful because they can't afford to be prideful, because a choice between pride and food will end in death. Ruti sighs, conceding the point and bringing up another. "And what happens if I can't sing the magic she needs?" It's another niggling doubt, the fear of failing at this new task. "What will she do to us?"

Kimya shrugs. Better to have food now and worry later, Ruti knows. But this is a risk that she's wary of taking. The Heir isn't kind, and she despises Markless just as much as any noble. To step into her domain is a bad idea, especially without an exit plan.

Still, she's just as tempted by the promise of food. If she weren't, then she would have left for a ship hours ago instead of lingering in front of the shop, waiting for their summons.

Markless boys roam the street, spotting them and giving them a wide berth as they recognize the shop. There are others out, too, ragged Unbonded who have never found their soulbonds. Even the poorest of the Bonded won't venture into the filth of the slums, but the Unbonded who lurk here are different. There are some Markless who have lived long enough to have children of their own, Ruti knows, children born with marks most of the time. Those Unbonded wear Markless shame and feel deep resentment toward the Markless. Few outside the slums will raise their palms to touch the palm of a Markless spawn.

Those Unbonded are the ones Ruti is most wary of. Their rage is as strong as their hunger, and they will destroy without fear of retaliation, will attack even a witch without thought of the consequences. Ruti's eyes flicker past those with half moons unfinished on their palms. Today, she keeps to the shadows with Kimya, waiting for Orrin to return.

He appears in the distance, clomping through the streets. His lips are thinned so that they disappear beneath the scant hair under his nostrils, making him look sourer than ever. A few Markless see him from afar. They let out jeering shouts, hurtling toward him as though to attack, and Orrin raises a thick-fingered hand and blasts them away without a second thought.

For all his idiocy, he's *lethal*, and the Markless boys are thrown back, shaking violently in the aftermath of the blast. They twitch on the ground, their skin blackened by the energy, and Orrin scoffs and walks past their bodies as though he's done so a hundred times before.

"You," he grunts, stopping in front of Ruti. "Follow me."

Ruti and Kimya follow him silently, Ruti's fingers fidgeting in the gloves that the Heir had given her. They're soft and expensive, a fabric unlike any Ruti's touched before, and they feel out of place against the coarse-spun ecru of her shirt and her mismatched, faded blue pants. Still, they'll conceal the fact that Ruti is Markless in the palace.

Her face, though, will still be a problem. "Doesn't the Regent want me dead?" she points out. "How are you going to hide me in the palace?"

Orrin doesn't spare them a glance. "The Heir has private chambers in the palace where others are forbidden to enter," he says brusquely. "You will be housed there." He leads them to a decrepit stable where a royal animal cart is waiting. "Get in."

"Sure you won't catch a disease from our Markless hands touching it?" Ruti says.

Orrin gives her a dark look. "The Heir will not find your little gibes amusing," he says, his voice low, his diction stilted. "You will find that she doesn't suffer fools gladly."

"She seems fine with you," Ruti retorts. Kimya tugs at her shirt in warning, but Ruti sits back, smug in her tiny defiances. Orrin won't do a thing to her now, she knows. The Heir needs Ruti, and she won't be forgiving if Orrin dispatches of her instead of bringing her to the palace.

Orrin sneers at her, but doesn't attack. Instead, he hisses, "You are a filthy *nothing,* Markless. And I have the love of the future queen. Do you know what will become of you when I become her consort?"

"You will shower me in gratitude for making your position possible?" Ruti suggests. She wonders where his soulbond is, if the girl had died or simply fled when she'd met Orrin. Ruti wouldn't blame her.

"You will do what the Heir orders of you," Orrin says, his smile cold. "And you will keep that gaping maw of yours *shut*, or I will make sure that you languish in the dungeons until you starve to death. Markless *brat*."

He turns away from her, pulling at the reins of the cart, and they ride in silence through the night.

Once at the palace, they're brought in through a hidden entrance watched by a woman wearing a guard's heavy black-and-silver shirt, a spear held tightly at attention. Orrin passes them each a delicate ash-colored cloak to conceal their ragged, slum-filthy clothes, and Ruti ducks her head as he says gruffly, "Private delivery for the Heir."

The guard doesn't examine them for more than a second, but sharp eyes flicker over them from under her heavy brow. She steps aside, allowing Orrin to walk them into the courtyard. It isn't the courtyard where Ruti had been put on trial. Instead, it's the courtyard behind the palace, and inside of it are the lush, spreading plants of the wet woods, insects alighting on large fronds and buzzing in front of them as they walk. They are uncultivated here, growing wild and trimmed only to create a path, and Ruti basks in the sensation of the cool mud against her bare feet.

Too soon, they've passed through the gardens to the inner palace, and Orrin leads them to a heavy stone door that he has to grunt to pull open. Inside, there are well-made metal pots and pans in front of her, and a fire burning in an oven just across from the door. A multitude of servants bustle through the kitchens, hands crusted with moistened flour and white clothes splotched with grease and other stains. They pay the new arrivals no heed, busy with their dinner cleanup, and Ruti's mouth waters as she takes in the scents of freshly baked food and meat–*meat*–fried in oil. Ruti's never even *tasted* meat before.

There's more food than she's ever seen. There are fresh mangoes diced into precise squares and unripe tamarinds that smell tangy and sour. A tall boy stirs coconut milk into an eggplant curry at a counter near Ruti, the smell so strong and rich that her stomach turns, overwhelmed. There are luscious pastries with warm chocolate oozing from them and fluffy, soft loaves of wheat bread with a scent that overpowers all others on their side of the kitchen. The food in this palace could feed the entire population of the slums for a day, maybe longer.

Kimya's long-fingered hand flashes out from her cloak in a glimmer of gold to snatch a creamy pastry topped with berries from a discarded plate, and Orrin makes an irritated sound but doesn't stop her. Happily, she eats her pastry, and Ruti wishes for the first time that she could be as careless as Kimya, as quick to brazenly steal what she wants.

They're led from the kitchens up a staircase, and from there down a hallway to a wooden door marked with textured golden ornamentation shaped into a circle. Orrin raps on the door once, then takes a step back. "No men may enter the Heir's chambers," he says grudgingly. "Not until she is wed."

Ruti says, "So we can go in but you can't?" It's a childish taunt, one she can't resist, and Orrin's glower deepens.

The door opens just in time, sparing Ruti the burning of a lifetime. "Ah," a square-jawed woman says in a silvery voice, beaming at them and pressing a tanned, strong hand to each of their gloved right palms. "Come in! Come in! Oh, you're a *mess*," she says critically, eyeing Ruti's grimy face and narrow build and then Kimya's slight figure and the long, tangled hair spilling from the hood of her cloak. "And you're just a child. How old are you?" Kimya uncurls seven spindly fingers. "Inside," the woman says briskly, her wide violet pants swishing against the floor as she moves. "Quickly."

She slams the door behind them, cutting off Ruti's last sight of the outside and Orrin's put-off face.

The woman takes them in, eyes flickering over the tattered cloth beneath their cloaks and their dirty faces while Ruti takes in the room. They are in a wide hall with a ceiling that stretches many feet higher than any she's seen, a polished ebony table across the middle of the room, and a few gold-trimmed chairs with ornately shaped legs against the walls. The most impressive sight in the room is a window that stretches across the far wall, large and wide, offering a view of the Inner Circle and the tamed, colorful gardens of the front of the Royal Square. At the center of the window is an altar to the Spotted One, fresh with herbal offerings upon it that fill the room with the sharp scent of peppercorns and the sweetness of fig tree sap.

There are various doors on both sides of the hall that all lead to narrow corridors, but only one has a black-clad female guard standing beside it. The others are hubs of activity, guards and other women passing through them and out the door to the main hall, carrying colorful clothing and linens in expensive fabrics with shimmering highlights, or other items to be cleaned or put away.

Ruti glances back at the square-jawed woman, who cleared her throat. "I am Kalere," she says. Her words are business-like, her movements quick and sure, and she speaks with a confidence that lacks unkindness. "The Heir's Master Attendant. These are the Heir's chambers." She points to the guarded hallway, and Ruti can see a two-doored archway just beyond it, the woodgrain dark and sleek and the knobs that meet in the center gleaming silver. "Under no circumstances may you enter that room. Otherwise, you will be confined to these chambers for the duration of your stay here."

They are attracting stares, and for the first time, Ruti is self-conscious about how she must look: a filthy child dressed in rags, too small for her age and with the weathered meanness that the slums sharpen on every Markless's face, with none of the finery expected in the palace. Kalere sighs, seeing her gaze wander. "We'll have to clean you up before you see the Heir," she says disapprovingly. "Where did she find you?"

She leads them down one hallway to an enormous round tub with walls that go nearly to Ruti's chest, the heat steaming the glass mirrors that line one wall and plastering sweat against Ruti's face. "Mikuyi, put out the fire," Kalere instructs, and a Bonded attendant hurries forward to extinguish the low flames burning beneath the tub with a wave of her hand. "I want these two bathed and presentable," she orders. "Naima!" Another attendant steps up. "Find them new clothing. None of this will do."

Ruti and Kimya are undressed, each of them guided into one side of the tub. The water is hot, and Ruti lets out a little hiss when it touches her skin. "Is everything all right?" Mikuyi says worriedly.

"It's just . . . hot," Ruti says. Her skin feels warm now, too. She's never experienced a bath in anything but the cool, muddy River Somanchi, so this is a new experience. She closes her eyes, lifting a hand to slide with effort through her tangled, matted hair, and then she hears a choked gasp.

Oh. Her unmarked palm is visible to the attendants, and she bites her lip, uncertain how this will play out. Kalere speaks, her brow furrowed. "You are . . . does the Heir know of your . . . condition?"

"That we're Markless, you mean?" Ruti says, no patience for artifice. "She certainly called me *Markless scum* enough times when she ordered me here."

Kalere and the others all exchange dubious glances. Finally, Kalere straightens. "We will do as the Heir commands, of course," she says airily. "Get to it."

Mikuyi kneels again, reaching out to take her hand with some trepidation. Ruti shuts her eyes again, and this time, Mikuyi takes a rough, short-bristled brush and begins to scrub it along her arms. "This might hurt," she says. "You're . . . well, it's going to take a while." She sounds apologetic, scraping at Ruti's shoulders and back. Kimya whimpers on the other side of the tub, and Ruti's eyes snap open to check on her.

Instead, she catches sight of herself in the mirrors. An attendant quietly combs through her hair as well, tugging through knots and pulling out dirt and twigs. It feels as though she's being scrubbed raw, as though every last inch of her skin is being cleaned of filth, and she turns obediently and lets the attendants work over her body without fighting it.

Her feet are massaged, the rough skin of her soles scraped with a porous stone until they're soft as a baby's, and attendants knead a soapy mixture that smells of pricey jasmine into her hair. By the time they're finished, the water is brown with filth and Ruti feels fresh-faced and new, like a delicate noble instead of the Markless from the slums that she is.

One of the attendants is a Bonded with earth skills. She dips her hands into the water and swirling dirt is pulled to her fingers, chunking together into a solid orb of brown mud that she drops into a bin. The water sparkles, fresh as the River Somanchi in the morning sun, clear and cleansing. Mikuyi heats the water again, and Ruti lies back in it, finally clean.

"Come," Kalere says briskly. She wraps Ruti and Kimya into matching brown linen, thick and warm with textured diamonds strewn across them. Kimya looks different now, her lengthy hair wound by the attendants into a mass of tight little jet-black coils that hang down her back to her waist. Ruti's hair hasn't been braided or wound, but it falls free in soft curls past her shoulders. She hardly recognizes herself in the mirror, with her silky skin and defined cheekbones; the color of her hair now almost amber instead of a shade of mud. They both look suddenly noble, wealthy Bonded instead of scruffy Markless, and Ruti gulps when Mikuyi brings in satin, gleaming dresses for them to wear with their golden gloves.

"We'd be robbed in an instant if we stepped back into the slums looking like this," Ruti mutters, and Kimya giggles silently. There's a strange feeling to sitting in this room, dressed in finery. She feels like someone else, like this is all a terrible jest at her expense.

It only gets worse when Kalere leads them into the hall of the Heir's chambers. The Heir stands by the big window, speaking to another attendant, and Ruti catches only the tail end of the conversation. "The first prince is due to arrive next week. We can only plead with the spirits that he will be my Bonded," she says, a wry note of irony in her voice. The attendant doesn't catch it, nodding vigorously, and the Heir says, "And I have some—who is this?"

Her voice is sharp as she turns to face them, but her eyes are startled, and they sweep over Ruti slowly, taking in her gown and then moving up to her face. For a moment, her eyes flicker down again, a second once-over, a gleam of interest in her eyes.

Ruti says mockingly, "Have you forgotten me this quickly?" Kimya grabs her wrist in warning.

The Heir's eyes clear and narrow as she recognizes Ruti at last. "Markless lackey," she says, dismissive, and the spark of interest is gone, replaced by a dark tint at her high, strong cheekbones. "I see Kalere has taken care of you."

Kimya makes a motion with her hands. Ruti says, "Not completely. We haven't been fed."

"It's the middle of the night," the Heir snaps. "Dinner is over."

Ruti stands her ground. The Heir made them promises, and Markless can't afford to let promises of food slide because of mere etiquette. No one is ever going to like them, so the most they can aim for is satiated, not beloved. "My assistant is hungry. You offered us food and drink."

The Heir fixes her cold eyes on Ruti, a rumble of thunder in the distance. "Don't make yourself difficult, Markless. I will do as I please." But she turns, finding Kalere beside them, and she snaps, "Give them some old bread. And get this eyesore and her *assistant* out of my hall."

She turns around, sweeping toward the guarded hallway, her white gown moving with her. Ruti watches her for a few seconds too long, eyes tracing the curves of her body for an unconscious moment, and Kalere says, "Watch yourself, Markless." Her clear voice isn't harsh, only knowing, and Ruti flushes.

"I wasn't–" She *hates* the Heir, and her eyes are only seeing what is on display. She can't stop herself from *seeing*.

Kalere tuts. "I say it for your own good," she says. "Not for hers." Ruti sputters, humiliated at the very implication, and Kalere puts an arm around Kimya's shoulders. "Come, child," she says. "Let's find you something as delicious as that smile of yours, shall we?"

They stroll off toward the kitchens, Ruti trailing sulkily behind them.

K alere leaves them in a room as vast as Ruti's entire shop in the slums, set with a sleek-topped table against one wall and two beds with springy mattresses and thick blankets that smell like they've been freshly washed. Ruti takes one bed, motioning for Kimya to take the other. Kimya shudders and vigorously shakes her head, curling up against Ruti on the bed beside the window. She's asleep in moments, a lump beneath warm blankets, and Ruti lies back on the soft bed and struggles to sleep.

It's hard, harder than she'd have imagined. Everything about this new world she's been thrust into is dizzying, most of all the Heir at whose beck and call she seems to be. In the slums, at least she'd been her own master.

She'd been only eleven when she stumbled across a grey-eyed man who had sung a vine to bloom, little red fruits blossoming and growing before her eyes. He'd offered her one, but she'd been even hungrier for the song. In it, she had heard power, and power meant survival.

He must have seen something in her eyes that made him think she might have the skill for it. He taught her the song that day, helped her modulate the key and chant until she'd been able to feel the spirits responding to her call. Her chanting is only a cry to them, and she has learned, bit by bit, the highs and lows that each song needs to offer the spirits, how each chant might work or might not. The spirits need nothing from the Bonded that they endow with their magic. They have everything except for song, and Ruti's voice is something that they crave enough to reward her for.

She has never been very good at chanting food into being, not like the old man. Her vines grow, but they rarely bloom. Instead, her first composition had been for the paint. She'd learned how to paint half marks and full marks on her palm, and the song had held one in place for a long time. For weeks she traipsed out to the elaborate estates and the horse-drawn carriages of the Inner Circle, wandered through the color and shouts of the Merchants' Circle, and even glimpsed the multicolored flower beds of the Royal Square. A family found her and she lied, told them that she was an orphan, and they took her in without question.

She lived that lie for almost a week, basked in their care and their love and pretended that her endhi sign was too muted to express itself uncontrollably, and then one morning, her mark had been smudged. She'd been thrown from the house, watching affection turn to disgust, and she swore never to paint herself again with that chant.

There had been other chants since: protection chants that grow deeper and louder like thunder as they progress; healing chants that follow a gentle, flowing melody; and other songs that have brought people to her shop. Occasionally, she even got a few nobles, people who looked furtively around before whispering to her for a bright little chant for luck, a guttural and raw chant for children, or a song whose tones matched the cadences of the supplicant's voice for finding their soulbond. She'd been able to find the song for each one, calling to the spirits and offering them poultices of herbs that they might require in a more demanding song.

The Heir doesn't understand this magic, knows only the easy magic that the spirits present to the Bonded without conditions. What the Heir wants is something far beyond anything she's done before. It's a spell that will have to undo the very magic of soulbinding somehow, that will take away a power beyond any human comprehension. Soulbinding is a gift from the spirits, and they will not take well to her plea to be free of it. Ruti doesn't know how she can sing that request; which threads, colorations, modalities, or rhythms it might take; and what offerings might satisfy the spirits.

She shudders to imagine the Heir's wrath if Ruti proves useless. The Heir sees Ruti just as all the Marked see Markless—as nothing at all, as abominations that are less than human. If Ruti fails, she has no doubt that the Heir will punish her exactly as she promised. There is no mercy for the Markless. Even Kimya will suffer for Ruti's failure.

The thought of Kimya strengthens Ruti's resolve. She's just going to *have* to succeed, somehow.

She sings in a low voice, aware that only a curtain separates her room from the other attendants' rooms in the hallway. Slowly, she threads together a plaintive, regretful dirge of apology with a brassy chant for protection. Into that, she forms her lips into a circle to add the wistful, echoing tune that she uses to make her paints stay on a Markless palm. She reverses it gradually, changing the key from major to minor, as though to cast out the permanence of a mark instead of sealing it into the skin.

There is nothing. The slightest twitch of interest from the spirits, perhaps, but Ruti feels oddly removed from her own song in this comfortable bed high above the ground, in a room where there is no nature but a faint breeze–

A breeze. The curtain is rippling, and Ruti sits up, tugging her blanket to her. She's no longer in the gown that Kalere had given her; instead, she and Kimya had changed into long red tunics that are worn for bed. She feels the sudden urge to hide as Kimya does, a second lump beneath the downy weight of the blanket, but she resists it.

Instead, she returns to her song, turning away from the door deliberately. She winds together a braid of offerings– wheat, goat hairs, a length of reed from the River Somanchi– and joins the ends together to make a loose circle. The melody rises and falls with the motion of her hands; but still, it isn't quite sparking the magic that Ruti needs.

A voice cuts into her song as it wanes. "Does that work?"

Ruti doesn't look up. "I don't know yet."

The Heir's voice lowers. "Show some respect, Markless brat," she bites out. "Rise."

Ruti grits her teeth. The Heir says, "You will *kneel* when I enter your room. You are not my equal. When we are together in public, we will have to appear companions. But in private, you are *nothing*. Kneel."

Ruti glares at the wall. The breeze has become a full-blown wind, whipping around the room and pulling at Ruti's gown. She thinks of Kimya beneath the blanket and slides slowly out of bed. The Heir watches her, eyes as barbed and cutting as those of a Winged One, and Ruti makes a very gradual descent to her knees.

The wind slows. "Good," the Heir says. "Stand."

Ruti stands, glaring at her. The Heir contemplates her for a long moment. "I have told my uncle that I have chosen a new companion. The search for a soulbond can be a long and arduous task, and I will need a friend to help me through it." She smiles mirthlessly. "My uncle will not recognize you. You looked like a demonness when you were brought on trial. And my attendants are discreet."

The Heir scrutinizes the room, her hard eyes landing on the untouched bed beside Ruti's. "Where is the little one?"

Ruti doesn't answer. The Heir snaps, "I asked you a question, Markless."

"She's here," Ruti says irritably, gesturing at the lump under the blankets. The Heir's eyes flash, and Ruti adds, reluctant, "*Your Highness.*"

The Heir's lip curls. "We are going to have to do away with this attitude of yours, Markless. There are other witches in Zidesh."

"Not as good as I am, Your Highness," Ruti retorts, foot falling to one side so her hip can jut out in a semblance of confidence. Maybe it's a lie, maybe not. She's never met another witch. "You need me."

The Heir doesn't respond for a moment, her face sculpted like those of the Spotted Ones that sit at the entrance to the Merchants' Circle. "We shall see," she says at last. She wears white even to bed, a gown with a gold thread that ripples down the front. Her hair has been divided into five sections and braided, a few loose curls at the sides, and she wears no paint or jewelry. Even without it, she's a vision, and Ruti remembers Kalere's words and looks stubbornly at the wall instead.

The Heir says, "You will keep your gloves on at all times. Speak only when necessary outside of my chambers. Breathe no word of your true purpose here to *anyone.*" Her glare is probing, digging deep into Ruti and taking hold of her. "Have you finished your composition for me yet?"

"I'm *trying*." She can hear the petulance in her voice. It makes her sound less capable than she is, and she rephrases. "I'm too far from nature here. I can't feel the spirits."

The Heir regards her, studying her as though she might be able to see Ruti's lies with only a glance. "Very well," she says at last. "Come with me. You will rest when we are done."

Ruti half expects to be brought down to the dungeons now, already written off, but instead the Heir takes her down the stairs and through the quiet kitchens to the back courtyard. Ruti slides the offering around her wrist and hurries to keep up, inhaling the scent of the wet woods as they walk down the path through the trees and flowers and vines.

The Heir turns, stopping abruptly, and Ruti nearly crashes into her. She slips instead, tumbling back to her knees, and the Heir smiles, satisfied. "Good. Keep that up."

Ruti scowls. "I hate you," she snaps, climbing back to her feet. Her red tunic is soiled at the knees now, brown with mud.

"You don't have to love me," the Heir says coolly, "only obey me." She straightens, staring at Ruti with distaste. "Well? Sing."

Through her clenched jaw, Ruti bites out, "Yes, *Your Highness*." She scowls, and it takes a moment before she can collect her chants again. She clears her throat and her mind, holds out the offering that she'd woven together, and begins the lilting melody that she had sung in her room.

Now she can feel the energy that it sparks, the magic that seems to flow from the spirits to her as she follows the lines that wind through the world, calling to the spirits for guidance and assistance. She asks the Spotted One again for persistence, calls on the Scaled One's speed and agility, cries to the Toothed One for power, and the Maned One for dignity. Each listens, and each gives her a little piece of itself, and she can feel the power floating around her as she lifts her hands to take the Heir's–

The Heir recoils, repulsed, and Ruti is jolted rudely from the song. "Don't *touch* me, Markless," the Heir snarls, thunder rumbling around them.

Ruti straightens, flushing. "Do you want me to stop your soulbinding or not?" she demands. "I thought that you, of all people, would be less . . . less prejudiced about it," she says resentfully. The Heir only glares at her, delicate hands tucked together away from Ruti. "You don't want to be Bonded. I can't be Bonded. There's nothing to be afraid of."

The Heir stares at Ruti's hands. Ruti had tucked the gloves under one arm when she'd begun her song, and now she twists her fingers together uncomfortably, sliding them through the untaken offering to return it to her wrist. The Heir's eyes are drawn to Ruti's blank palm. "It's unnatural," she says.

Ruti scoffs. "Strong words for someone who wants to resist her own soulbond. At least I was born not to bond."

The Heir's eyes flash, but she doesn't reprimand Ruti this time, and Ruti plunges on, digging the hole around herself a little deeper. "Don't you think it's kind of selfish to leave your Bonded to be alone forever?" she challenges. "With an uncontrolled energy around him for eternity instead of the powers he was born for?"

The Heir is not impressed. "He'll survive," she says curtly.

"What about Orrin's Bonded? She must already know him, if he has his powers." Ruti hasn't thought about Orrin, Bonded and in love with someone else, until now. The thought of a Bonded choosing someone else is scandalous, a story to whisper in the dark and giggle at, but hardly a real experience. "How can you take away her soulbond?"

The Heir is silent, standing rigid, and she says at last, "Orrin and his soulbond don't know each other. He was born in Kîaene, in the south. He was bonded at only three to a girl in his village. My father had young Bonded children collected and trained. Her family refused to let her go and left Zidesh. Orrin was brought to the castle. He has no connection to his Bonded. And he loves me." She says it with grim certainty, with no joy or affection in her eyes. Even in love, she is emotionless.

"Of course he does," Ruti says scornfully, if only to get a reaction from the Heir. "You're the Heir. You're powerful and you're pretty and . . ." Her voice trails off. The Heir blinks at her, and Ruti isn't imagining the amusement in her eyes this time. It gentles them, makes her look like a girl instead of an imperious royal. "But he doesn't belong to you," Ruti finishes too late, her cheeks hot.

The Heir stares at her, her gaze growing cold again, and she holds her hands out to Ruti. They waver in place, betraying anxiety, and her wrists stiffen to quell the trembling. "I think we should begin now," she says abruptly, and Ruti reaches out to hold her hands.

They are warm, warmer than Ruti would have expected, and they are delicate in Ruti's grasp. The Heir's jaw works beneath her skin as Ruti's palm touches hers, but she is silent this time, eyes fixed on Ruti's face. They drift closed as Ruti begins to sing, her breath emerging in quiet little puffs, the lightest whisper.

Ruti sings a larghetto barrier between the Heir's mark and anyone who touches her, and hopes that it will be enough. She is asking too much of the spirits, can feel their displeasure at the request, and she infuses her desperation into the song, begging them only to give her this.

There is a sharp movement from the Winged One, who reigns above the others in the sky and thinks little of the small humans and their pleas from the ground. Ruti feels talons rake into her skin as she sings, a warning that she asks too much. The invisible mark they leave stings, but she persists through the pain, turning her cry to the mighty spirits of the land.

At last they answer, and the offering is pulled apart and blown away into the wind. The Heir's hands glow and she opens her eyes again, staring at Ruti. Ruti stares back, mesmerized by the way that the Heir's skin seems to almost shine like fire in the light of the magic, an orange tinge to her face, and the air feels heavier as their gazes lock, harder to breathe through it.

Ruti chants more, again and again singing her request, and finally, reluctantly, the spirits grant it. Magic washes over them both. The Heir shivers, her hands trembling in Ruti's, and she looks less imposing for a moment, more like that girl Ruti's age again. The magic engulfs her as Ruti sings, and then, at last, it seems to retreat, leaving behind an invisible barrier.

"It should stop your mark from touching the mark of another," Ruti says, her voice throaty with the effort of singing and the force of the Heir's eyes on hers. "I don't know how long it'll hold."

The Heir hesitates a moment, eyes closing as she takes a deep breath, and when she looks at Ruti again, her gaze is ice and steel. "Your life will depend on the answer to that question," she says, and Ruti lets the Heir's hands go.

They had been so warm, and Ruti's cold hands—to her chagrin—feel their loss at once.

7

After a morning meal in the windowed hall, Ruti is brought, sleepy-eyed, to stand before the Heir again. "You will join me in my daily routine," the Heir orders. She wears white again, the color reserved only for royalty, this dress with an elaborate gold midsection. Her temples have been painted with a gold ochre highlight, the color glowing against her brown skin, and she looks particularly regal today.

Kalere dressed Ruti in a matching dress of brown-gold, and Ruti only realizes that when she sees the Heir. She scowls, and the Heir catches it. "Is that a problem?" she says, her voice low and dark, and Ruti shakes her head.

"No," she says, and tosses out a mocking, "*Your Highness.*" Behind the Heir, Mikuyi winces at her tone. The Heir's eyes flash.

She's distracted by Kimya, who moves to stand beside Ruti, her eyes inquisitive as she slips a hand into Ruti's and signs. "No," Ruti says immediately, recognizing her request. "You aren't coming along."

Kimya frowns at her. Ruti lowers her voice. "*Stay*, Kimya. Kalere will look after you." Kimya has never been *looked after*, not in the sense that Ruti knows Kalere will.

Kimya looks unimpressed at that. Kalere sweeps in, crouching beside Kimya. "Today, we wash the linens and clean these chambers," she says. "Do you think you could help with that?"

Kimya bobs her head, distracted, and Ruti straightens. The Heir gives Kimya a cool glance and then turns to Ruti. "Your sole purpose here is to provide comfort to me," she says. "No one you meet will ask you for any more than that." She glances at Ruti's hand, her nose wrinkling. "Just your name will suffice."

Ruti tilts her head. "You're going to have to come up with a better name for me than *Markless filth*, then," she says. Mikuyi, again, looks faint at her boldness.

But the Heir barks out a startled, throaty laugh, her eyes lighting up like jewels against her skin for an instant. She looks to regret it a moment later, thunder rumbling and her expression settling back into its emotionless façade. "Shame," she says dryly. "It suited you so well."

She walks toward Ruti abruptly, and Ruti stiffens as the Heir approaches. She blinks and the Heir has walked past her to the door of her chambers. "Keep up," the Heir orders, and Ruti twists around and trails after her, already annoyed.

Outside, Orrin awaits the Heir, as though Ruti isn't irritated enough already. "Her," he says, looking at Ruti with deep dislike. He presses his palm to the Heir's in greeting, but ignores Ruti's gloved one. "Has she proven useful?"

The Heir turns her right hand over to regard the semicircle sign of sewa on her palm. "Only the spirits know," she says. "Come." Her hand slides over Orrin's for a moment, an instant of tenderness that Ruti nearly misses. Orrin smiles at her, his distaste for Ruti forgotten. When he watches the Heir, it is without the grip of ownership that Ruti has seen from boys in the slums, only attentiveness. "I must change. I have lessons this morning."

The Heir keeps a structured day, moving through the palace grounds with Orrin trailing behind her. The Royal Square is in fact a hollow, one-story rectangle, with guards' rooms and barracks and servants' quarters in the rooms within it. Inside the rectangle are a series of courtyards and gardens and temples for the spirits, well protected by the guards, and in the center of the rectangle is a tall, squarish castle that holds the Heir's quarters and the Regent's as well. There is a large banquet hall that they pass through on their way out, busy with servants who tidy up for the next meal, and a main hall beyond the banquet hall that leads into the front courtyards.

Ruti recognizes the far courtyard as the one where her trial had been. To the right of it, she sees a staircase leading below the rectangle of barracks into the dungeons, and she shudders. The Heir sees it. Her eyes are on Ruti when Ruti looks up, and her smile is thin and sharp.

They're walking through a different courtyard, toward the outer rectangle, when the Heir pauses. She looks unhappy, her fingers pressing against her palms, and Ruti watches her warily. The Heir is unpredictable, and she seems to revel in it, in the fear that threatens their interactions time and again. Ruti refuses to let fear consume her. She has spent a lifetime learning to sing so she could live a life without fear, and no royal will change *that*.

The Heir's fingers twitch again, and Ruti's wariness begins to shift to curiosity. "What?" she says, staring at her.

Orrin says gruffly, "Do *not* speak to the princess in that tone."

But the Heir doesn't respond to Ruti's tone, only stiffens as a look of sheer frustration crosses her face. Finally, she bites out, "Well, what is it?"

It takes Ruti a moment to understand, and when she does she can't stop the laugh that escapes her lips. "Your Highness," she says, and it feels *good* to be this smug, to talk down to the most powerful person in the kingdom. "Are you asking for my name?"

The Heir's lip curls and she refuses to respond. Ruti prods further. "I know *your* name, Dekala," she says. It's daring to say it like that, bordering on treasonous, but the Heir appears too stymied to respond to it. "It's rather rude to subjugate someone and bring them into your palace as a companion without even learning their name."

She's dancing on a fine line, hovering above the ground with her life in the Heir's hands, and she should be *sensible*. And yet there is something addictive about the cold murder gleaming in the Heir's eyes right now, her discomfort at having to *ask* something. "How will you introduce me as your companion?" Ruti wonders aloud. "Witch? Brat? A girl you picked up from the slums?"

The Heir turns on her heel and marches toward an open door in the rectangle. Ruti hurries to catch up, Orrin left a distance behind them, and says, "I go by Ruti. Your Highness."

The Heir doesn't respond. Ruti says, irritable, "You're *welcome*."

"Insolent brat," the Heir says at last, the wind remarkably cold around Ruti. "*Ruti.*" Her voice seems to caress Ruti's name, lingering at the final note of it for a moment before she lets the syllable drop. Ruti swallows, an odd warmth washing over her. Kimya doesn't speak, and there are few others who call her by name. She is known as *witch*, as *Markless*, as *girl* and nothing more. The youngest Markless make friends, and the friends who live until adulthood have allies and power because of it. But the solitary ones survive by keeping to themselves.

There is a power to names, but Ruti never understood the depth of that power until now, as the Heir speaks her name into existence. If Ruti were Unbonded, she thinks, the world's energies would be thrumming around her right now.

The Heir doesn't notice Ruti's reaction—or if she does, she doesn't comment on it. Instead, she steps through the open door and is greeted by a smiling man named Tembo, who instructs the Heir on stick fighting.

Ruti says in surprise, "*You* fight?"

Tembo blinks, looking startled at her appearance. He presses his palm to her gloved one, and Ruti sees that he is Unbonded, the sign of ashto on his palm.

"Of course," the Heir says, and she flicks her wrist. The stick in her hands moves with shocking dexterity, a blur in the air as she maneuvers and twists and stands in defensive position as Ruti scrambles back from her. "A queen must know how to defend herself." She moves again, leaping in a dance with the stick that has Ruti composing a new song to it in her mind, and Tembo takes another stick and matches her movements.

By the time they're done, the Heir is drenched in sweat and retires to her chambers for a bath. In the afternoon, the Heir sits patiently through lessons with a tutor, discussing kingdom policy and geography while Ruti tries not to doze off. "Prince Torhvin's farmers have been bringing in paltry harvests this year," the tutor says. "Hardly anything to watch."

The Heir shakes her head. "But Rurana is flourishing. You said that they've been rebuilding their old palace in Byale and have made a new treaty with the Diri pirates. How can that be possible if the harvests are bad?"

The tutor raises her hands helplessly. "We can't ascertain why. Prince Torhvin's palace is impenetrable. Even our spies learn only what Torhvin wishes them to." She brightens. "Perhaps he will share his methods with you if he arrives to court you."

Orrin grumbles under his breath. Ruti whispers, "He sounds very capable," if only to watch Orrin's glower deepen.

Her tutor's words are enough to displease the Heir, and she rises abruptly. "It is time for the evening meal," she says. "My uncle the Regent awaits me."

Ruti tenses. Once they're outside of the tutor's chamber, she hurries to walk beside the Heir and says, "Wouldn't it be better if I ate in your chambers?" The thought of seeing the Regent again makes her nauseous, aware of how tenuous her safety here is.

The Heir gives her a cool look. "You will eat the evening meal as my companion," she says in a tone that brooks no argument, and she strides down the staircase, Ruti trailing behind her.

Still, there's a tense thunder that sounds as the Heir walks into the banquet hall, each step accompanied by a dull roar. The Regent sits at the head of a long table, his wife at his left and an empty seat at his right. The Heir stands in the doorway, Ruti hovering behind her with a sick feeling in her stomach.

But the Regent doesn't recognize the grimy girl from the slums who now stands in front of him in royal-made finery. "Who is this?" he says, his eyes narrowing as he takes her in. Ruti gets the sense that her worth is being assessed beneath his glare, and she is found wanting.

"Uncle," the Heir says calmly. "I have chosen a companion." She looks pointedly at the courtier seated beside her empty chair, and the woman scrambles to her feet, hurriedly taking a seat at the far end of the table. "This is Ruti, cousin to the king of Kaguruk. We have been exchanging letters for a number of years, and she has been so kind to offer to comfort me throughout this . . . ordeal."

"A companion," the Regent repeats, and cocks his head. "I did not know that you had a friend." He says it with a note of curiosity, apparently genuine. Ruti doesn't trust a word from his mouth, and she stays stiffly beside the Heir and awaits her cue.

The Regent stands, raising his hand, and the Heir nods Ruti forward. "A pleasure to meet you, Ruti," he says, still with a glimmer of suspicion in his eyes. "I don't think your cousin has ever mentioned you."

"Disappointing," Ruti says as she presses her hand to the Regent's. Her heart races as she struggles to keep a calm demeanor. "He always told me that I was his favorite." She knows nothing of Kaguruk, but she can tell from the curious eyes on her that no one else here seems to, either.

The Regent eyes her gloved hand. The Heir says, "It is the custom in Kaguruk to wear gloves until soulbinding. The people choose to search for their Bonded *before* their bonding." There's a murmur at the table, and the Regent's glare turns to his niece. "Imagine," the Heir says dryly, "having a choice in your bonding."

"An idiotic waste of time," the Regent counters, pulling his hand from Ruti's and sitting back at the table. The Heir takes the seat beside him, Ruti sitting with her and noticing with spiteful pleasure that Orrin remains standing. "As is you bringing this girl all that distance for what will be a quick soulbinding with no complications."

The Heir lifts her chin. "Orrin thought it might calm me." She shoots a rare smile at the bodyguard behind her. His chest puffs out and Ruti makes a face at her plate. There is food on it already, a thick piece of meat and flat cornbread and a mixture of fruit, and she begins to eat.

She hears a gasp. When she looks up, she sees horrified, scandalized faces fixed on her, and she notices suddenly that every other plate is untouched. Orrin bends down to hiss, "Wait for the princess, you boor!"

The Heir sighs loudly. "Well?" she says, turning to Ruti. The Regent looks livid. The Heir ignores him, her eyes boring into Ruti's but her lips curved into a polite smile. "Is it any good?"

Eyes are fixed on them, awaiting Ruti's punishment. Ruti shrugs. "I've had better," she says, an outrageous lie that only one person at the table will recognize for what it is, and the Heir lets out a little huff of laughter and takes a bite.

The courtiers relax, turning to their food at last. The Regent still looks thunderous. "Orrin," he says, seizing on the last thing that the Heir had mentioned. "That boy spends too much time around you."

Orrin stubbornly stays where he is, three feet back from the Heir's seat. The Heir says, her voice sharp, "He is my bodyguard."

"But he is *not* your Bonded," the Regent reminds her. "Forgetting that will cause you nothing but heartbreak." A cool breeze whips around him.

The Regent's wife speaks up. Ruti remembers that the Regentess Adyana had been a third princess of Guder before she bonded with the Regent. She is plain-looking, not nearly as radiant as the Heir, but her smile has a brightness that brings warmth to the room. "I once thought I was in love," she says. "I had a dear friend in my city with whom I was sure that I would spend my life. But when I met your uncle, Dekala, everything changed. I knew before our palms ever touched that he would be my Bonded." She touches her hand to her glass and water fills it, clear as crystal. "It will be like that for you as well."

The Heir's voice is cold, a sharp contrast to her aunt's words. "It will never be like that for me," she snaps, thunder rumbling through the banquet hall.

The Regent's voice is just as sharp. "Very well," he barks. "You wish to *get to know* each suitor before you attempt the soulbinding? I will grant you that. But you *will* attempt the soulbinding." He impales his meat with a sharp fork, cutting it vigorously.

"I don't want to be Bonded at all," the Heir says irritably. She sounds younger in the presence of her guardian, closer to her twenty years. Ruti focuses on her food, unwilling to attract the Regent's attention again.

The Regent pops a piece of meat into his mouth. "An Unbonded girl can hold no kingdom," he says definitively. "You are weak and uncontrolled." He chews, the food visible in his mouth. "Perhaps Prince Kobe of Machajabe will change that when he arrives next week."

The air in the room grows abruptly thin, as though they have all scaled a great peak and can hardly breathe. The courtiers choke, as does the Regent, spitting out his meat onto his plate as the Heir glares at him. Ruti struggles for breath, but it comes in jagged bursts.

The Heir's fingers dig into her palms, and she grits her teeth. Slowly, the air level returns to normal. "You see?" the Regent says, satisfied. "You are incomplete Unbonded. I simply can't give you your kingdom like this."

The Heir stands, knocking her chair back into Orrin. "I will take my leave," she grits out, and she twists around and walks from the banquet hall.

Ruti casts a wistful look at her meat, juicy and delicious and hardly touched, and follows.

The Heir is in a foul mood in the days that follow. When Ruti is in a bad mood, she tends to take it out on debris in the streets or Markless kids fool enough to harass her. Ruti likes to *fight*, to get out her anger until there's nothing left.

The Heir is different. She bottles up her anger and lets it simmer, emerging only in wisps of uncontrolled power. Though the Heir has sewa, by far the least destructive of marks, Ruti is beginning to understand exactly what it's capable of when she wakes up for the third night in a row because thunder is crashing around her. This time, even Kimya stirs, and she sits up and squints around while Ruti lies stubbornly in her bed with her eyes clamped shut. She knows who has come to visit again, and she refuses to acknowledge her until forced.

"Stop," the Heir says, and she sounds frustrated. "Stop making those motions; I don't *understand* you." The bed creaks again, and the Heir says, "I ordered you to *stop*." Kimya lets out a little whimper.

Ruti rolls over, ready to tell off the Heir for being cruel to Kimya. But when she opens her eyes, she's startled to see the Heir crouching in front of Kimya, her dark eyes searching Kimya's gaze for something. "You're cold," the Heir finally guesses, and Kimya nods vigorously. The Heir crooks an eyebrow. "That's my doing," she says dryly. "I tend to bring my presence wherever I go."

Kimya jabs a finger at the door, a clear dismissal, and Ruti tenses. But the Heir only laughs lightly, the thunder calming around them. "I will leave in a moment," she promises. "I have need of your witch sister." Ruti snaps her eyes shut a moment too late, caught watching them, and she sees an instant of the Heir's rueful regard. She opens them again, and the Heir still has the ghost of a smile on her face, painting little lines into the skin beside her eyes. Ruti stares. The Heir purses her lips together, the smile fading. "Well? What are you waiting for?"

Kimya waves at them as Ruti follows the Heir from the room, and Ruti looks between them. "What?" the Heir snaps.

Ruti shrugs. "Just wondering if you're going soft." It's meant to provoke, as most of what she says to the Heir is.

The Heir scoffs. "In my uncle's fantasies, perhaps." A low chill falls over Ruti as they creep out of the Heir's chambers.

"A caravan has arrived outside of the Royal Square, and Prince Kobe must be with it. I want you to strengthen your magic on my mark."

Ruti sighs. They've followed the same routine every day since Ruti has gotten here. In the morning, the Heir practices with Tembo. She departs at lunch to sit with the Regent in judgment, but in the afternoon Ruti is expected to join her with her tutors. They dine with the court at dinner and Ruti makes up new outrageous statements about what happens in Kaguruk, and then she's free to wander the Heir's chambers with Kimya until bedtime.

And every single night, without fail, the Heir has roused Ruti in the middle of the night and commanded her to do some paltry magic on the mark. At least tonight Kimya managed to distract the Heir from insisting that Ruti kneel first. "It's strong enough," Ruti says. "I can't make the spirits give me more than they've offered."

"Then I will find someone who can," the Heir snaps.

"You keep saying that, but you haven't replaced me yet," Ruti points out. "Is finding a witch harder than you thought?"

The Heir gives her a dark look. "Ntuka has three witches. Aelin has eight. Somanchi's Merchants' Circle alone has a dozen witches who would be happy to serve their future queen. Zidesh has no shortage of witches."

Ruti blinks at her, startled. The Heir says it with confidence, no lie in her voice, and it occurs to Ruti for the first time that the Heir *means* it when she says that Ruti can be replaced. "Then why pick some Markless girl from the slums?"

The Heir says, "No one will notice your disappearance." It's coldly calculating, a cruel thing to say, and Ruti does her best to shrug it off and fails.

"So that's it? You brought me here to . . . what, die after I've served my purpose?" Ruti pieces it together with sudden dread. "If you never find your Bonded because of what I've done—what you've had me do—then I'm the only one keeping that secret," she says. The Heir regards her silently. "And you can't leave anyone behind who might know it." She stops in the middle of the hallway to stare up at the Heir, aghast at her betrayal. It hits all the harder after she just saw that glimpse of the Heir's unexpected gentleness with Kimya. "You're going to kill me no matter what, aren't you?"

She remembers, very suddenly, exactly how good the Heir is at combat, exactly how many guards are around them at any time, exactly how close the dungeons are. She's known that she might die if she fails, has pushed herself night after night to ask the spirits for more because of that, but it hasn't crossed her mind that even success will doom her.

She spins around, ready to turn back and grab Kimya and flee, but a hand lands on her arm, restraining her. "My life is in your hands," the Heir says, and she sounds more subdued now, the coolness tempered with an emotion that Ruti can't read. "My future is yours. If I have to take precautions, then. . . ."

Ruti clenches her jaw, furious and terrified, and the Heir murmurs, "I will have use for a witch in my court when I am queen. If you give me no reason to silence you, then I will not." It is distant, disinterested, and that infuriates Ruti even more.

"So either I die or I'm yours forever? Will I never be free of you?" She cherishes her freedom, power, and agency because she's scraped and fought for them for years. Now, in a flash, they've been stolen away from her.

The Heir straightens, looking down at her with eyes that have frosted over again. "I will be your queen," she reminds Ruti coldly. "You are mine by definition."

Ruti snorts. "You'll be the queen to the merchants and the farmers and the craftworkers. Never to the Markless. We don't exist in your world. You've all made sure of that."

The Heir glowers at her. "Run," she says.

Ruti stares at her. "So now you're just going to . . . what, throw me out of the palace? Is this some sort of test?" She can't make heads or tails of the Heir, and it's growing more and more frustrating. "Are you going to send guards after me and have me tried as a–"

"*No*, you *idiot*," the Heir hisses, and she seizes Ruti's hand and yanks her away from the staircase they just descended. Ruti opens her mouth and the Heir claps a hand over it, pulling her into the shadows beneath the stairs just as voices sound nearby.

"It's right past here, Your Highness." One of the Regent's main attendants is speaking, his voice low. "We are so thrilled to have you here. The princess has been so hopeful that you might be her soulbond."

"As am I," a man's full, booming voice responds. He makes no attempt at quiet. Ruti cranes her neck to peer past the staircase at him. He's considerably older than they are, past thirty years with a paunch only a royal could have, and he wears a gaudy velvet robe. *Prince Kobe*, she guesses. He speaks their language with the practiced accent of well-educated royalty. "I am the third son of a second son, and I have little chance of amounting to anything without a Bonded."

"I'm sure that's not true," the attendant says soothingly.

"I hear that the princess is a great beauty," Prince Kobe says, licking his lips. "And young, too. Does she have child-bearing hips? We are the land of the Toothed One, you know. The princes of Machajabe are as big-headed when we emerge from the birth canal as our patron spirit. My poor mother was bedridden for years after having me." He guffaws. The attendant is looking more and more uncomfortable by the moment.

Ruti twists around to glance at the Heir. The Heir is flattened against the staircase, wind flying around her, and she looks absolutely petrified. Her eyes are wide and horrified, and she turns her palm, staring down at the mark on it. "He seems nice," Ruti whispers, suddenly enjoying herself.

"I will have you cut to pieces and buried beneath the flower beds in the courtyard," the Heir snarls in a low voice. The prince and his entourage are retreating, moving past the kitchens to a complex beyond them.

"I mean, he was empathetic," Ruti says, grinning. "He was very worried about your . . . hips." She glances down at the Heir's hips, which are very nicely shaped indeed, though probably not for a big-headed Machajabe baby. "And he thinks you're beautiful, so he isn't unconscious."

"Must you continuously do that?" the Heir demands, glaring at her. She is discomfited, a new look on her that Ruti thoroughly enjoys. Ruti has been confined in the palace for long enough that it's a treat to see the Heir looking just as trapped as she feels.

"Do what?"

"Mock me," the Heir bites out. "Put me in a position where I have no choice but to execute you for your insolence. You overestimate your worth, Markless brat." But her words lack the smooth certainty that usually accompanies them, and Ruti realizes that the Heir is truly afraid.

She might deserve a soulbond like Prince Kobe, but Ruti isn't mean-spirited enough to wish him on her. "My magic will hold," she says firmly, and she struggles to muster up the confidence she wants to feel in it. "And there's no way he's your Bonded. Isn't a bonding supposed to be between two perfectly matched souls?"

The Heir watches her for a pained moment, the air in the hall very thin. Then she exhales, a breeze on Ruti's skin, and straightens. "Yes, of course," she says, her arrogance returned. "He will be an excellent test of your abilities, though." She turns, heading back to the stairs.

"Wait," Ruti says, puzzled. "I thought we were going to go outside to strengthen the magic." She pauses for a moment, piecing together what she knows of tonight, and says, "Did you know they'd bring the prince through this room? Did you just drag me out of bed to *spy* on him?"

The Heir raises her chin. "I couldn't bring Orrin," she says coolly. "He would be outraged on my behalf and pick a fight." Ruti is about to agree when the Heir adds, "And he needs his sleep."

"More than I do?" Ruti says dubiously. "At least I'm *useful* to you. He's a boor who spends all day hovering behind you." Orrin's only redeeming quality, as far as Ruti sees, is his unwavering loyalty to Dekala.

"Watch your tongue," the Heir snaps. "He is your future queen-consort."

"Not mine," Ruti reminds her stubbornly. The idea of Orrin being ruler of anything is laughable. He exists to linger in Dekala's shadow.

The Heir swoops close to her. Ruti stands her ground as the Heir places a finger beneath her chin to pull it up, glaring down at her with those sharp, imposing eyes. Ruti is wordless, caught in the Heir's stare, and she isn't sure if it's fear or defiance that stops her breath. "We shall see," the Heir says, her voice dark, and she drops her hand and stalks past Ruti and up the stairs.

The Heir is formally introduced to Prince Kobe at dinner, where he is seated between the Regent and the Heir and eats half of the food off her plate while he talks about his family's great fortune. "And I'm the heir to one quarter of one portion of that," he says self-importantly. "Nearly six farms and a large estate."

The Regent's eyes narrow. "I was told you were a favorite prince of your land," he says.

"Well, I'm certainly not the least favorite," the prince says heartily. "That would be my cousin the king, who nearly disowned me because of a few *tiny* card debts when the message came from your kingdom that you thought I might be sweet Princess Dekala's soulbond." He puts an arm around the Heir's seat. The air chills. "I love this quaint little idea she had to have a chat before we bond. She's going to be such a delight in our kingdom, I imagine."

The Regent looks a little ill. The Heir says, "I am ready for the soulbinding." She stands.

The Regent blinks at her, startled. "This was enough time for you?"

The Heir smiles, thin-lipped and cold. "When you know, you know," she says, turning to face Prince Kobe. "Why don't we go for a walk in my gardens?"

Orrin's eyes are thunderous from behind the Heir, and Ruti is nearly enjoying herself as she observes him. But still, there's a pit in her stomach as she stands up to follow them, the Heir sandwiched between the two men and nodding slightly to keep Prince Kobe speaking.

"I have to say, I was a bit surprised when I heard that Princess Dekala's scholars thought I might be her perfect match," he says. "After all, you are practically a child, and a headstrong one, from what I hear. Hardly an appropriate match for a man of my intellect. But you are so lovely." He puts a hand on her back. Orrin steams. Even Ruti has to fight the urge to shove him away. The Heir is untouchable, aloof, and the role she plays tonight–demure and sweet and innocent–doesn't sit well with Ruti. If she's uncomfortable, though, she doesn't show it.

"Perhaps I need someone like you to remind me of the lighter things in life," the prince says, and he turns to face the Heir. "And perhaps you need someone like me to keep you leashed."

He raises his hand, palm out, and the Heir lifts her chin as though to gird herself for battle. She holds out her hand to match his and Ruti steps back, watching through the leaves as the Heir's hand hovers in front of Prince Kobe's. Carefully, in a low voice, Ruti chants to the spirits.

One last time, she begs them. *One more time. Hold the magic.* Prince Kobe presses his hand to the Heir's, and Ruti feels the magic straining between her and the Heir, the spirits undecided. Ruti sings and sings, calls to every spirit she knows, and there is a sheen of light over the Heir's palm that is so faint it's nearly invisible.

Prince Kobe's brow furrows and he presses a little harder. The magic shatters, the spirits retreating, and the light vanishes from between their joined palms. Ruti lets out a quiet curse and Orrin looks sharply at her. "It failed?" he hisses.

"I don't–" Ruti wrings her hands and sings again, a low, desperate chant, but there is nothing but silence in response, nothing from the spirits but a flash of claws and teeth in warning.

The Heir stands stiffly. "It doesn't seem to be taking," she says at last. Ruti has been lucky, even with the shattered magic. There is no magic joining their hands, no glow between them. They are no match. When the Heir pulls her hand back, her palm still carries only the half circle of sewa.

The prince frowns. "That can't be. I was certain you were my match," he says. "And you were certain you were mine."

The Heir gives him a regretful look that doesn't quite mask the darkness in her eyes. "You would be a magnificent match," she lies blatantly. "But I must be Bonded. Farewell, Prince Kobe." The Heir turns away from him. "I hope you'll leave me with my disappointment."

When Prince Kobe is gone, Orrin surges forward to enfold the Heir in an embrace. She closes her eyes, allowing him to hold her, and Orrin murmurs, "He was *hideous*."

"And this is whom the scholars select for me," the Heir says grimly. She stands comfortably in Orrin's arms, her own hands resting at his sides as he holds her. Ruti watches them from her spot behind the leaves, her eyes sharp and curious as she takes them in. Orrin's affection is unmistakable, as is the gentleness with which the Heir leans against him.

The Heir is *never* gentle, never any less than sharp-carved steel, and perhaps that's why Ruti is transfixed at the sight of them, even knowing what will come next for her. Because her magical barrier *failed*, because the Heir could have been *bonded*, because the spirits refused her request–but all she can do is stare at the Heir, the other girl's eyes drifting shut for a moment as Orrin tucks his chin over her head.

And then, inevitably, the Heir's eyes snap open, the moment of tenderness forgotten. "Markless *traitor*," she hisses, twisting around to glare into the leaves. "Show yourself."

Ruti panics. Years of being hunted by other Markless, of being attacked by guards, of being a handbreadth from death–they all kick in at once. Ruti moves by instinct, her heart thrumming with fear of what might happen to her now.

She twists away from the Heir and runs, runs from the Heir and from Orrin, runs from the gardens, and flees at a breakneck pace from the punishment to come.

9

She makes it nearly to the back entrance of the Royal Square before she remembers Kimya and makes an abrupt turn. There are sharp commands somewhere behind her–"Orrin, *faster*. Find her!"–that sound like a Fanged One's sibilant hiss, and Ruti ducks down and flattens herself against a tree.

Orrin tears past her, his big angry face twisted into a sneer, and he peers around in the dimness, searching for Ruti. Ruti closes her eyes and sings a silent chant to the Scaled One for stillness, imagining its long snout and deceptively stubby legs barely visible beside logs in the river.

The Scaled One grants her request without need for an additional offering, and Orrin twists around without noticing her at all. Ruti burrows into the trees, closing her eyes and thanking Kalere privately for choosing a dark green gown for her today. She blends into the dark, and soon Orrin is calling, "She's gone."

A rustle through the trees, a crack of thunder, and the Heir says coldly, "I refuse to accept that. Send out guards to find the Markless witch. Tell them not to return without her." Her voice is clear, her words deadly, and Ruti shivers as thunder rumbles above the palace.

She's been caught before dozens of times, and she knows that the best way to run is not to run at all. Stay put, wait as your pursuers search outside for you, and you can steal away once they've given up. She'll have to go retrieve Kimya, and the two of them can hide out in the massive palace while the Heir fruitlessly tears apart Somanchi in search of her.

Ruti waits until the Heir is gone, the wind quieting around her and the thunder fading, and she regards the door to the kitchens with some suspicion. The cooks and servants in the kitchens know her face by now, have seen her in the Heir's chambers and in the banquet hall. If they see her in the palace after she's supposed to be gone, her entire tactic will fail.

There's only one real option. She can't walk through the palace without being seen. Kimya is up in the Heir's chambers, safely ensconced in their room—unless the Heir has already taken her to the dungeons. But Ruti doesn't think so. Kimya is good at blending in, at being forgotten and overlooked when she needs to be. In the weeks they'd spent together at the shop, she'd spent most of her time out of sight, picking through ingredients and cleaning the dark corners of the shop. If the Heir returns to her chambers in a fury, Kimya will slip away before the princess thinks to arrest her.

Now, Ruti has to get to her.

She slips around the corner of the castle at the center of the palace, squinting up at the large window that she knows marks the Heir's chambers. Four windows to the right will be Ruti's room, and if Ruti can somehow make it there, she can climb inside. The windows of the bottom two floors of the palace are shuttered for security, but when it's cool outside, the attendants open the windows in the Heir's chambers to let some air into the rooms.

Ruti just has to climb.

She sings in a whisper as she begins her climb, calling to the spirits for even more help–too much, enough that she must be trying their patience–and imagines monkeys swinging through the trees above mighty beasts as the Winged One soars over them. They are quick and nimble, strong and daring, and she borrows their bravery as she reaches up to the next jutting brick, kicking off her sandals so her bare toes can wrap around the cool, weathered foothold.

She is halfway up and can see more bricks jutting out above her. Carefully, she seizes the next, pulling at it as she sings herself more agility, squeezes her fingers around it, and moves.

The brick slips from the wall, and Ruti nearly slips with it. She slaps a hand against the wall unsteadily, adrenaline and terror surging through her, and she regains her balance and makes a terrible mistake.

She looks down.

She's flat against the wall, halfway between the first-floor windows and the second, and she's as good as suspended in midair. One wrong move and she'll fall, break her legs or her neck or worse, and several of the tan bricks she used to ascend have already fallen to the ground. There's no going back, not this way, and she'll have to make it to her room or drop.

She takes a shuddering breath. No matter. She's survived worse situations. This is only a *wall*, and she has magic. She sings another chant, one she composes on the spot, another plea for agility that lets her dig her hand into the gap left behind by the fallen brick and hoist herself up higher.

Her gloves are gone, discarded with her sandals. Her hands are scratched and her arms and legs ache from the strain of the climb, but she ignores them all to reach higher still until finally–*finally*–she's just below the shutters to the window of her room.

The shutters are unlocked, and Ruti slides them open a sliver to see Kimya curled up on her bed. It's gotten late, and Kimya has been sleeping earlier in the palace than she used to in the slums. Kimya's eyes are open, though, and she watches the window with quiet attention.

She's been expecting Ruti. Ruti breathes a sigh of relief, pushes the shutters open all the way, and tumbles through them to the floor of the room. "We have to get out of here," she says breathlessly. "I'm in trouble."

Kimya only sits silently, watching her without signing, and Ruti notices two things that she hadn't before. First, Kimya's hands and feet are bound with rope to keep her from moving.

"That seems a common dilemma for you," a voice says crisply, and Ruti lifts her head to stare at the other bed, the one they don't use.

They aren't alone.

Of course. Ruti should have known that the Heir would immediately anticipate what Ruti would do next. She sits on the second bed, leaning against the wall as though the bed is her throne, and watches Ruti with inscrutable eyes.

"Oh," Ruti says numbly. "It's you."

She could run again, flee and hope that Orrin isn't standing on the other side of the door to the Heir's chambers, but she won't be able to free Kimya in time for them to have a chance. Instead, Ruti stands very still, staring at the Heir as the Heir stares back.

"Kneel," the Heir says coldly, and Ruti obeys without question this time.

She drops to her knees, heart thumping with dread, and the Heir rises to stare down at her, looking for all the world as though she holds more power than a witch. Ruti matches her stare, unflinching, prepared to face her doom at last. The Heir circles her once, then speaks. "Who sent you to sabotage me?"

Ruti blinks. Of all the orders and questions and demands that the Heir might make, she hadn't expected *that*. "I . . . what?" she asks, incredulous.

"Who sent you?" the Heir demands. "Was it my uncle? Was it one of the courtiers? Was it Rurana's prince? Is this a political coup? Who had you sabotage your magic on me?"

"Sabo– No one!" Ruti says, disbelieving. "No one brought me here but you!" The Heir stares down at her, her face stiff and dark, and Ruti says, "I failed, yes. But I *tried*. I put all I could into my magic. I *begged* the spirits again and again, I swear it." She gazes up at the Heir, beseeching. The Heir watches her, a flicker of doubt on her face. "I did all I could."

"I don't believe that," the Heir says darkly. "I saw you summon a Spotted One. I saw you burned and scorched into something monstrous at the market, and you healed yourself in just hours. And *this* is too much for your magic? A simple mark?"

Ruti takes a deep breath, remembering the spirits' disapproval at her plea. "The spirits thought . . . they thought it was unnatural to resist it," she murmurs, and the Heir sags in front of her. This will be Ruti's death, now that she is condemned to uselessness, and there is nothing she can do but tell the Heir the truth. "Soulbinding is their gift to humans. It is the gravest of offenses to reject the gift of the spirits. So they refused to keep you from trying to bond with the prince. I'm sorry."

The Heir turns away from her, thunder crackling around them, and Ruti stands, hurrying to untie Kimya from her bonds. Kimya hisses at her, frustration in her eyes, but she doesn't push Ruti away.

"I knew you'd return," the Heir says, her back still to them. "I knew you would come back for your sister. It doesn't make you a good person," she says, but her voice lacks bite. "It makes you weak."

"It can be both," Ruti counters, and the Heir turns back, her eyes black pits. "What will you do with me now?" Ruti whispers. She is afraid. There is something thrumming in the air around them, something unpredictable hovering around the Heir, and Ruti has endured enough threats to know that her admission of failure will end in her suffering.

She has to protect Kimya, who sits beside her stiffly and refuses to look at her right now. Kimya is angry, and Ruti can guess a dozen reasons why. She will negotiate with the Heir, find a way to trade some songs for Kimya's protection within the palace. Kalere likes her, the attendants dote on her, and Kimya is a hard worker. Kimya can be safe here, instead of alone in the slums. If the Heir wills it. The Heir will decide their fates right now, and Ruti can do nothing but await her decree.

But instead the Heir sinks to her knees in front of Ruti, bowing her head and closing her eyes. Ruti gapes, dumbstruck.

"I lied to you," the Heir says quietly. "I don't know how many witches there are in Ntuka or Aelin. I have only seen one witch in Somanchi's market, and he was a fraud. I led you to believe I have options, but I have none. Only you. And I saw your strength and I thought you might be. . . ."

Ruti stares at her, at the quiet, desperate humility from a ruler who raises herself so high above everyone else. The Heir looks up at her, and now her eyes are pained, a raw vulnerability within them. "My life is in your hands, Ruti of the Markless," the Heir whispers. "I can't be bonded. I can't be chained down to someone I didn't choose."

"I know," Ruti says, and she's surprised at the frustration she feels on the Heir's behalf, the sudden empathy she feels with someone who has done little to deserve it from her. "I'm doing all I can. Maybe there's another way, a better way, but I don't know how."

The Heir lets out an irritable sound that she quashes, rising to sit on the bed opposite Ruti again. "Will you try?" she says, and she still sounds . . . less imperious, perhaps, a plea tempering her words.

Ruti hesitates. The Heir says swiftly, "I can offer you coin. Protection. A space in the Merchants' Circle–"

"How about we start with a promise that you aren't going to kill me if I fail?" Ruti says. The Heir blinks at her, a ghost of a smile on her face. "And that I'm not *yours*. No more kneeling or–or waking me up in the middle of the night just to *talk* or. . . ." The Heir's lips are curving upward, and it has Ruti flustered, discomfited at the Heir's amusement. "I don't care if I have to work to earn my keep here. But I want my freedom. Mine and Kimya's. *And* that coin you just offered," she says hastily, because she isn't *naïve.*

"I will give you everything your heart desires," the Heir promises. "Please, I only need. . . ." Her voice trails off and she looks very, very lost. "I want to be free, too."

"Okay." Ruti puts out her hand, palm out in the way that she's seen traders make deals. It's a challenge, and the Heir accepts it, pressing her palm to Ruti's unmarked one.

The contact sends a tingle through Ruti, and the Heir startles a bit as though it's done the same for her. "If I do find that you are playing me for a fool, though," the Heir warns her, "I will not look lightly upon that. Any sign of treachery and all our deals are off."

Ruti stares at her, unpleasantly reminded of why she dislikes the Heir. "I *told* you I'm trying," she says irritably. "Is it really this hard to trust me?"

The Heir retreats, her eyes closing off again and her back straightening. "I would be a fool to trust a Markless," she says scornfully. "Particularly a Markless who has control over my fate."

Ruti turns away from her, disappointed with no reason for it. "I will try, Your Highness," she bites out.

The Heir doesn't respond, only stands, turning to walk to the door. Ruti watches her leave, the sour feeling returning with the Heir's aloofness. But the Heir pauses at the doorway, and she says, "Dekala."

Ruti stares after her. "What?"

The Heir doesn't turn. "If we are to be free companions, then it is best that you call me by my name," she says smoothly. Her back is still to Ruti, and Ruti glowers at it, her stomach tying itself into knots at the offer.

"If we are to be free companions, then I think I'll make that decision by myself, *Your Highness*," she shoots back, and the Heir's shoulders shake in what Ruti is unpleasantly certain is a silent, mocking laugh.

"Very well," the Heir says–and there is *clearly* laughter in her voice–and she steps out of the room.

Ruti groans. "I hate her," she says, untying Kimya and stretching out beside her. But Ruti's heart is beating quickly, a bubble of air somewhere within it. She'd *won* somehow, had run off and been found and had still managed to get more than she'd ever thought she might. Maybe the Heir will renege on her word, but she'd still *given* it, had admitted that she needs Ruti more than she'd ever let on before. The Heir can't afford to do more than level empty threats at Ruti, and she's willing to compromise in order to get what she wants.

And what she wants might be beyond Ruti, but she wonders if there might be someone out there who can help her. If Ruti can–

A sharp poke to her ribs interrupts her thoughts, and Ruti rolls over to face an unsmiling Kimya. "What?" Ruti demands finally. "I came back for you, didn't I?"

Kimya shakes her head and her eyes flash, lips twitching with frustration. "Tell me," Ruti says, forcing herself to focus on Kimya instead of the insufferable Heir.

Kimya signs. "It's long," Ruti translates, and Kimya nods. "Tell me," she murmurs again.

Kimya signs, and it *is* long, a convoluted explosion of emotions that takes Ruti some time and guesswork to fully understand. "You're angry because I left?" she finally asks, bewildered. "I was going to bring you with me."

Kimya's hands fly, her eyes accusing. "We have food at home, too," Ruti protests, watching Kimya's hands. "We're safer there, too. We're–"

Kimya slaps her palm, a vicious little motion that Ruti has seen her use before, followed by the curve of her hand against her heart that means home. "We're Markless at home," Ruti repeats, and Kimya looks at her with such loss that Ruti's heart cracks. "Kimya, we're Markless here, too."

Kimya signs a word that she's only ever used for Ruti before. *Friends.* Here, Kimya is comfortable, surrounded by attendants who make no mention of what lies beneath her gloves. She folds linen and helps prepare food and is treated like anyone else, like a favored child instead of a monster, and Ruti slips her arms around Kimya and tugs her close. "I made you a dreamer, didn't I?" she whispers. She's spent so long railing against Markless dreamers, against children who believe that they can someday become just like all the Marked people out there, that she hadn't thought about what feeding and sheltering a Markless child might do to her.

Kimya shakes her head, then nods, just a short little motion that breaks Ruti's heart even further. "I'm sorry," she murmurs, pressing a kiss to Kimya's temple. "I wish . . . I wish you could have this everywhere. But we had a good life in the shop, didn't we?" Kimya refuses to answer.

Ruti sighs, kissing her hair again. "You heard what I told the Heir. I'm going to try to help her. We'll stay here for as long as she needs us," she promises, and Kimya presses a hand to Ruti's upper arm, a silent sign of gratitude. "As long as I don't kill her first," Ruti mutters wryly.

Kimya's head bumps against her laughingly, followed by a sign that Ruti recognizes. "I do *not* like her," Ruti says, horrified. "She's a monster."

Kimya shrugs, offering Ruti a sign that she uses to mean *gift*. Swiftly, she digs into her robe and emerges with a neatly-wrapped paper that she opens as Ruti stares in bewildered surprise.

Sometime tonight, before the Heir tied up Kimya and used her as bait to draw Ruti in, the Heir had taken a moment to offer Kimya a little chunk of chocolate. Kimya signs again, grinning, and Ruti translates it in her head: *Well, I like her.*

Ruti glowers at her. Kimya smiles, her anger receding, and breaks off a piece of the chocolate to place into Ruti's hand.

Ruti pops it into her mouth, still scowling. It's the sweetest candy she's ever tasted.

Nothing changes very much after that evening. The Heir is still snide and distant, and their rare conversations begin and end with questions about Ruti's progress with her song. Ruti begs out of afternoons with the Heir now, focused on mixing offerings and testing out new chants to see if they might appease the spirits.

Thus far, she's had little luck. The spirits remain stubbornly immobile as they have never been before for her, and she fears their patience may run out. Soulbonds are destined to be Bonded.

Ruti senses the Heir's impatience growing with each day, and when she's awakened in the middle of the night, she fears the worst. "You promised," she gasps out before she even opens her eyes. "If you lay one finger on me, I'll sing you to your death."

"Calm down," the Heir says disgustedly. She stands over Ruti, the light of the sun's rise haloing her as she snatches her hand from Ruti's shoulder. "I'm not here to kill you." Her eyes narrow as Ruti sits up, squinting at her through the bright light. "I need your help. My uncle only just sent word. A new prince is arriving today."

"I'm doing my best," Ruti says, but dread suffuses her at the thought of trying to persuade the spirits with what she's done so far. "There's no way that I'll be able to–"

"I know," the Heir says abruptly. "But there is another option." She raises her voice. "Kalere," she calls, and Kalere hurries into Ruti's room. "Can you do it?"

"Do what?" Ruti asks, but suddenly Kalere is running her hands over Ruti's hair, cupping her face, eyeing her with calculating eyes.

"I think we can," Kalere decides, and pulls Ruti unceremoniously from her bed and herds her toward the bathing room without another word.

"Wait, what?" Ruti says, keeping up with Kalere as the Heir gives her a cool once-over and slips out of her nightgown.

Ruti stares, averts her eyes, then stares again, her face very hot as her eyes flicker over the Heir's smooth skin. The Heir, for her part, seems unbothered by her own nakedness, accustomed to being touched and bathed by the attendants around her.

The Heir steps into the bath and says, "The only option I see is that this new prince believes we are trying the bonding when we aren't. You and I are about the same height, even if you're too light-skinned," she says, assessing Ruti. Ruti still feels heat passing through her as the Heir's body disappears beneath the water. "I think with some styling and heavy makeup, we can make you look like I do in paintings."

"You want me to pose as *you*?" Ruti repeats, the full import of what the Heir is asking finally settling in. "How am I supposed to–"

"I haven't met Prince Kedron of Phecia," the Heir says. "He won't know the difference. And you've spent enough time with me to do a crude facsimile of me. It will be enough, at least until dinner with my uncle."

Mikuyi urges Ruti into the bath, tugging the gown off her shoulders, and Ruti feels the Heir's eyes lingering on her torso. Ruti flushes, self-conscious of what she knows is nowhere near the smooth perfection of the Heir's skin. She is scarred from various fights and bad weather in the slums, and she's always been a little too scrawny, even after weeks at the royal palace. Her ribs are visible, her figure uneven, and she wants to cover herself the moment the Heir sees her.

But she leaves her hands at her sides, stubborn and prideful in all the ways the Heir brings out in her. The Heir watches her, lower lip trapped for a moment in her teeth, and she looks away when she sees that Ruti has caught her. Ruti slides into the bath opposite her, their bare feet bumping together, and Ruti can't stop a new flush at *that*.

She clears her throat. "I can certainly do a *Princess Dekala*," she says, her voice slyly mocking. "All that involves is treating everyone around me as though they're below me and I am *forced to put up with them*." She heaves a long sigh and affects a cool expression. "It is my fate, as heir to this squalid kingdom."

"Perfect," Kalere says, grinning. The Heir glowers at them both.

Mikuyi applies a liberal amount of golden ochre onto Ruti's face, enough to conceal the disparity in her skin color and the Heir's from all but the most acute of eyes. Ruti's hair is twisted tightly into a facsimile of the Heir's customary coils. The Heir, for her part, has her hair teased out into soft curls much like Ruti's, and she wears a simple red gown.

Ruti is dressed in white and gold and sent out into the hall for her first test. Orrin falls in place beside her without a second glance and says, "You look lovely today. Will we at last have a morning without that Markless urchin?"

"I wouldn't count on it," Ruti says brightly, and Orrin recoils. The door opens again, the Heir gliding out in Ruti's clothing and a hood placed carefully to conceal her face. Orrin looks between them with faint horror.

They do not go about their daily routine, which is a relief for Ruti, who had been afraid she would have to attempt stick fighting with Tembo. Instead, they're brought to the main courtyard by the Regent's attendants, men who don't look twice at Ruti or the Heir as Ruti stumbles in her long dress and the Heir slips an arm in her gloved one to keep her steady.

"Prince Kedron will arrive shortly," the attendant, a man named Obasi, informs them. "Your uncle will be watching your meeting to guarantee your–"

Ruti draws herself up to her fullest height, frowning at Obasi. "I hope you aren't implying that I would *ever* flout propriety," she says, mimicking the cadences of the Heir's voice. The Heir's arm in hers shakes ever so slightly, a little ripple of thunder above them sounding like soft laughter.

Obasi stumbles over his words. "Of course not," he says hastily. "I only meant–well, you have expressed a. . . ." He looks around wildly. "Your uncle is waiting," he says, nodding toward the twin thrones at the end of the courtyard.

This is their next test, and Ruti's heart beats quickly. She is wearing the gold ochre in elaborate swirls marked by diamond blots across her face, specially shaped to conceal her identity from even the Regent, but one word from her mouth might be enough to expose her. She walks in tiny steps toward the Regent, who watches her with deep disapproval.

"You will spend the day with Prince Kedron," he says curtly when she sits, the Heir and Orrin arranging themselves beside the throne. "He is the heir to Phecia, a suitable match for you and for Zidesh. I want you to try bonding with him within the day."

Ruti watches him, keeping her eyes cool, and she is careful not to respond. "You saw the last prince as a humiliation," the Regent says, his voice gentler. "I have ensured that this one is far more deserving of you." His manipulations are as subtle as the note of kindness in his voice, and Ruti peeks at Dekala out of the corner of her eye. The Heir's lip is curled, and Ruti does her best to mimic that expression.

The Regent makes a disgusted noise and turns away, the simulacrum of caring gone from his expression.

Prince Kedron arrives with an entourage: first, a crowd of Bonded guards, with faces and chests painted to mimic their Maned One patron, who create a show with lightning and fire and wind in the courtyard. Then a trio with power over form create grand, lifelike images in the air, telling stories of Phecia's greatest triumphs through picture and dance, and Ruti watches with fascination as they move through the courtyard. They sing in a language like Zideshi but different, though Ruti can catch a few words here and there, and their song isn't magic but it feels like it should be.

"And now," calls one dancer in Zideshi as they tumble over each other, clearing the center of the courtyard. Together they raise their hands and form a great pathway across the courtyard, the earth rising like a bridge toward the Heir's throne. "We present our prince."

The doors to the courtyard open and Prince Kedron saunters forward, flanked by guards as he walks lazily up the bridge toward the throne. He has a narrow Phecian nose and a handsome shape to his face, Ruti supposes, though she is hardly one to note such things. There is a slyness to his smile that makes it nearly a smirk, and it's this that makes her wary of him.

"Your Highness," he says in lightly accented Zideshi, kneeling before her and raising his hand to hers.

Ruti stretches out her hand. Kalere used a lotion on her arms that is a slightly darker brown than her olive skin calls for, and Mikuyi gave her a carefully painted mark in anticipation of this. Once they touch palms, this farce will be over at last. But Prince Kedron only presses a kiss to the back of her hand. "Your uncle told me of your wish to delay soulbinding," he says, his smile still lingering on his face. "Please, show me your grand palace."

Ruti stands stiffly, her eyes flickering to the Heir's. The Heir nods almost imperceptibly, and Ruti allows the prince to help her rise. Under the Regent's eagle eyes, Ruti walks with Kedron down his earth bridge and toward the two-arched, gold-inlaid doors to the palace.

Once she's put some distance between them, Ruti finally feels as though it's safe to speak. "These are my companions," she says, gesturing to Orrin and the Heir as they catch up with them. "Orrin, my lumbering bodyguard, and Ruti, who is the best of us all."

The Heir's eyes narrow. Prince Kedron laughs. "The stories of your comeliness have spread across the land," he says, "but the tales have made little mention of your wit."

"The tales would have me quiet," Ruti says boldly. "A queen to be seen and marveled at with a king ruling over her. But I will be ruled by no one." It is true of the Heir, who has proven to be a force to be reckoned with. Her uncle underestimates her, and even the people of Somanchi speak only of her beauty.

The Heir, walking beside her, gives her an odd look that Ruti can't quite decipher. Prince Kedron extends his arm for Ruti to take. "A princess of your might should bow to no one," he says easily.

His words are sweet and sly; Ruti feels her distrust grow. She shows him the palace as well as she knows it, the Heir silent beside her and Orrin glaring at them both, and the Prince is nothing but complimentary toward her and Zidesh. Still, his words reek of insincerity.

"When we are Bonded," he says as they watch the guards do their exercises in the courtyard, "Zidesh and Phecia will be joined as well. Have you ever seen Phecia?"

The Heir speaks up before Ruti can answer. "Of course the Heir has journeyed to Phecia a number of times while you were away at war. A terrible shame you've never met before, as you two are becoming such close friends today." Her eyes are narrowed.

Kedron looks taken aback at her hostility. "I suppose it is a shame," he acknowledges. "I feel quite certain that you are my soulbond. They say that your uncle selected the most experienced scholars in the land to calculate who might be yours." He looks at Ruti, who smiles thinly. The Heir stares daggers through them both, which seems very unfair to Ruti. She's only doing what the Heir *wants*. "I understand that your kingdom will never accept an Unbonded woman as its queen," he says gravely. "But our joined kingdom will be mightier than any other in the land."

"I feel quite certain that you are my soulbond as well," Ruti says, glancing down at her palm to make sure the paint hasn't smudged. Thunder rumbles in the distance, and Kedron smiles.

They walk through the coral hibiscus shrubs of the front courtyard, past the sky-flowers and the plumerias toward the wild gardens of the rear courtyard. Kedron is followed by his shirtless, muscular bodyguards, and Ruti is followed by the Heir and Orrin. Kedron tells them all stories of his home. They are stories of Phecia's might and Kedron's skill in battle, and they stretch on and on until Ruti nearly dozes off. She is sitting beside the Heir just outside a mass of wide green fronds, and her head has only just touched the Heir's shoulder when the Heir jabs her in the side and awakens her.

Ruti jolts back up. "How wonderful," she says quickly.

Kedron looks bewildered. "A famine is wonderful?"

Ruti blinks. "Wonderful that your people have a prince like you, of course," she says. The Heir lets out a quiet breath of laughter. "You seem to care so deeply for them, and you are . . . both wise and beneficent."

Kedron's eyes clear. "I am, aren't I?" he says serenely. Ruti disguises her bark of laughter as a coughing fit.

The more time she spends with Kedron, the more unbearable he becomes. The sun rises and curves across the sky, and it is beginning to set when Kedron suggests they join the others for dinner. "Your uncle was most eager for us all to get to know each other," he says, leading Ruti toward the castle. "I think this alliance will benefit us all."

"Particularly your people," Ruti says, raising her eyebrows. "You did mention that famine, didn't you?"

Kedron scoffs. "Hardly a famine anymore. We have been in recovery for years now, thank the spirits. Zidesh's fertile farmland combined with Phecia's new income from fishing and trading will be a force to be reckoned with. As will you and I," he says, stopping suddenly to take Ruti's hand in his.

Abruptly, Ruti notices that they are alone. Kedron's pace has been swift, and he's been leading her through the winding hallways of the palace. Ruti was focusing so hard on not tripping that she hadn't realized until now that they'd lost Orrin and the Heir along the way.

For the first time since she'd been painted with ochre and dressed in the Heir's clothing, she is afraid at how vulnerable she is here. Kedron's fingers run along her hand and he presses her wrist to the wall, her painted palm exposed to him. "We are to be Bonded," he says, his voice pleasant. "Why delay?"

"Why delay indeed," Ruti echoes, a flash of trepidation weakening her words. Kedron, she is suddenly afraid, will not take it well when nothing happens. And she has no protection. She would even take Orrin right now. For all his grumbling and posturing, she trusts him more than she would ever trust Kedron.

Kedron's hand on her wrist is firm, clamped around her in possession instead of courtship. He lifts his right hand, holding out his sign of ashto, and presses his marked palm to Ruti's painted one.

Nothing happens, of course, and Kedron does it again, this time pressing her hand with more force. Ruti's knuckles scrape against the wall, and Kedron slaps his hand hard against hers, forcing her hand to his. The paints will run if he continues, and Ruti is afraid. "Stop," she hisses. "*Stop*. It won't work!"

"Shut your mouth," Kedron snaps. He is no longer smiling. His eyes are dark and angry as he stares at her. "You were meant to be mine. *Zidesh* was meant to be mine."

"Apparently not," Ruti says, and she feels fury bubble up beneath the fear, the anger that comes with someone trying to force her into being something she isn't. "Zidesh belongs to–"

"Zidesh belongs to someone with the power to rule it," Kedron bites out, pressing her to the wall with his lithe body. "Not a foolish Unbonded girl. You are a laughingstock amongst the princes, did you know that? A child who believes she can rule with the great men of the land. No prince comes here to be subordinate to *you*."

Ruti wants to sing, wants to chant away this vile prince, but she can't risk him finding out who she is–or worse, telling the other princes that Princess Dekala is a witch. But she isn't defenseless, even without her songs. "You underestimate me," she manages, and brings her knee up between his legs as she has done to attackers a hundred times in the slums, using her free arm to elbow the prince in the face.

He staggers back and then comes at her again, his eyes narrowed and mean. "Bitch," he snarls, a painting on the wall lighting on fire. "You will never–"

Ruti punches him in the gut and he deals her a glancing blow, slamming her head against the wall. "You could do with some *rule*," he says, his voice low and dangerous. "And I shall–"

A wind rages through the hallway, hurling into him with roaring force. Orrin is there a moment later, pinning the prince to the wall as Ruti sinks to the floor. The Heir rounds the corner as Kedron rages at Orrin, shouting for his own bodyguards. "You will pay for this humiliation!" he snarls. "Phecia will not sit lightly after this!"

The Heir stares down at him, her eyes very cold. "You threatened our Heir," she bites out, her deep voice sharpening like a knife. "You will be very fortunate if she chooses to spare your head." She turns, bending to kneel beside Ruti. "Did he attempt the bonding?" Ruti offers a jerky nod, her head still pounding from the last blow.

The Heir lifts her hand and Ruti squints down at it. Her knuckles are scraped and bruised, the blood seeping from them red and black with dirt, and the Heir says, her eyes on Ruti's hand, "Orrin."

Orrin looks up. "Yes, Your–" He hesitates, unsure of what to say, Kedron still pinned beneath him.

The Heir doesn't wait for him to come up with something. "Bring that feckless little princeling to the banquet hall," she orders. "Tell the Regent what transpired. Phecia can reclaim its worthless royalty at once." Her gaze is still on Ruti's knuckles, and she straightens. "Can you stand?"

Ruti nods. Orrin drags off the prince while Ruti stumbles to her feet, head still spinning, and she manages, "I can chant my skin healed," as the Heir stalks with her down the halls.

"Not here," the Heir shoots back, glaring around them. They emerge into the main hall, mostly empty but for guards from both Zidesh and Phecia, and the Heir ignores them all and leads Ruti toward the kitchens. "You'll need to wash out the dirt first."

"I've never done that before."

"You've been living in squalor for a lifetime," the Heir says curtly. "It was only a matter of time before you bled black and died."

"Touching," Ruti says dryly, but she follows the Heir obediently, still a little dazed from the blow to her head. She can't even think of a fitting jab to provoke the Heir, and she sits when the Heir orders her down.

The Heir has taken them to a corner of the kitchen where only a few servants cast a nosy eye toward them. Ruti is still dressed as the Heir, but the Heir stands over Ruti with the regal bearing of a princess, making their interactions all the more curious. "Here," the Heir says, bringing her a wet cloth. She swipes at Ruti's knuckles, making them sting, and Ruti lets out a little gasp of pain. "Don't be a child," the Heir says briskly.

"Don't be a sadist," Ruti grits out. It *hurts*, hurts like her knuckles are being rubbed raw, and tears of pain spring to her eyes.

"Good," the Heir says, satisfied at the bloody mess she's made of Ruti's knuckles. "Now you can sing." She is still holding her hand up, her fingers streaked with paints that have washed off of Ruti's palm, and Ruti feels suddenly hot again as she surveys their joined hands.

Carefully, shakily, she begins to chant in a whisper, leaning back against the wall as she sings to the spirits. The tears still streak down her cheeks, over the ochre and down to her ears, and she feels the spirits accept the tears as an offering and grant her request.

She exhales, singing again and leaning forward, and notices that the Heir is still watching her, eyes fixed on Ruti's as her skin begins to heal. Ruti flushes, staring back at the Heir as her heart thumps rapidly, and the Heir whispers, "Keep singing."

She had stopped without realizing, struck dumb by the Heir's gaze on her, and she curses herself silently and resumes her desperate call to the spirits.

11

They do not try dressing up as each other again when the next man arrives. Instead the Heir puts him off, manufactures an outrage and refuses to try bonding with him altogether. He is a minor noble, a grandson of a king's brother, but the Regent's scholars are insistent that he fits the profile for a potential soulbond and the Regent pushes until the Heir finally, irritably, presses her palm to his.

They aren't a match, and Ruti exhales when she sees that. She has yet to find a chant that will do the trick for the Heir, and pure luck and the scholars' incompetence are the only reasons why the Heir isn't bonded yet. "I don't know what else might work," she admits one afternoon. The Heir has had shelves and closets put into Ruti's room for her ingredients, and Kimya is sorting through them on the spare bed, squinting down at dried beetles and dried dung in an attempt to figure out which is which.

The Heir wrinkles her nose and turns away from Kimya. "Find something," she snaps. "It's been weeks. Every day, the scholars find another potential match for me. Every day, they swear that another royal is my perfect soulbond."

"I'm *trying*. There might just . . . there might not be any way to stop a bonding," Ruti admits. "Have you ever heard of it being done before?"

The Heir glowers at her in silence, then deflates abruptly. "No," she says flatly. "I haven't. But I refuse to believe that there is no alternative."

"Maybe not," Ruti says, and she stares at a closet shelf packed with little bags of offerings for the spirits. "I just don't know it. There might be some other witch out there who does know, but I don't know them, either. The only witch I've ever met was an old man in the slums who disappeared soon after."

"You've met another witch?" the Heir says, her eyes suddenly focused on Ruti again. "You never mentioned him before."

Ruti shrugs. "He's dead, I assume. It's been years, and he was old even when I saw him. He taught me my first song."

The Heir is undeterred. "Take me to him."

"I haven't seen him since," Ruti protests. "I have no idea where he is, let alone if he can actually help you . . . and you want to go to the slums? You? The princess? Do you have any idea how dangerous that is?"

"I've been there before," the Heir points out. "Orrin searched for you and then brought me to you. And I can hold my own."

Ruti scoffs. "With a stick, maybe. The Markless kids in the slums aren't competing to see how skilled they are. Plenty of us can't afford to give up the chance to steal some coin. And the biggest ones–the ones who've survived long enough to help us find that man–they aren't going to hesitate."

The Heir rises, drawing her gown around her. "I can hold my own," she repeats. "I will have an animal cart prepared for us. If my uncle asks, we will tell him that we're journeying to the river for a brief excursion." She glides from the room without waiting for Ruti's response.

Ruti glares into the cabinet. "She's unbearable," she mutters. Kimya signs a denial, and Ruti turns her glare on the other girl instead.

Yet again, the Heir has decided what will be done next, but this time, Ruti knows the Heir will regret it. One journey into the slums and out again is nothing compared to spending a lengthy period of time there, surrounded by Markless and misery. Ruti knows the slums as well as any Markless who's lived until eighteen, and she still isn't fool enough to stride through them now as though she owns them.

The slums are unpredictable, and Kimya scowls and protests but ultimately stays behind as Ruti and the Heir ride together toward them. "You'll need to purchase a new cloak,"

Ruti says, peering over at the Heir in the seat beside her. The Heir is wearing blue today instead of the royal white and gold, but they both stand out regardless. "We look rich. No one rich makes it out of the slums with their possessions intact."

The animal cart only goes as far as the Merchants' Circle, where Ruti finds a pair of roughspun brown cloaks. "This is a rag," the Heir says, scowling. "You paid coin for this?"

"Not very much, don't worry," Ruti says wryly. The Heir drapes it around her shoulders, somehow managing to wear it like royal robes. Ruti reaches over to rearrange it, letting it fall haphazardly around her.

"What about a cloak for Orrin?" the Heir asks, nodding to the bodyguard behind them.

Ruti shrugs. "I don't care if he gets robbed," she says. Orrin glowers at her.

The Heir lets out a little puff of laughter. "He *will* be my consort one day," she says. "Must you provoke us both?"

"This is provoking?" Ruti wrinkles her brow. "I thought we were getting along."

The Heir flicks a finger against Ruti's shoulder. Outside the Royal Square, she veers from wary to light, still cold but less domineering. She smiles more, is quicker to laugh at Ruti—the only way Ruti can ever get her to laugh—and she offers more information. "I came out to the Merchants' Circle the first time because I thought my uncle was lying to me," she says. "He claimed that the people were starving in Zidesh and we needed a strong ruler to bring them back to order."

"The only people starving in Somanchi are Markless," Ruti says grimly. Somanchi is built on the convergence of river and forest, the most bountiful of places in the land, and all that is needed for someone to flourish is a mark on their palm.

"So I saw." The Heir purchases a third cloak for Orrin and arranges it on his shoulders with care, mimicking the way that Ruti wears it. It looks awkward on him–he is too boxy and well built to look like a beggar, and Ruti watches the Heir as she takes care with the cloak, offering Orrin a smile as she helps him.

Something unpleasant thrums in Ruti's stomach, and she turns away with a pang of uncertain melancholy. "We should hurry if we want to have a chance of finding the witch before nightfall," she says abruptly. "Keep up."

She strides through the Merchants' Circle, paying no attention to the Heir or Orrin. She might not care for either of them, but Orrin in particular is so *distasteful*. She can't comprehend the Heir's fascination with him, and she says so when the Heir strides forward to catch up to her. "What does he have that the princes courting you don't?" she demands. Orrin is keeping pace with them, a few feet back. "Why is he worth fighting the spirits for?"

The Heir says, "I don't expect you to understand."

"He's devoted to you," Ruti says, moving faster. "But any soulbond would be devoted to you. He isn't particularly wise or strong or any other trait that might make him a good ruler. Why would you fall in love with *him*?" A thought strikes her. "Is it that he is the only man you know well who isn't your uncle? Because you have much better prospects than *Orrin*."

The Heir's voice is sharp now. "Bite your tongue, Markless girl," she snaps. "Remember whom you address. My choices are my own, and they are right."

"By virtue of what, *Your Highness*?"

Wind slams into Ruti's face. "By virtue of the fact that I am your *queen*," the Heir hisses. "I will treat you as a companion if you wish. I will allow you to fail and fail again and withhold punishment. But you will *not* question my decisions. I have my limits, even for you."

There is danger in her voice, a warning that sends a chill through Ruti, but she refuses to answer and concede the point. Instead, she stalks away from the Heir, leading the way toward the slums without looking back.

She knows that Orrin has fallen into step with the Heir. Of course he has. The Heir has given him no reason not to.

Ruti's shop is already gone. The two rooms where she'd once squatted have been taken over by a group of Markless adults who come to the door with knives when Ruti tries to come inside. "Stay back," one barks out. "This is ours."

Ruti steps back, feeling oddly forlorn. The shop had been the only place that was hers, a shelter when she'd never had one before. Now it's been possessed and remade in an instant, someone else's dwelling with no sign that she'd ever been there. In the slums, no one leaves a mark on the world, and all are forgotten as soon as they disappear. She just hadn't expected it to happen to her, too, at least so quickly.

The Heir is watching her, and Ruti looks away, afraid of what emotion she might have revealed to her. "Wait," she says, staring at the men. They are a group, old and powerful enough that they will have had the run of the slums instead of hiding in the closest shadows. "I'm looking for someone. An old man."

"In the slums?" one says incredulously. "No one grows old here."

"That's not true," one of the other men calls out. "I saw an old man once, out by the Wastelands. Decrepit old coot. Claimed he was a witch." They laugh raucously, and the man says, "Never saw *him* again."

"He was probably our age," another calls out. "Just ugly." More laughter, and the man at the door gives Ruti an assessing glance. "You look pretty well off for a Markless," he says, eyeing her bare palm. She'd slipped the gloves off once they'd reached the slums.

Ruti ignores him. "Where in the Wastelands did you see him?" she calls out, but there is no answer from the men inside. Instead, their eyes run over Ruti, calculating and hungry, and Ruti stands steady and tall. To flinch back now is to tell these Markless that she's an easy target. She might not like them, but she knows that Orrin is waiting for the opportunity to blast them with his lightning.

No one deserves Orrin.

After a few moments assessing Ruti, the men relent, slamming the door to their home shut. Ruti sighs, turning around, and the Heir and Orrin melt out of the shadows. "We'll need to search the Wastelands," she says.

The Wastelands are at the edge of the city, near where Somanchi hits forest, in the worst part of the slums. The land is so miserable there that no trees will grow. Instead, there is only wreckage and dry, cracked land, ravaged by people who don't have a next generation to worry about. They say that even the spirits won't roam free there, in a land too desolate to rest in. Ruti has never spent much time in the Wastelands, where only the most desperate of Markless hide.

She leads the Heir down the road, past little Markless children who stretch out their hands as Ruti walks by. The Heir looks perturbed as she watches them. "I thought my father opened orphanages here."

"He did." Ruti avoids the eyes of the beggars, conscious of her own weakness when it comes to little ones. "But the orphanages need coin to provide food. They make for safe shelter at night for the little ones, but children still have to find their own food to survive out here."

"All for being Markless," the Heir murmurs. She crouches suddenly, her gown and cloak sweeping against the grimy ground, and drops a coin into the hands of one of the Markless children. The others clamor, rushing to her with their hands outstretched, tugging at her cloak and her arms with desperate need.

The Heir stumbles back, overwhelmed, and Orrin charges forward. Ruti moves before she can think it through, stepping between Orrin and the crowd of children with her eyes flashing. "Out of the way, Markless," Orrin grits out.

"Lay a hand on them and I'll kill you," Ruti snaps back. The Heir is still beset by children, but she's passing out coin to them, her brow knit as she takes them in. Few of these children will survive for long, Ruti knows. Fewer still will make it somewhere they can use their new coin. "Go," Ruti orders them. "Run and find food before the older boys take your coin."

The little ones understand *that*, even if they'll never understand who it was who just fed them for a week, and they scatter. The Heir tucks away her purse, still looking deeply perturbed, and Orrin mutters, "It's a waste of coin." Ruti might have thought the same thing, but she glowers at Orrin nonetheless.

"When I am queen," the Heir says abruptly, and raises her chin. "The slums are a blight on Zidesh and its capital city. The only solution is to fund the orphanages."

"I agree," Ruti says, but she's startled–both at the unexpected humanity from the Heir, and from the unexpected humanity toward the Markless.

The Heir turns to look at her, Orrin ignored, and her eyes are sharp. "Kimya was on this line once," the Heir murmurs.

"How did you–"

"She told me." The Heir motions with her hands, a lazy gesture that is Kimya's exact sign for *collecting*. Ruti gapes at her. Somehow, in all the free time that Kimya's spent wandering around the Heir's apartments and after all the chocolate that Kimya has been sneaking into their room, it had never occurred to her that Kimya had been teaching the Heir her speech. "Would she have survived here?"

"No," Ruti says immediately, then reconsiders. "Maybe. She was good at surviving. I think she might have made it past seven."

"And how much longer after that?" the Heir asks, and Ruti has no answer for her.

They continue their long walk down the Beggars' Road and slowly, rickety little shops begin to grow more and more sparse, replaced with old wreckage and fallen buildings that have never been rebuilt. They reach the edge of the Wastelands, and Ruti shivers and glances around.

It is nearly dusk, and she has the sense already of haunted eyes fixed on them. The Wastelands are different than the rest of the slums. Everywhere else, there are people *surviving*, struggling to get through the impossible just to live another day. But there is no food in the Wastelands, no shops with coin to steal, nothing to strive for. There are no threats in the Wastelands, either, because anyone who still has the desire to live is far outside of them.

Markless come to the Wastelands to die.

"I thought about coming here once," Ruti whispers. The Wastelands are too quiet to speak aloud. "When I was very little. There was no food and nowhere to go, and it seemed . . . this seemed the most peaceful way to starve to death."

The Heir is silent for a moment. "What changed your mind?" she murmurs. Her eyes flicker over the devastation of the Wastelands with wariness, and Ruti knows that she must feel the same haunted gazes on them.

Ruti shrugs. "Stubbornness, I guess. I wanted to live. So I did." It isn't so simple, but she doesn't think the Heir would understand the gnawing hunger she'd once known, the instinctual desperation to eat, stronger than any other conscious thought. She had thought about food for so long that the Wastelands had felt like an impossible sacrifice. Setting a single foot into the Wastelands alone would have been a surrender to starvation that Ruti hadn't been capable of.

The Heir shakes her head, and for the first time she looks just as haunted as Ruti feels. "If my uncle had wanted to frighten me into bonding, he should have shown me this," she mutters. There are tiny Markless here, little things who might be as old as Ruti scampering away into the shadows like mice. Next to them, the hungry wanderers of the rest of the slums look fat and sated. Everyone here is starved, and the sky is grey as though the sun never quite reaches this land.

Even Orrin looks uneasy. "Dekala, are you sure you want to–"

"Look," the Heir says, and points off to the distance, into the dusk.

Beneath the grey skies, so deep in the Wastelands that Ruti isn't quite sure that they're even in Somanchi anymore, a little hut still stands. It's just a bit higher than the wreckage around it, but it stands out by virtue of two things: the roof, a curved marvel in this dead place; and the vines of greenery that wind around it. It looks as though the vines are bleeding at first, but Ruti knows immediately what it is.

Fruit. Small, red fruits, the kind that the witch had sung into being as Ruti watched them blossom with envy. "That's him," Ruti says, and she quickens her pace.

It feels as though the hut is right in front of them, but Ruti is running for minutes and she still hasn't reached it. The Heir is right behind her, the Wastelands growing dark now, and Ruti fiddles in the pockets of her clothes to find a speckled feather and a vial of star anise. She douses the feather with the anise and chants to the spirits until the Horned One seizes the feather from her, letting it flutter away in the wind. In its place is a glowing ball of light in front of them to illuminate their way. Orrin looks put off by this, and he flexes his wrist so that lightning glows bright in the sky, shining down on them.

Arrogant posturing, Ruti thinks grumpily, but she continues on, moving for an eternity toward the hut until finally she is close enough to make out the fruits on the vines. She plucks one off the vine and tastes it. The Wastelands and their pervasive hunger have made her ravenous.

"Careful!" the Heir snaps, and she actually sounds worried for a moment. "They might be poisonous or cursed or—"

"They're just food," says a voice from the doorway. It isn't an old man. It's a boy, not much older than Ruti, and he regards them with curiosity. "No one who makes it all the way out here is coming with ill will. Who are you?"

The Heir doesn't speak. Nor does Orrin, so Ruti says, "I'm Ruti." She raises her hand, displaying her empty palm. "I am looking for the witch."

The boy raises his own unmarked hand. "I am Adisa," he says. "The witch is dead." He touches the doorpost beside him. "I stay in his home because of the magic that keeps me safe here. I don't dare venture out into the Wastelands."

Ruti stares at him, processing this new revelation. "Are you a witch?"

"No." Adisa ducks his head. "I did not have the talent for it. I kept Fahim's home while he was alive and learned from him how to make ointments and offerings to the spirits. But I can't sing. Fahim said that he had only once met another Markless who had that skill." He eyes Ruti for a moment. "A girl, he said. I had heard word of her in the slums, selling magic for food."

Ruti smiles, a bittersweet pleasure filling her at the thought of the old witch knowing what she'd done with his lesson. "May we enter?" she asks.

Adisa steps back, his eyes narrowing as he takes in the rest of her entourage. "Your Highness," he says, and bows low as they file inside.

The Heir blinks, startled. "How did you know?"

Adisa shakes his head. "No great feat," he admits. "I only see the way you walk and the mark of sewa on your palm. A strong mark," he murmurs, examining it. "The strokes of the mark are dark. You will be formidable when you become Bonded."

"I will not be bonded at all," the Heir says coldly. "We came to see if your master could help us with that."

Adisa is taken aback. "Ah," he says. "I don't know if that's . . . it isn't done," he says finally. "It's. . . ."

"Unnatural," Ruti finishes. "The spirits say it's unnatural. They refuse to grant me this request."

Adisa contemplates them. His hut is small, about the size of Ruti's old shop, with shelves along one wall and a bed against the other. A table is behind him, a dozen half-finished poultices atop it, and Ruti doesn't recognize the ingredients within them. "An unnatural request," Adisa says slowly, "requires an unnatural offering."

Ruti leans forward. "How can an offering be unnatural?"

"There is a place," Adisa says, and lifts one of his poultices, inspecting the objects within. "A lake that can turn a man to stone. It is known as the Lake of the Carved Thousand, and it is deep in the south of Guder, where it meets Rurana and touches the Southern Sea. If you can bottle its water, the spirits may grant you even the most impossible of wishes."

The Heir pounces on that promise. "*May* grant it? So even if we voyage there, we might still be without hope?"

Adisa looks at the Heir for a long while before he speaks. "If you seek to destroy your mark," he says quietly, "then you are already without hope."

12

The arguments begin before they make it back to the Royal Square, and they're still squabbling over their new quest the next day in Ruti's room. "You are not bringing Kimya," the Heir says definitively. "She'll be safer here."

"She's a Markless in the royal palace," Ruti shoots back. "I'm not leaving her here alone for *days*. Maybe even weeks. No one in this palace can be trusted."

The Heir looks irritated. "I'll be here," she says, which silences Ruti at once. "What?" the Heir says at her expression. "Did you think I could go off on a journey for weeks without my uncle raising an alarm? I can't join you." She rolls up the scrolls she's been examining. "I will have my tutors put together a map for you, and I will give you all the coin you need. But Kimya stays here. There is no need for her to join you."

Kimya makes an annoyed sign from the bed, a *pay attention to me!* that has them both looking at her. She wants to go, and she makes it clear with her next signs, but the Heir remains immobile. "One girl traveling alone will move much faster than a girl and her little sister," the Heir reminds Kimya. "And time is of the essence."

"No, *I* am of the essence," Ruti says irritably, picking through different roots that the Heir had brought her. "And I want Kimya with me, *Your Highness.*" She says it in the tone that she knows annoys the Heir, the inflection almost an insult.

The Heir's jaw works beneath her skin. "We'll revisit this later," she says abruptly, and stalks from the room, leaving behind a surge of wind that blows the roots off the table. Ruti mutters something uncomplimentary and goes to collect them.

"You're coming with me," she promises Kimya. "I won't ever leave you behind." Kimya bites into her chocolate sullenly and doesn't respond.

But the Heir is just as intractable the next day. "My tutors have plotted this map for you," she says, setting a scroll down on the table. "The Lake of the Carved Thousand is within an island accessible by sea. You'll have to travel through Rurana in order to reach the lake, and Rurana is. . . ." She pauses. "Prince Torhvin keeps his land strong and difficult for outsiders to penetrate. I don't know how he'd take to a Zideshi Markless wandering through it." She points at one of the red circles on the map. "Here are people we know have hosted royal emissaries from Zidesh before. I will give you enough coin that they will consider it again."

Ruti stares down at the map, overwhelmed. "I've never even left Somanchi," she manages.

The Heir considers her. "Do you need an escort? If need be, I can send Orrin."

"That's fine," Ruti says swiftly, alarmed. "I'll be all right. I don't need any escorts–except my assistant, of course." She gestures at Kimya.

"No," the Heir says, a crack of thunder punctuating her comment as though it is purposeful.

And so it continues. Ruti prepares for the trip with her teeth gritted. She learns to recognize the names of the places written on the map. She practices the Ruranan dialect of Zideshi, the harsher *R* sound and the flimsy *Kh* that is indistinguishable from *K*. She makes lists of herbs for offerings she'll have no use for, only to gain more time before she leaves. For three days of preparation, the Heir returns each day before dinner with exotic ingredients and more information about the lands Ruti will travel through, none of it good. "We know very little about the treatment of Markless in Rurana," the Heir admits one day. "My tutors believe that they aren't easily ignored as they are in Zidesh. If you can paint your hand each day, or if there's a more permanent option–"

"No." Ruti's most recent attempt at a protection poultice falls apart in her hands. "I don't do that."

"Don't or can't?" the Heir prods. Even Kimya is eyeing Ruti curiously. "If it'll make this trip go faster–"

"I don't do that," Ruti bites out again. Fish scales crumble in her fist, and she stares at her hands and refuses to meet the Heir's eyes. "I think we're late to dinner, Your Highness."

Ruti is still expected at dinner with the courtiers and the Regent, even as she plans for a trip that is going to be an ordeal. The Regent eyes her with distrust, but he ignores her as often as he glares at her, focused on his niece. "The scholars are certain now that they've found your soulbond," the Regent says abruptly. "A prince who is as powerful as you will be, and who has the will to match yours. We have sent word, and he is willing to meet you."

"Willing?" the Heir echoes. "How kind of him. You offer him my kingdom on a silver platter and he deigns to accept."

The Regent's eyes darken. "Your spurned suitors have been speaking amongst themselves," he says. "There are not many who are willing to come see you any longer. We are fortunate that the spirits have granted us a prince prepared to give you a try." He clears his throat. "It will be a week's time before he arrives. During that time, you will familiarize yourself with the common etiquette that escapes you. And your bodyguard will be replaced with one of my own." He looks at Orrin with distaste.

The Heir sneers at her uncle. "If you so desperately want to keep my throne, then muster your army and prepare your coup d'etat," she says abruptly. Forks clatter to plates, and there's a gasp in the room. The Regent only shakes his head. Ruti herself gapes at the Heir, startled at the calm way she speaks, the surety with which she makes her sudden accusation.

The courtiers look appalled, and the Heir rises. "I take my leave," she says, walking close along the table as she departs. Courtiers choke on their drinks and lurch forward, freezing up as the Heir walks past them. The Heir inspires fear, but Ruti knows that fear and dismissed it long ago.

She follows the Heir from the room, Orrin jostling her as they head through the doorway at the same time. "Do you really think the Regent wants to control the throne?" she asks. He isn't a kind man or a great leader, but it has been over a decade since the king and queen died and he's never made that power grab before.

"I think he wishes to control me," the Heir says. She is walking toward Tembo's training room, crossing the courtyard as wind whips around her. "I have tired of weak men who believe that I require *control*. I am sewa. Do I look like I can be ruled?"

Ruti stares at her–really stares at this formidable princess who will someday rule Zidesh. There are some who claim that each mark is a sign of how the one who bears it is deep down. Ashto is fire, for people who are passionate and temperamental. Majimm, water, for the calm and intro-spective. Endhi is earth, for those who are grounded and compassionate. And then there is sewa, the rarest of the four signs. Sewa is air and wind and sky, distant and untamed and free, and the Heir can never be ruled by any man.

"No," she murmurs, and there is something in her voice that seems to calm the Heir, to help her find her balance. "No, I don't think you could ever be ruled."

The Heir steps into Tembo's empty room. She lifts a stick and moves it in a blur. She dances with it, whirling it around faster and faster before hurling the stick into a target and lift-ing another to leap with it. "Sing," she orders, and Ruti blinks at her. "Sing me," the Heir repeats, and Ruti begins to sing.

When she sings, she usually has a request in mind, but tonight she has nothing. *Sing me*, the Heir says, and there is only the Heir before her, rising and falling and spinning like a cyclone. Ruti sings as the Heir moves, her voice dancing with the Heir's movements, and she can feel power simmer-ing between them, a new magic that rises from singing to someone else.

The Heir leaps and Ruti's voice leaps with her. The Heir whirls around, bringing the stick down on an invisible enemy, and Ruti crescendos, her voice falling as a waterfall. Every movement of the Heir's is fluid music, and Ruti strains to resist it at first, to keep control of the dance. She fails with the swoop of the Heir's neck and the power that permeates the room.

The Heir seems to glow, the sheen of sweat on her face making Ruti warm as she sings to her movements. There is beauty in how the Heir fights, and Ruti feels her own voice rising to the occasion. Magic permeates every inch of the room, leaving Ruti drunk with it, teetering on unsteady feet as she watches the Heir.

The Heir is lithe and tall, and her braids swing in the opposite direction of her body, her eyes bright and exhilarated. She moves faster than Ruti's ever seen her, somehow more agile than before, Ruti's song giving her power as her dance gives Ruti the same.

Ruti doesn't know how much time passes as she sings. Dusk has come and gone, leaving only the lamps burning in the corners of Tembo's training room as their light source. Orrin lurks by the door, alternately gazing at the Heir in adoration and Ruti with distrust, but Ruti hardly notices him. The Heir spins, faster and faster with the stick moving between her hands, dangerously close to Ruti's position. Ruti chants and chants, the song coming in spurts that seem to speed up impossibly as the Heir approaches, and the Heir is so close that she's going to crash into Ruti–

Ruti stops the song abruptly and the Heir comes to an instant halt, the stick raised between her hands and nearly pressed to Ruti's chest. They're close, close enough that Ruti can see the Heir's chest rising and falling and feel rapid breaths against her cheek. Ruti swallows, her stomach knotting itself up and her heart pounding with the force of the song. The Heir is watching her, their eyes locked, and they stand frozen opposite each other.

It's Orrin who breaks the silence between them, moving toward the Heir to place a hand on her back. She whirls around, still on edge, and she has him pinned against the wall in an instant, the big bodyguard immobile beneath the stick to his neck. "Orrin," she says. She sounds dazed, and it takes her an extra minute to drop the stick. "I. . . ."

She turns, her eyes seeking out Ruti again, and Ruti is frozen by her gaze. It burns like an icy winter wind from the tales, the kind of wind that has never reached Somanchi. Ruti is scorched by it, and it takes all the strength that she has mustered in song for her to duck her head and say, "Your Highness?" in a light tone.

The Heir exhales, raising her chin, a low rumble of thunder in the distance. "Well sung," she says, and she dips her chin and walks outside to the courtyard.

Ruti follows her, oddly numbed by the entire experience. "Did you . . . did you feel the–"

The Heir holds up a hand. "Look," she says, her voice hushed.

Ruti casts an eye across the courtyard, squinting at movements that she can barely make out on the other side of it. They're near the entrance, and there are tiny flames cupped in hands, a few careful lights that shine only for their bearers. Whoever is coming into the Royal Square doesn't want to be seen, and Ruti's breath catches in her throat as one flame-bearer comes close enough to a figure for his face to be visible.

It's the Regent, and the man bearing the flame wears unfamiliar dress, the clothes of a different land. Ruti's eyes narrow, and she ventures, "*Is* he trying for a coup d'etat?"

"No," the Heir says, her deep voice as low as a Fanged One's hiss. "No, he isn't. Those men are from Rurana. Prince Torhvin's men." There is a chill in the air, seeping into Ruti's skin. "He lied to me at dinner. The prince isn't coming in a week's time. He's already here."

She squeezes her hand. "If he's right about this one. . . ." She is silent for a moment, staring down at the dark pattern on her palm. "I can't be bonded," she says, quiet urgency in her voice. "I can't stay here while my uncle passes me off to a man he believes will tame me."

She turns to face Ruti, her dark eyes gleaming with new desperation, and Ruti can only think to say, "We're bringing Kimya."

The Heir looks at her, and Ruti thinks for a moment that the Heir might slap her for her insolence, for pushing an agenda when the Heir is afraid and desperate. But the Heir only nods.

"So be it," says the Heir. "I will have Kalere prepare an offering to the Spotted One for safe voyage. We leave before dawn."

13

They take four donkeys loaded with food and everything else they might need. "They're slower, but they won't be noticed like the royal horses," the Heir points out as they depart. Kimya fits easily on hers, and Ruti is amused at the sight of Orrin, far too bulky for even the largest donkey in the palace, hunched over uncomfortably on his steed.

Ruti has never ridden before, but the donkeys keep a calm pace as they ride southward. "We're looking at three or four days in Zidesh before we reach Rurana," she reports, squinting down at the notes that the Heir's tutors have written for them. "Then maybe another week in Rurana until we reach Guder's peninsula."

The Heir nods, riding beside her in the light of dawn. "We will have to be careful in Zidesh," she says. "Too many know my face. And my uncle won't rest until he finds me."

"What will you say when you return?"

The Heir pauses, considers. "That's a question for the way back," she says at last. "Then, if the magic holds, I will be in control of my own destiny. And if my uncle resists, I will take control by force." Thunder rumbles to punctuate her declaration, and Ruti shivers.

"What about your tutors? They must know where you're going."

"They won't breathe a word to my uncle." She says it with certainty, and Ruti persists.

"How can you know–"

The Heir puts up a quelling hand. "My tutors are mine and mine alone. One day they will be my advisors. They would die rather than betray me." She shakes her head. "No more chatter. We must ride on."

They ride for hours and hours through narrow, springy trees that drip water when they are rustled. Snakes hang down in looping shapes just above them, and the chirping sound of monkeys and crickets echoes around them until Ruti can't recall a time before the noise. The air is fresh and damp, the scent of the wet trees strong in her nostrils, and she is covered by a sheen of sweat only from sitting within it. Eventually Kimya is keeling over on her donkey, arms wrapped around its neck in an attempt to stay on while dozing off.

By the next afternoon, they're beyond the wet woods and into drier forests with tall trees whose branches are narrow and conical. There are fewer animals here, without the boldness of the snakes and insects of the wet woods, and the air is thinner and cooler. The ground beneath them grows higher and rockier, and they ride up and down mountains that stretch for miles between Somanchi and Rurana's border. "There are few cities in the mountains," the Heir says. "Only Lubasa, and small settlements here and there. We can't stop in Lubasa. My uncle will have soldiers stationed there."

There has been little conversation until now, only silent riding, and it's a relief to slip off the donkey when the Heir gives the order. Ruti's thighs ache, unused to the way the donkeys move, and she collapses against a tree as Orrin helps the Heir dismount.

There is tenderness in his motions, a care toward the Heir that has her stroking his arm, and Ruti feels as though she's witnessing a private moment between them. She attributes her displeasure to dislike of Orrin, though it doesn't explain the lump in her throat when she watches the movement of the Heir's fingers and the way the Heir watches him with attentiveness, as though his words are precious to her. She turns away, listens instead to a high-pitched, distant chirping—a single bird, calling out in the hollow thrum of the night—and watches Kimya crawl to her as Orrin and the Heir speak in quiet murmurs.

When they part, Ruti finally dares to look back at them, wrapping an arm around Kimya. Orrin glances around critically, raising his hands to blast small branches from the trees around them. "Firewood," he explains at Kimya's wide-eyed stare. "We will need a fire to keep away leopa–" He freezes, staring around in alarm. "Spotted Ones," he amends.

To call a predator of Zidesh by animal-name instead of spirit-name is to summon its displeasure. Perhaps that isn't a fear in the Royal Square, where the people are well-guarded, and there's a savage kind of pleasure in seeing the fear that Orrin's words have evoked in both his own heart and the Heir's. *Spoiled*, Ruti thinks.

Kimya nudges her as though she knows exactly what Ruti is thinking, and she gets up suddenly, her legs unsteady. Carefully, she makes her way through the clearing where they've settled down. She picks up a few small branches from the ground, offering them to Orrin.

Orrin looks startled, and his eyes flicker to Kimya's unmarked palm with wariness. But he takes the branches and says, "Thank you," setting them down with the ones he's already collected. "Can you find some rocks now?"

Ruti helps this time, picking through the rocks until they've set up a border between them and the fire. When the site is ready, Orrin presses his hands to the branches and lightning crackles from his palms. The branches glow faintly, fire barely licking at them. It's dim, carefully controlled so it illuminates only a tiny patch of land. It smells sharper than an ordinary fire, of charred metals instead of the pleasant scent of burning wood, but Ruti can feel its warmth from where she sits in the shadows.

They eat from the rations they've brought along. Ruti is ravenous, spoiled by her time at the Royal Square, and she has to actively slow herself down so she won't devour her meal to the point of sickness. The bread has gotten hard and tasteless after the changes in humidity, but Ruti still savors it. Kimya does the same, eyes closed, and the Heir sits beside her and eats her own bread in silence. Everyone is quiet, focused on their food and exhausted.

Kimya is the first to fall asleep, curled onto Ruti's lap, and Ruti settles her down on one of the bedrolls. Orrin is tending the fire while the Heir stares into the flames, and the Heir says suddenly, "Did she ever speak?"

Ruti shakes her head, stroking Kimya's hair. "Not since I've known her," she says. "A lot of Markless little ones don't speak. Sometimes it's about survival. Sometimes they've just . . . been through something that took their voice." She'd met a Markless once who'd been kept by his family for a few years, hidden away behind the doors of their home and abused and used within it. When he'd finally fled to the slums, he hadn't spoken a word.

The Heir blinks at her. "Not since you've known her?" she echoes. "I thought she was your sister."

Ruti shrugs. "I've had a lot of sisters over the years," she murmurs. "Little ones come to me and don't leave. But Kimya has survived the longest." She laughs dully. "Markless don't have *siblings*. You'd need a family for that."

"That's true." The Heir is quiet for a moment, contemplative. "So you never knew your family?"

Ruti shakes her head. "I must have lived with them when I was very little. The mark can take up to a year or two to appear. They probably held out hope until then. My earliest memories are all of the orphanages in the slums. There was never enough food and too many children, and eventually I ran away and went to find food on my own."

When she looks up from the fire, the Heir is watching her, her eyes flickering orange from the reflection of the flames. Ruti wraps her arms around herself, self-conscious in her vulnerability, and says, "What about you, Your Highness? You barely knew your family, either."

The Heir's lips quirk downward. "Stop calling me that."

"Sorry. Is *Your Majesty* more appropriate now that you're planning to overthrow your uncle?" She means it to be snide, but it comes out too light, almost teasing. Instinctively, Ruti glances across the fire to where Orrin is tending the flames, his gaze distant.

The Heir ignores her gibe. "I remember my parents," she says finally. "My father was a good and noble ruler. My mother was tender and cared for all of her people. They passed on to the spirit world when I was seven."

Ruti's brow furrows. "You talk about them like a subject, not their daughter."

The Heir rolls her eyes. "I was adored and pampered," she says. "It isn't something I'd like to discuss with *you*." She reaches for Ruti, her palm closing over the back of Ruti's hand, and turns their joined hands together to display Ruti's bare palm. Ruti is staggered into silence, her heart thumping against her chest, and the Heir reaches over to trace a pattern into Ruti's bare palm. There is no more fear when she touches it, none of the wariness of that first night at the palace. Instead, she runs her finger over it with fascination.

The fire crackles, and Ruti murmurs, "It isn't your fault that I'm Markless. It isn't anyone's fault. This is just . . . how things are."

The Heir says, "Not in Niyaru." Ruti looks at her, taken by surprise. "Tembo was born up north, did you know? He told me once. . . ." Her eyes are distant, her finger still running along Ruti's palm as her voice falls into a deeper, huskier storytelling lilt. "There aren't cities in Niyaru's deserts. The people live in little villages where every hand is needed, marked or not. Most Markless stay with their families. They even marry Unbonded sometimes."

Ruti's heart clenches so hard that she has to take a moment before she can respond, blinking away traitorous tears. "It sounds like a fairytale," she says finally. "I don't believe it."

"Maybe it was," the Heir whispers, but she turns to look at Ruti, her ever-unreadable eyes suddenly penetrating, and Ruti feels the heat of the flames as warm as the heat of the Heir's gaze. "Tembo is prone to exaggeration."

Orrin clears his throat before Ruti can respond. "We'll need to set out again in a few hours," he says, and the Heir drops Ruti's hand, shifting away from her incrementally. "The Markless girl should sleep now if she's going to take the second watch."

Ruti glowers at him, irritated at the interruption and at his careless designation of her. The Heir nods. "I can take the third," she says, moving to the far side of the fire. Ruti sets up her bedroll and stretches out on it.

Her last sight before she slumbers is of Orrin wrapping an arm around the Heir's shoulders, and her dreams are full of turmoil.

By the next day, Ruti's legs are numb, the pain from riding a dull ache that she can hardly feel anymore. As the days continue, there are only the tall pines of the mountains, the scent of goats in the air, and the howls of the wind through the trees.

At night, Kimya is the one to find them shelter. Ruti lights a tallow candle that smells of cardamom and plumeria for the Spotted One and sings for them before she sleeps, a chant she puts together that might enervate and sate them with artificial strength from the spirits. The Heir watches Ruti one night as she sings, her eyes glowing, and when Ruti is finished, the Heir says, "You sing beautifully."

Ruti ducks her head. "It's the magic," she says, biting her lip. The Heir somehow makes her more nervous when they *aren't* squabbling.

"Not only the magic," the Heir says, and she tilts her head and smiles.

It's the most remarkable thing that Ruti has glimpsed in a dull life free of shine, and she is struck speechless by it. She can't respond, can't come up with anything snide to say, and she instead stretches out on her bedroll and watches the Heir, the smile that softens the sharp edges of her face and brings a glow of warmth to her cold eyes.

The terrain is less uphill the next day. There's a pass between the mountains that tower above them, a rocky route through a low-running river. The donkeys walk through the water easily, moving faster than expected. "We'll reach Rurana by nightfall," the Heir proclaims, running a finger along their route as they ride. "Beyond that, I don't know what we'll face."

"The visitors at the palace were from Rurana," Ruti recalls suddenly. It had meant little to her then, another name of a place she'd never gone, but now it seems relevant. "Is it safe for us to travel through it?"

"We have no choice," the Heir says grimly.

"Have you ever been there before?"

"I never met Prince Torhvin," the Heir explains. "Rurana has never invited outsiders, but the older princes of Rurana came to Somanchi a few years ago. Prince Torhvin was the third son. Not likely to be any more than a noble with a city to rule, back then."

Kimya signs the same question Ruti speaks aloud. "What happened?"

"A coup." The Heir's donkey shifts, rising and falling as it climbs over a rocky protrusion. "The king died a year after that visit. The oldest son, Prince Jaquil, was meant to rule, but the second son, Prince Serrold, made a power grab. There was deep unrest in Rurana for months, culminating in what should have been the fatal injury of Prince Jaquil. But he didn't die. Doctors managed instead to keep him in a deep sleep. After that, the people of Rurana rose up against Serrold."

It's safe to assume that Rurana treats Markless with disfavor, but it seems an unpleasant place even to be Marked. "And Prince Torhvin saw his chance."

"Prince Torhvin was put into place as the new Regent of the throne. He had Serrold put to death and rules in Jaquil's stead. He is a strong leader, one who will probably lead his people forever as prince, not king." The Heir looks pensive. "That is all we know."

Ruti pieces together another part of the puzzle. "That's why he was so willing to come to Zidesh," she says. "He's smart. He knows that if he bonds with you, he can take your throne and become a king. Then he would have full authority over both Zidesh and Rurana."

The Heir scoffs. "He will never bond with me. I won't be some power-hungry ruler's tool to gain even more." She rides carefully, her donkey stepping up above the river as Ruti and

Kimya follow. Orrin leads them, but there is space here for the rest of them to ride side by side. The river turns, and they continue straight across sparse mud and dirt that is thin and gritty like sand along the mountains.

"You'd rather be Orrin's," Ruti says snidely.

The Heir gives her a dark look. "Orrin doesn't want the throne," she says. "He only wants me. There have been Unbonded queens in Zidesh's past. Two hundred years ago, there was even a queen who ruled alone. The people then didn't question her."

"A lot has happened in two hundred years."

"Yes," the Heir agrees. "But the people are more malleable than my uncle believes. If I am a strong ruler and the land is prosperous, no one will care about what is on my palm or yours."

"Mine?" Ruti says, casting her a look. The Heir has spoken before of aiding the Markless in the slums, but never of anything as dramatic as *acceptance*. It's an oddly idealistic concept for her. "I think we'd have a better chance of getting the people to accept you as a queen who rules a–*ahh*!"

She lets out a strangled cry. Out of nowhere, her donkey's front hoof has slipped, tilting him downward and sending Ruti tumbling to the muddy ground. Ruti struggles to stand, but it's as though she's being restrained, as though the mud itself is holding her down.

She looks down. The mud *is* holding her down, as though it's being controlled by a Bonded with matching endhi signs. But there is no one in sight, and the more she moves, the deeper she sinks into the ground. *Quicksand*, she realizes dully. She's never experienced it in Somanchi, but there are stories of mud that swallows people whole near the sea.

The Heir sees her. "Ruti!" she cries out. "Orrin, *help!*"

Orrin turns around, looking in alarm at them. Ruti sinks deeper into the mud with every movement, her legs and hips encased in it now, and she screams. She can't help herself, the terror of being devoured by the earth too great to think, to sing, and the Heir calls her name desperately, on her knees in front of the quicksand and reaching for her as the wind whips against her face.

Orrin bounds over, his eyes taking in Ruti's terror, and he steps back cautiously. There is indecision in his eyes, a reluctance to risk himself over a Markless he dislikes so deeply, and Ruti is certain for a moment that he will leave her to die.

"Stop struggling," Orrin says at last, and his shoulders straighten, resolve settling on his face. "You're going to trap yourself even deeper." He spins around suddenly, seizing Kimya as she makes a desperate leap for Ruti. Her eyes are narrowed with ferocious determination as she struggles against Orrin's arms.

"Kimya, stay back!" Ruti bites out. "Hold her, don't let her–" She feels claustrophobia begin to envelop her, her heart racing as she stops moving at last. She isn't sinking anymore, the mud somewhere around her waist, but she can't seem to move either, to lift herself from the mud.

"We need water," Orrin says curtly. "Pour water in and lie still and the mud will release you." It's the Heir who grabs a flask and flies down to the river, running back to them with her chest heaving from the speed and incline as she pours the water into the mud. The pull on Ruti's legs is a little less now, and the Heir reaches over the pool of mud to take Ruti's hands.

"Careful," Orrin warns her, but she's already pulling Ruti forward with all her might. She is strong, muscles built from years of stick fighting, and she is able to yank Ruti from the quicksand with a single protracted pull. Ruti tumbles into her, free of the mud, and the force of it is enough to knock the Heir off her feet.

They roll down the rocky slope together, bruised as they bounce toward the river, and Ruti has the presence of mind to press her hands to the back of the Heir's head, protecting her from the rocks. The Heir follows suit, the two of them entwined as they tumble to the river, banging down into the shallow water after a few moments.

Ruti, stretched out in the river and coated in mud and bruises, can only laugh helplessly, the fear gone and the adrenaline that remains almost like hysteria. The Heir stares down at her, her lovely face streaked with mud and her travel clothes caked in it, and Ruti laughs some more, high and endless and so utterly overwhelmed at it all.

The laughter only fades as Ruti takes in their position at last. The Heir is atop her, her hands still cradling Ruti's head, her legs tangled with Ruti's in the river. There is a breathless fear still in the Heir's eyes, and her body is pressed to Ruti's, and Ruti freezes, the mood shifting to something very solemn. "You saved me," she whispers, and there is no more hysterical laughter in her voice.

The Heir blinks down at Ruti, her eyes glazed over, and murmurs, "Well, I couldn't lose my witch *now*, could I?" Her hands move, letting Ruti's hair fan out in the shallow water, and she presses a hand to Ruti's cheek with the same tenderness that Ruti has seen Orrin granted. Her head dips down and Ruti stops moving, her skin burning with desire that she can't, she *can't*–

Orrin says from above them, his voice strained, "Dekala."

The Heir jolts, rolling off of Ruti and landing in the water. There is still mud on her knees from where she'd crouched and pulled Ruti from the quicksand. Ruti notices it with a dazed sort of wanting, sees the water washing it away. "Come," Orrin says. "I saw–just over the edge of the mountain–"

Ruti rises to her feet, her thighs and arms trembling as Kimya signs enthusiastic motions that Ruti only halfway comprehends. Orrin leads them all past the quicksand to the dip that their donkeys had been climbing before their distraction, and Ruti gasps at what stands below them.

It is a lush forest, the mountains descending to closely packed trees of green and tan. Grasslands stretch past the forest into the distant horizon. The land is different here, the sun shining down on low grass dotted with clusters of gentle, hooved animals grazing ahead, and the tall mountains of Zidesh are no more.

They've reached Rurana.

14

They clean their clothes in the river before it winds away toward the sea. Ruti is in a fresh set of tunic and pants, and the Heir wears a deep purple set that fits her perfectly. "We can't follow the river much longer," Orrin warns them. "The sea this far south is infested with Diri."

"Diri?" Ruti asks.

"Pirates." The Heir straightens, draping her wet clothes against a tree branch to dry. The sun is stronger here, near the bottom of the mountains and the green forests ahead, and the clothes are hardly dripping.

"There are more cities near the sea, anyway," Orrin says, gesturing toward the distance. "The woods are safer for us. We can't be seen."

Ruti shields her eyes to peer at the sun flickering through the greenery ahead of them. Now that they're at the foot of the mountains, she can see the thick forest that stretches between them and the grasslands. It looks safe and cool, the air temperate and the underbrush packed with a riot of colorful flowers and berries beneath long-branched, sweet-smelling trees that shield the land from the sun.

The animals they find are easily startled by visitors. They're smaller than the creatures in the wet forests or the grasslands, chittering long-armed monkeys hanging by their tails and spiders as large as Ruti's hands, and Orrin even fells a few fat, short-winged birds for them to eat when night falls.

"The grasslands will be more trying," the Heir observes. "If only because we'll be more easily seen. Orrin can fight off any predators that attack us in the woods." Orrin had frightened off a single Spotted One the day before with a lightning bolt that had crashed right in front of it. Today he fries several Fanged Ones as they make their way through the forest, and Ruti can feel the spirits' displeasure in the air. "It's Ruranans I'm worried about."

"Do you think your uncle has given up?" Ruti wonders. "Or is he still searching for you?"

"He will have sent messengers to all the major cities, I'm sure." The Heir looks pensive. "And perhaps claimed that he is awaiting a ransom. But he must know by now that I left of my own free will. My attendants will have confirmed it when they recall how we left my chambers fully dressed for travel. He will never admit it to the people and suffer that humiliation, though."

"So he's waiting for you to come back."

The Heir scoffs. "Waiting to hear of my death, no doubt." She unrolls her bedroll, just a thick rectangle of cowskin, onto flat dirt with a coating of moss over it. "It's getting dark. Kimya is already drifting off." She nods to the area near the fire where Kimya's eyes are half-closed, her mouth still chewing mechanically. It's been rare that they've had food they don't have to ration out, even burnt food struck by lightning. "We should sleep here for as long as we can," she says, her voice drowsy as dusk glows dim around them, shining through the leaves of the large tree that surrounds them. "It won't take more than a day to cross this forest."

The Heir's eyes close and Ruti glances across the fire at Orrin, who looks just as exhausted. These days spent riding are taking their toll on them all. Ruti's legs are stronger than they've ever been, but they ache still when she's off her donkey, and she's eating less now than she did at the palace.

Still, if Orrin is tired enough that he won't be able to stand watch at the first shift, she has to stay awake. She struggles to sit up, humming a little plea to the spirits for energy that helps marginally. For a few extra minutes, she fights off her tiredness. It's long enough to lean back against a tree trunk, yawning, and watch the others toss and turn in their sleep.

The Heir lets out a little noise and Ruti looks blearily over at her, incapable of fighting an odd surge of fondness that has begun to make itself known each time the Heir does something even a tiny bit less than obnoxious. Her heartbeat quickens at the sight of the Heir, and she refuses to think about what the warmth she feels might mean. The Heir is. . . .

The Heir is in love with Orrin. The Heir is willing to fight destiny itself to keep Orrin, and Ruti is here to facilitate that. Maybe she's attracted to the Heir, just a little bit. There have been other girls before, Markless drifting past her shop with an aimless desire for companionship. But always brief, always gone soon after. Not like the Heir, who has dominated so much of Ruti's life for weeks now.

It's nonsense to think about, and Ruti brushes it aside, ignoring the pang of her heart as she dismisses it. The fire has all but gone out, and Ruti must build it again without Orrin's lightning. She leans forward, brushing at the flame with a branch, her other hand supporting her as it lies flat against the ground.

The fire extinguishes entirely, and Ruti lets out a frustrated noise. She'll have to wake up Orrin. It's cold in the woods without the fire, dark beneath the stars, and the moon is behind a cloud. She can't quite make out the lump across the clearing that is Orrin, passed out sitting up, and she tries to lift her hand to pick herself up.

Her hand doesn't lift. In fact, there's an odd pressure on it, something she's never felt before. The moon emerges from the clouds to light up the night, and Ruti screams.

A tree is growing through her hand.

A *tree*, fully grown, directly impaling her palm where there is no mark, stretching high above her as though it's always been there. *No*, she realizes in quiet horror. It's the same large tree that they settled beneath in the first place, but its branches droop now, digging into the ground as though they're taking root.

Another branch has landed directly on Kimya's neck, thin, spidery roots spreading around her as they burrow into the ground. The Heir is crawling with roots, creeping down her body to lock her within them, and Ruti screams again.

She can see Orrin now, also covered in the roots that sprout from the branches, and the grass seems higher now, thicker and stronger. "Wake up!" Ruti shouts. "Wake *up*!"

The Heir is the first to wake, and she struggles against her bonds as her mouth opens wide in horror. Behind her, Ruti sees that the donkeys are unharmed, peacefully grazing on the newly grown grass. "Kimya!" Ruti cries out, and Kimya gnashes her teeth and windmills her arms as she sees the roots holding her down.

Something brushes Ruti's shoulder. Another branch, waving in the sudden wind, and Ruti flinches as roots slither from it to slide down her arm. Desperately, she draws her breath to sing.

The trees seem to sway with her song. She's dizzy, and she doesn't know if she's dreaming or not, but the Heir is yanking helplessly at strong roots and Orrin is howling and Ruti can't feel the spirits at all.

Instead, she feels the trees. They're *alive*, alive in a way that plants have never felt before. They rustle around her, her song echoed and reflected by them, and she's surprised when a deep, husky voice begins to sing with her. The Heir, her eyes glazed as the trees conduct their music.

A crackle of lightning. Orrin has hit the tree directly at its center, and the branches rot and fade, the roots no longer binding them. But suddenly it doesn't seem to matter very much at all, and Orrin's voice joins theirs, his lightning fizzling.

Ruti has always been the singer of her chants, the one controlling what she's singing and why. Even in the exhilarating moment when she'd sung the Heir's dance, she'd still felt the thread of the song in her will, in her choice to follow the Heir's dancing. Here, there is no choice. Their lips are parted, sounds vibrating from their vocal cords in perfect harmony. They rise together, Ruti's motions jerky as she follows the movements of the trees.

She stumbles forward, moves with the trees and pitches her voice low with them, and Orrin and the Heir gather beside her. Ruti sees terror on the Heir's face, and she knows her own face must look frightened, too. But neither of them can stop singing. The wind rushes in time with them, vibrates with the trees, and the woods echo a mournful, intoxicating melody with them.

Then Ruti hears the voice of a figure in the trees, who never quite materializes into a person. The group is moving swiftly through the woods now, so quick that they're nearly being carried, and she hears the chorus of song around her, the forest and the Heir and Orrin and Ruti an organ of the magic of the woods.

And as their voices crescendo, Ruti sees where they're going. The woods climb higher in front of them, a final remnant of the mountains at Zidesh's border, and they stop abruptly at a cliff forested with tall pine trees. There is a drop before them, a sheer fall onto rock down below, yet Ruti's soprano soars joyously with the trees as her heart beats with terror.

Ruti's foot touches the edge. Her whole body arches to leap when something hits her. She doubles over, nearly slipping forward. The same thing that hit her now seizes her, yanking her back and shoving a mixture of leaf and dirt and underbrush into her mouth. She chokes, her song muffled and then stopped, and she hurls herself forward again as she realizes what the Heir is about to do.

What *she'd* been about to do. The trees are still singing, but their power has lessened, and there's a blur of energy passing Ruti now, tackling the Heir to the ground and then Orrin. The one unaffected member of their party stuffs more underbrush into their mouths, and Ruti stumbles back, dumbfounded at how close she'd been to death.

Kimya moves as quick as lightning, darting between them and wrestling with all three as the trees still harmonize. She holds up a warning finger as the Heir attempts to sing past her gag, and she reaches out and claps her on the head, hard.

The Heir looks at her in outrage, then slow comprehension. The truth is beginning to dawn on Ruti, too.

Kimya makes a quick sign with her hands, a command they both recognize. *Run*, her hands say, and the girls run.

Orrin follows behind them, all four of them stumbling through the woods as the forest coaxes them to sing again. Ruti *wants* to, craves it as much as she knows it will be her doom, but Kimya slaps her the moment she manages to pull some of the leaf from her mouth and shoves in more. *Run*, she signs again, and they run down the side of the mountain, slipping and sliding and utterly lost and terrified, until they tumble down in front of a large, absurd-looking structure.

It is a house built three stories high of gleaming metal that winds through the trees of the forest, the branches still growing. There is no brick or clay or mud to hold it together, only solid metal with no gaps even where it touches the trees. Ruti skids to a halt in front of it, and a woman steps outside and stares at them.

"*Ahi'ataka*," she says, and at their blank stares, switches to a thick Ruranan dialect of Zideshi. "I thought we might have some visitors for the guest house tonight."

Ruti tears the gag from her mouth. It is quiet here, the singing trees giving the metalwood monstrosity a wide berth, and she says, spitting out dirt, "Guest house?"

"I'm one of the proprietors," the woman says, kind eyes swallowed by smiling round cheeks and stubby-nailed hands smoothing down the colorful fabric of her tunic. She waves them toward her as though they aren't ragged, terrified strangers covered in dirt. Ruti sees ashto and endhi joined on the woman's palm, the odd mixture that gives its Bonded mastery over metal. "Come in, come in!"

15

Inside, the metal house is just as odd as the outside. The trees that make up its walls are alive, creatures moving in and out of the house through knots in the trees and scampering past them. The tables in the main room are tree stumps, and there is a winding metal staircase in one corner that is surrounded by leaves.

The woman who brought them in is a pleasant-looking Niyarumi named Yawen, plump and cheerful and fully awake, as though it isn't the middle of the night. "We've talked about building a proper inn here, but there just aren't enough visitors to justify all that effort," she says, shaking her head. "*Aeil'ita'ya*–the Murmuring Woods–is the end of most travelers."

Kimya signs a question to her and glances over to Ruti to translate. But to Ruti's surprise, Yawen says, delighted, "Ah, you've been taught the hand-language of the Niyaru!" She signs in response, her hands flying so quickly that Ruti can't follow her words. Kimya answers, her own hands just as fast. Ruti had thought herself skilled at Kimya's language by now, but she is left with the uncomfortable sensation that she's been utterly ignorant all along.

After a few minutes, Yawen looks up again as though she's just remembered the rest of them. *Kimya*, she signs, as slowly as one might speak to a toddler, and simultaneously speaking out loud, "says that you came close to an end of your own in the woods."

The Heir, looking dignified with her face cleaned and only a few stray leaves trapped in her braided coils, says, "We were nearly sung to our deaths."

"Legend has it that a witch-prince with the powers of majimm and endhi combined was once killed by a tyrant king in this place," a voice says from the stairs. A second woman descends, tall and pretty, her puffy hair streaked with an odd red that looks like the glint of steel when it's heated. "Where he died, greenery grew to create the forest, and at night, he still seeks his vengeance. The spirits roam free here, and they protect only those who make them offerings before they sleep."

They stare up at her and she smiles, extending a hand. "I am Adimu. With my wife, I maintain this guest house," she says, and Ruti sees on her outstretched palm a mark that matches Yawen's. "I have been tracking your donkeys from above." She gestures vaguely upstairs. "When they arrive, of course, we can settle the matter of payment, but why don't you enjoy something to eat first?"

Her hand still dangles in front of them, waiting for them to press their palms to hers, but no one has moved yet. Finally, Kimya stretches out her dirty gloved hand to Adimu's, and Ruti blurts out, "Are you *Bonded*?"

Never has she experienced such a thing before, two women with matching marks who exchange an indulgent smile at her disbelief. "Yes, darling," Yawen says. Kimya signs a question to her, and Yawen signs back in a rush of information of which Ruti only gleans a quarter. "It is not altogether uncommon for two men or two women to be bonded to each other."

Adimu's eyes are sharper. "If this is a shock for you, perhaps you will be best served in the woods tonight."

"No, not at all," Ruti hastens to explain. "I just . . . I've never seen it before. Not *Bonded*." The idea of being with another girl had always seemed like a relationship unique to the Markless, to Unbonded who hadn't found their match. Ruti has always thought that destiny must not look kindly on those who will not breed, and she hadn't imagined that. . . .

Beside her, the Heir stares at the women's marks, the same look of disbelief on her face. "My tutors . . . my teachers say it's impossible," she says at last.

"And yet, here we are," Adimu points out.

The Heir is uncowed by Adimu's hard eyes. "You share a mark," the Heir concedes. "But so do thousands of others with metal skill. It means nothing."

"It meant something when we touched for the first time and our hands glowed," Yawen says serenely. "And then we were Bonded. Not every soulbond is between a man and a woman. Not every soulbond is romantic, either. I have met a woman who bonded with her own son, her life entwined with his forever. We once hosted soulbonds who were traveling companions, a blind man and a deaf one, who guided each other on their travels and were not in the least bit attracted to each other. Or so they said. The person your soul craves to bond with can serve many purposes for you, my dear, and the most shortsighted of them is marriage."

Ruti gapes at them, lost. "I've never heard any of that before."

"Well, you are Zideshi," Adimu says, her eyes sweeping over their garb. "The Zideshi prize some limited traditions, if you'll pardon my saying so. We are from Niyaru, where the Fanged One roams free. Even speaking aloud can draw her fatal interest, and life is too short to dwell on old customs."

"We aren't Zideshi," the Heir lies. "We are travelers from the sea." But it is clear that they aren't, from their colorful dress to the lack of bands around their necks. The people of Rurana wear plain colors, greys and browns, and their ornamentation is in their jewelry.

Adimu lifts one dubious eyebrow. "In Niyaru," she says, "Bonded women can live where they wish, though the land is far more dangerous than it is in this place. Rurana is more like Zidesh, but no one bothers us here. We are protected by the trees and by the Fanged One herself." She gestures at the walls around them, and Ruti notices for the first time that there are gaps in the walls, openings in which Fanged Ones lie dormant. Their scales gleam in the light, and Ruti sees one enormous, lazy eye open to watch them and then close again.

Ruti shudders. Adimu exchanges a glance with Yawen. "Come," she says. "Eat something. My wife will fetch your donkeys."

Yawen disappears out of the house while Adimu prepares a warm soup for them on heated metal. "Ruranan soldiers gifted us this stove while they were traveling," she says. "It never cools."

"*Kuduwaí*," the Heir breathes, staring at the stove. "I've only ever heard rumors."

Ruti is bewildered. "What's kuduwaí?"

"Magic. Of sorts." The Heir sits down at a table as Adimu brings them soup. "There are stories that the Ruranan witches have crafted a way for Bonded to keep their powers alive even after they're gone, with the blessing of the spirits. That a Bonded with mastery over water might keep the waves flowing long after he has departed, that a Bonded with mental powers could keep a whole city floating with kuduwaí. It is a jealously guarded secret, if it is true. Only Ruranan royalty and the generals of their army know how to create kuduwaí. It's said that it is how the Ruranan navy is so strong."

"I have seen it in action," Adimu says soberly. "We are all fortunate Rurana keeps to itself rather than attacking its neighbors. And for my stove, of course." The soup is hot, and the metal still glows red when they're done and Yawen has returned.

"The guest house is small, but it should serve your purposes," Yawen promises them, leading them up the staircase to the top floor. "There are two bedrooms. I will bring you some water once you're settled in."

She leaves them at the top of the stairs. Ruti ducks under the doorway of the low ceiling to survey the room on the right. It's a small room, one large bed in the center of it and a dresser beside the bed. A small wooden chair is against the wall, though it looks hard bottomed and uncomfortable.

The Heir, Ruti expects, will take a room with Orrin. She brings her bags into the right room and surveys the wide bed. It could fit four, maybe five women in it, and she supposes that it's meant for multiple guests. Kimya and Ruti will fit in nicely.

But the Heir follows her into the room, eyeing the bed and then the little chair expectantly. "I'm not sleeping on the floor," Ruti says at once, looking at her askance. And then, because she can't help herself, "Aren't you going to share with your *future consort*?"

Orrin and the Heir both look scandalized. "She's the heir to the throne," Orrin says from the doorway, scowling at Ruti.

"I can't share a bed with a man, even one I intend to marry." The Heir casts an eye on the bed. "There's space for us all in there."

"Is there?" Ruti's stomach flips, something within it fluttering to the point of distraction.

Yawen offers them a few ornate bands that fit around their necks.

"If you wish to travel unmolested through Rurana, you will need to look the part," Yawen says, smiling at them. "And my wife sent you some cloaks as well. No need to attract attention in the grasslands. From Maned Ones or . . . others." Her eyes flicker over them, and the Heir thanks her graciously and offers her more coin. She refuses it. "Consider it a gift," she says, her eyes lingering on the Heir for a moment. "I think we are all best off if you blend in on your journey." There's a note of significance in her voice, a hint that she might be aware of whom she houses tonight, and Ruti says so as they prepare for bed.

"Word must have spread all the way here that I'm missing," the Heir says. She's fully clean again, in the set of clothes they'd washed in the river, and she climbs onto the bed and beneath the covers. Kimya curls up beside her in the center of the bed, and Ruti tries to feel relieved at that. "They might suspect, but they don't know."

Kimya signs her trust for the woman who speaks her language and a dismissal to any new paranoia. "We'll be gone soon," Ruti agrees, "and the Regent won't think to search the woods for a guest house made of metal."

She climbs into the bed gingerly, tucking her feet in under the blanket. The Heir tugs at it. Ruti yanks it back. There is *plenty* on the other side, and the Heir is just provoking her. It's easier to be annoyed with the Heir than to feel any other way toward her, and Ruti gives her a dark look and holds on tightly to her side of the blanket.

It's a mistake, though, because they both really do have too much blanket and neither will give up any, and so they're both pressed up against Kimya as she rolls over and falls fast asleep. When she's out, Ruti realizes suddenly that she is barely more than two handbreadths from the Heir, only Kimya their border, and she takes in a ragged breath.

She wants. . . .

Never mind what she wants.

The Heir's eyes are on Kimya, brown and alive as the wood of the trees in the wall behind them, and they regard her in silence for a long moment before the Heir says, "Are Markless capable of love?"

Ruti is taken aback, unsure of whether or not she's being insulted. "I love Kimya, don't I?"

"No. I mean. . . ." The Heir looks frustrated. "As Yawen spoke of. The sort of love that joins Bonded. If you aren't

Marked, then does that mean you have no capacity for love?"

This isn't an attempt to insult, then. Just sheer curiosity from the Heir, who has little insult in her lately. Ruti shrugs. "I don't know," she admits. "Not much time to fall in love in the slums. I've wondered sometimes about some of the allies who stay together from childhood. I think anyone can fall in love," she points out, and it pains her to add, "You and Orrin did it outside of your bonds, too."

The Heir's eyes close off from Ruti's again, as they do whenever she brings up Orrin. "If you are capable of love," she says slowly, "then what separates you from the Marked beyond the blank space on your palm?

"We are told that Markless *can't* love." Ruti bristles, and the Heir says, "But we are also told that every soulbond ends in marriage, that a woman will always bond with a man. Perhaps Adimu is right. Perhaps we over-care for tradition. Perhaps tradition is not truth."

"Perhaps," Ruti whispers. It's strange, the way tiny snatches of goodness from the Heir seem to take hold of Ruti and consume her, burn her alive from inside without leaving so much as a scratch. She yearns suddenly to take the Heir's hand, to clasp it in hers and trace the pattern of her half moon mark. She yearns suddenly to lift Kimya and move her behind them, to move closer and–

She sucks in a breath. "Or perhaps they're all right, Your Highness," she says, playful instead of longing.

The Heir sighs. "Stop," she says, scowling at Ruti.

Ruti smirks at her, the mood shifting. "I thought you liked reminding me that you rule me," she says, a hint of a taunt in her voice.

The Heir's scowl intensifies. "I offered you my name," she says. "I don't gift that lightly."

Ruti takes another breath, processing that statement. *I don't gift that lightly.* She had seen the Heir's name as another challenge, another mocking invitation that Ruti had been determined to eschew. Now she hesitates, thinking back to the interaction with renewed understanding.

It had been a gift from the Heir. An offering, not a challenge. Her name, gifted to Ruti, to use as though they truly are equals. And in this moment, lying in a bed with the other girl and seeing the quiet hurt that had come with Ruti's dismissal of her gift, it is suddenly impossible to think of her only as the Heir anymore. The Heir is an impersonal, distant role. It hardly defines the inimitable Princess Dekala. "All right," Ruti says.

"All right, *what?*" Dekala presses, and Ruti almost contemplates adding a *Your Highness* to it again. She likes the way that Dekala's eyes flash when she's angry, the little bolt of cold ice that comes with it. Never fire. Always ice, cold as a winter's wind.

But she stops short of baiting Dekala right now. "All right," she says simply, and Dekala lets out a little huff.

"*All right*," she says, her voice devoid of any amusement, and rolls over, away from Ruti. "Goodnight, Ruti."

It's the first time Ruti's slept in a bed in days, and she luxuriates in the simple, smooth suppleness beneath her, stretching out and tucking herself deep into the blanket. "Goodnight, Dekala," she murmurs, and she hears nothing from Dekala, no intake of breath or low laugh. But the wind blows across her face, gentle and cool, and Ruti is at peace.

In the morning, Kimya has squirmed over Ruti to her favorite place at the edge of the bed near the window, a lump beneath the blanket, and Ruti and Dekala have somehow breached the space between them in their sleep. Ruti's arms are wrapped around Dekala, her face buried in Dekala's shoulder, and Dekala's hands have burrowed in Ruti's hair, holding her close. Her face is peaceful in slumber, and Ruti stares up at her, struck with a yawning desire that she can never speak aloud, with the drowning sensation of Dekala's fingers against her skin and hair.

She takes in a shaky breath and disentangles herself from Dekala, her heart racing.

16

The grasslands are vast and endless. Day after day, their company rides through even land with few shifts in elevation, surrounded by swaying green and yellow grasses that look undisturbed moments after their animals pass through them. Cautious horned beasts feed in the grasses ahead of them, but they scatter and flee whenever they spot an intruder.

Ruti's eyesight begins to blur, hazy from too many days with little change in their surroundings. They follow the path of the setting sun and the stars to be sure that they aren't moving in circles, but it still feels as if they're meandering in place, never finding their way out of this savanna. The Ruranan band around Ruti's neck sits heavy and thick, a sheen of sweat collecting beneath it, though it looks like tasteful jewelry on Dekala's slender neck. The cloaks that

Yawen gave them are warm and rough, and they remind Ruti of the material sold in the Merchants' Circle back home.

On the third day, they begin to see a few parties moving past them in caravans, paying them little notice in their new Ruranan attire, but the land is so exposed that Ruti is itchy with constant paranoia. Anyone can see them, and the donkeys–perfectly suited for the mountains–move too slowly on flat land. When they sleep, her dreams are unsettled, and she awakens in a cold sweat more than once a night, certain that the Regent has found them.

On their sixth day riding through the grasslands, they encounter their first Maned One. A female without a mane, actually, and it's so silent that they don't catch it until it's leaping onto Kimya's donkey, claws outstretched. Kimya slips off and runs, a smaller target for the Maned One, and Dekala slides off her own donkey and grabs a stick as though she's about to fight off a Maned One with nothing more than that.

Ruti yanks Kimya onto her donkey and chants as she crushes an herbal offering between her fingers, calling on the spirits to subdue the Maned One and make it docile. The spirits yield to her song and the Maned One pauses, confused, short of devouring the donkey. Ruti sings more, the Maned One's head falling in sleepy concession, the spirits thrumming through Ruti–

A bolt of energy sparks from Orrin's fingers and chars the Maned One in a matter of moments, taking the donkey with it.

Ruti whirls around. "What are you doing?" she demands. "I had it under control!"

Orrin scoffs. "I saved us all," he retorts. "You were going to give it a nice nap before it came right back after us."

"It didn't need to be killed! I was sending it away!"

"You were slow." Orrin nods in satisfaction. "Lightning is fast."

"It was *mine*," Ruti mutters, and Orrin's eyes narrow, his gaze flickering to Dekala and then back to Ruti.

He says, his voice rough and harsh, "Nothing is yours, Markless *dog*."

"Enough," Dekala says, her voice commanding as she directs a cold look at Orrin. Ruti puffs up, just a little bit, until Dekala turns her glare on Ruti. "We don't have time for petty squabbling," she says. "And Orrin, we needed that donkey." Ruti tosses a cool glare at Orrin, who has bowed his head in apology.

"I erred," he says, and there is a flicker of shame in his voice, soon replaced with resentment. "The Markless girl brings out the worst in me."

Dekala turns away from him, casting an eye to the grassland that stretches out before them. "The maps have a village marked to our right, with a friendly innkeeper who might give us lodging if we have enough coin. Let's take an evening to rest."

It's a relief to ride into a quiet town, to haggle with an innkeeper and sit in a crowded tavern. For too long, she's been with her traveling companions, out in the open and raring for a fight. Now she sits in silence and drinks the sweet drink that Dekala brings her. It has chocolate with a hint of something stronger, and it makes her mind happily hazy. "How much longer before we leave Rurana?" she asks Dekala in a low voice.

"A day or two. We've been riding faster than anticipated," Dekala says, glancing down at the map. Ruti can't read the words on it beyond the few names she'd been taught to recognize, but she can see the line that runs between Rurana and Guder's peninsula, just a bit below where they are now. "Then it's only a few hours down to the Lake of the Carved Thousand."

"And then we travel back," Ruti says, eyeing the ground they've already crossed on the map. It's a long trip. It's *been* a long trip. "What if we–"

She stops abruptly when she hears Dekala's name. It isn't coming from anyone in their party. Instead, it's from a group of Unbonded at the next table, and Ruti puts a hand on Dekala's thigh and squeezes it before she can speak again. Dekala falls silent.

The Unbonded are gossiping. "I heard that Princess Dekala was *kidnapped*," a narrow-faced one says in a hushed voice. "That she wanted to marry Prince Torhvin so her jealous bodyguard stole her away and ran."

Orrin glowers at them. Another Unbonded says, "I heard she never even got a chance to meet our prince. The bodyguard took her in the night."

"I wouldn't mind marrying the prince," a third says wistfully, downing his drink in a single gulp. The Unbonded break into raucous laughter, each one chiming in with their own dreams of marrying Prince Torhvin.

"I *know* we're Bonded," another says, holding up her calloused hand to show the others. "Majimm and ashto. Imagine me with powers of the *mind*."

"Imagine the prince with them," Prince Torhvin's first fan says dreamily. "He deserves a strong Ruranan soulbond. Not some Zideshi royal brat."

The third chimes in again. "He says he won't rest until he finds her. That's true love."

"Or political expediency," someone retorts. There is more laughter, and the conversation shifts to a discussion of the unconscious heir to the Ruranan throne, King Jaquil. They debate his merits in comparison with Prince Torhvin's, and Ruti loses interest in the conversation. Dekala still listens, never one to turn away from political discussion, and Ruti sips her drink and talks to Kimya with the signs she's learned from her.

Orrin says irritably, "I know you're talking about me. I see my name." Kimya's sign for Orrin is to stiffen and raise her shoulders and wrinkle her forehead. Ruti hadn't realized that Orrin had recognized it.

Kimya ignores him, instead twisting her hands beside her head in the braided sign that represents Dekala. *Are you holding hands with her?* she asks silently, and Ruti snatches her hand from Dekala's thigh and shakes her head.

It's okay if you are. Kimya's signs convey plenty. *She's very pretty.*

Ruti makes a rude gesture in response. When she glances to her left, Dekala is watching them, eyebrows raised. Her hands move quickly, an amused response to Kimya. *So is,* her hands say, and she presses the tips of her fingers to her mouth from the side and does the arc from her mouth that represents Kimya's word for Ruti.

Ruti's eyes widen. Dekala smiles enigmatically. Ruti, flustered and lost for options, signs a sharp, harsh *be quiet.* Kimya laughs silently, Dekala's eyes sparkling, and Orrin mutters, "I'm going to bed."

He shoves his chair back and rises, stomping toward the steps, and Dekala sighs. "I'd better go, too."

She follows him, and both of their doors are closed and bolted when Ruti and Kimya make it upstairs later in the evening.

At about midday on the next day, Ruti sees her first sign that they're approaching the lake. It's a bird, wings folded as it lies on the ground. Or rather, it *was* a bird. It's blackened and brittle, the skin sunken into itself and the moisture squeezed from its body, and it appears made from stone.

"There we have it," Dekala murmurs when Ruti shows the bird to the others. "The first of many."

The closer they get to the Ruranan border, the fewer people they see. Ruti remembers from Dekala's lessons that the Guder people are based mostly in the Southern Sea, where they vie for naval territory with Rurana. It doesn't seem like the dry land at the north of the peninsula holds any interest to them, and the area around the lake is all but empty.

As they near the lake, more stone carcasses are visible. Many birds and bats that had flown into the lake without knowing what they'd encountered. A few large rodents that had run afoul of the lake's banks. "The lake must overflow during the rainy season," Dekala says, eyeing the most recent stone animal they pass. It's a large antelope, its knees bent and its face as blank as a statue. "That's why no one rides this way."

When they cross the border, they find something that stops them in their tracks. It's a body, shrunken into something black and empty, its face stretched into an eternal scream. Ruti stares at it in quiet horror. "Be cautious," she says to Kimya, riding with her on her donkey. "Do not get off of this donkey until I say so."

Ahead of them is the lake. Ruti can see it now, and she thinks at first that she's seeing the reflection of the sun distorted in the water. But *no*, the Lake of the Carved Thousand is an unnatural red so dark it's nearly purple, glistening in the sunlight like a pool of blood. Dekala takes in a breath, staring out at the water.

The donkeys lurch forward, mesmerized by the water, and start running. They're moving faster than they ever have before, and Ruti seizes the reins, pulling hers back before it charges into the lake. "Keep the donkeys," she orders Orrin when he dismounts behind her. "I'm going down there without them."

There is something in the air that makes animals mad, and Ruti can almost smell it herself. Birds screech from above and dive toward the purple-red waters of the lake, careening toward its center, and they don't rise again. Ruti feels the same odd compulsion to touch the water, to immerse herself fully in the toxic liquid and let it consume her.

She resists, walking gingerly toward the lake with her satchel slung along her back. Dekala follows from a distance, hanging back but never quite retreating to safety. Ruti feels the wind brushing against her neck, a reminder that Dekala's attention is on her. It is a strange comfort when she's all alone in front of this deadly lake.

She kneels down into a careful crouch at the shore of the lake, pulling out the two vials that she'd brought along for the water. It's a dangerous offering to hold on to, and she's leery of bringing too much back. One vial, and another for backup if the first fails. Slowly, she dips one vial into the water.

Even with spells in place to keep the vial secure, it still begins to turn to stone from the moment it touches the water, becomes heavier and harder as the water splashes into it. A droplet of water hits Ruti's gloves, and Ruti feels it burning through them, the soft cloth becoming hard and brittle against her skin.

She fills the second vial and caps it, slipping both back into her cloak and peeling off her ruined gloves to see the damage. Her hands are splotched with burns, and she hisses out a curse at the sight of them. "What happened?" It's Dekala, hovering nearby with her eyes narrowed at Ruti's hands.

Ruti shakes her head, stepping back and clearing her throat. All it takes is a quick healing chant and she's fine, the burning sensation gone and her skin whole again. "I'm fine," she promises Dekala. "Stay away from the water. Just a touch is enough to burn–"

She's cut off by the sound of frantic braying, then a jolt of lightning. "Orrin," Ruti snarls, twisting back to look for him. Instead, she sees their three donkeys, all racing away from Orrin at top speed. Ruti manages barely the beginning of a chant before she knows that it's too late, that she can't stop them in time. A witch's weakness is always time, the long moments until a spirit might choose to grant them relief.

The donkeys careen toward the lake, and Ruti glimpses with horror that Kimya is on the last. Orrin is still far back, sparking energy in his hands, and three hyenas are racing away from him at top speed. He must have used his power to chase the hyenas off, but the donkeys had been spooked.

Ruti runs at the last one, spotting Kimya hanging on for dear life.

The donkey bowls her over, a flash of hooves and brown fur and Kimya's mouth stretched round and terrified. Ruti takes a hoof to her head and topples over, helpless as the first of the donkeys reaches the lake.

It's a magic unlike any she's seen. The donkey's legs go first, as though all the blood is being sucked from them. They turn black and hard, the donkey braying in sheer terror, and it falls beneath the weight of its own body, keeling over to sink beneath the lake. The water envelops it, leaving dessicated, shrunken skin that hardens into something unrecognizable.

The second donkey is already nearly gone, and Kimya seizes desperately at the third's reins, slowing it down only incrementally. Ruti screams, "*KIMYA!*" She clambers to her feet, already beginning a new song for agility. There is a rock in the lake jutting up near where the donkey thrashes in the shallow start of the water, and if she leaps, she might be able to reach it.

A hand seizes her and yanks her back. "Stop!" Dekala snaps. "I'll go."

"You're not going!" Ruti says frantically. Stone is beginning to climb up the donkey's legs, making it totter in place, Kimya reaching for them. "I need to—"

"I'm stronger than you," Dekala reminds her. "You've seen me fight. Sing me there."

There's no time to argue. Ruti sings, her eyes fixed on Dekala, her voice rising and rising to impossible heights as Dekala takes a running leap across the lake. If she falls, Dekala will be gone, along with Kimya. She can't fail, can't lose them both, and she sings and sings and pleads helplessly with the spirits for the kind of strength and speed that she'd managed in the training room when she'd last sung Dekala. She is running out of herbs and offerings, and all she has to offer is her voice.

Dekala lands on the rock in a crouch just as the donkey is falling on useless legs. She snatches Kimya from the donkey's back, cradling her in her arms as though Kimya is an infant, and meets Ruti's eyes grimly. "I can't jump back," she says. "Not without a running start."

Ruti stops singing. They're maybe ten feet out, huddled on a tiny rock in the middle of a toxic lake, and they're so close that Ruti can almost touch them. But at the same time, they're unreachable.

Kimya signs, her eyes tired and afraid, and Ruti doesn't understand what she's saying at first. "Trees? Why do we need a tree? It'll just turn to stone." She glances around, spotting the few trees near the lake's shore, their trunks sunken and dead from the water.

"I only need a few seconds," Dekala says, her eyes following Ruti's. "Get Orrin."

Orrin. Orrin who had lost sight of the most important thing he'd been guarding, and now has left them at a deadly lake with no donkeys. Ruti narrows her eyes and turns to him. He's watching them, chagrined.

"Take down a tree," she snaps. "Quickly."

He doesn't fight her. It takes them time before they can find a tree that has grown high enough to stretch to the rock, and Orrin splinters it with some lightning. "At least that skill of yours is good for something," Ruti snaps, helping him lift it. They're far back from the lake, but Ruti can still see Dekala and Kimya, tiny figures in the midst of the purple-red water.

"Was I supposed to let the hyenas turn our rides into carrion?" Orrin shoots back. "They rarely attack people. These were desperate."

"You were *supposed* to protect Kimya!" Ruti snarls. "I don't care about anything else!"

Orrin scoffs. "Well, we both know that isn't true, is it?" His eyes gleam with resentment. "You could have taken her with you. But then you might be too distracted to sigh over *my–*"

Ruti's eyes flash. "Shut your mouth," she growls. Orrin calling Dekala *his* is enough to turn her stomach. "You don't know what you're talking about."

Orrin yanks the tree forward with a grunt of effort, dragging it down a hill toward the lake. "Dekala loves me," he says coldly. "And you are nothing more than a Markless brat she needs to preserve our love. Have you forgotten what this journey is about?"

He doesn't wait for a response. Ruti fumes, shoving the tree along, and they bring it in hostile silence to where Dekala is keeping a protective grasp on Kimya. "Drop it in," Dekala instructs them, her voice strained. "As soon as it hits the water, we'll have moments before it sinks."

Orrin strains to hoist the tree up and then lets it crash down toward Dekala, landing against the rock where she stands. Immediately Dekala races along it, Kimya in her arms, and she's on the shore before the tree breaks and sinks into the lake. She drops Kimya with a cry of relief and then falls to the ground. The cry of relief becomes a cry of agony, and Ruti and Orrin rush to Dekala as one.

"It's fine," Dekala says, twisting away from them. "I just– the rock was damp, that's all." Her sandals are hard, halfway to stone, and Ruti peels them off and gasps at the sight beneath them.

Dekala's feet are red and blistered, her soles burned. The purple-black of the burn is greying at the center, on the verge of turning to stone. "How did you stay standing on that rock when this. . . ." Ruti takes in a ragged breath, her fingers brushing against Dekala's soles. "Dekala," she manages, out of words.

Dekala grimaces, an uncharacteristic whimper emerging from between her lips. "I didn't really have a choice, did I?" she croaks. Kimya crawls over to her, wrapping her arms around Dekala and pressing her hand to Dekala's shoulder.

Ruti blinks back strange, unwanted tears at the sight of Dekala's pain. "Hold still," she whispers, and chants a new melody. It's haunting, a quiet dirge that sends shivers up her spine, and it holds less desperation than she'd meant for it to. There is something about the unstoppable, untouchable Dekala now brought down to earth, helpless and in pain for helping Kimya, that changes every song Ruti knows.

She sings, pressing her rough hand to Dekala's burned feet, and Dekala shuts her eyes but doesn't cry out. Instead, her throaty voice hums along to Ruti's song and she wraps her fingers around Ruti's wrists. They are entwined, holding on to each other, quiet comfort in the touch, and Ruti can feel it like strength in her song.

Gradually, Dekala's burned skin begins to heal, the blisters fading away and the red-black fading to a healthy brown. In the center of her soles, a tiny patch of stone remains, thin and impossible to heal. Dekala's eyes are squeezed shut for a long time as she is overcome with pain, and when she opens them, she whispers, "Why are you crying?"

Ruti doesn't know. Ruti can't answer. Ruti doesn't know, except that Dekala's hands are gripping her wrists and Kimya is curled against Dekala and the spirits are singing with her in a gentle chorus, and she aches for this, for it to last forever.

17

The outer skin is healed, but it takes hours before Dekala can walk barefoot without wincing. Ruti offers Dekala her sandals, but Dekala refuses them, walking along the rocky land with her head high. She has the stride of royalty even like this, barefoot and in a Ruranan cloak, and her upturned chin and grim gaze still grip Ruti's eyes and don't let them go.

They have no donkeys and no supplies, and there is no map to show them which way to go. Instead, they walk along the shoreline of the sharply pungent lake and away from it, moving forward toward the Southern Sea. "It won't be too far, even by foot," Dekala promises them. "And from there we can find a Guder ship that will take us to Somanchi. Guder has a thriving trade with Zidesh."

"How will we pay them?"

Dekala slips off a familiar silver ring with a gleaming red stone at its center, the one that Kimya had stolen from her in the Merchants' Circle, what feels like a lifetime ago. "This should grant us passage," she says, eyeing it critically. "My uncle gifted it to me for my seventeenth birthday. I won't be grieved to part with it."

By foot, the journey takes them almost three days. Unlike their trip through Rurana, their views are less uniform. First, there is the walk to the Southern Sea, and the dusty land is replaced with creeping green dotting the hard rock until there is grass everywhere around them. The trees rise high above them, windblown to a light tilt, and there are little creatures rushing through the trees over and around them, skittering through the underbrush and unbothered by their new visitors.

They sleep at night with the crickets and the monkeys singing their own songs around them, but the weather is cool and Ruti slips into slumber easily. Kimya curls against her in the evenings, wiggling her fingers into the ground so that insects can climb over her hand, and Dekala sits across from Ruti and speaks with Orrin about the state of the kingdoms.

"When I return," she says, and there is no uncertainty in her voice, "I shall put an end to the search for my soulbond. I will make it clear that I have been *excessively* tolerant of my uncle's intrusions, but I now have the magic that will stop them forever." The vials are a welcome weight in Ruti's cloak, and she pats them as Dekala's eyes flicker to her.

"He will say it is not enough," Orrin points out, his big forehead furrowed. "He will say that you are still Unbonded, and it makes you a liability. You know that he wants your crown."

Ruti remembers the time that the air had been sucked from the dining hall, that Dekala's untamed magic had nearly killed them all, and she privately thinks that Dekala's uncle might have a point.

Dekala does, too, if the tightening of her face is any indication. "Would you prefer I wed my soulbond?" she snaps, sharp and defensive. Orrin rocks back for a moment, looking stunned, and Ruti is taken aback as well. Dekala doesn't budge. "Shall I find the man who is my perfect match?" she demands. "Perhaps he might know his place."

It's cruel of her to lash out at Orrin, who has always been annoyingly loyal, and Ruti speaks up despite herself, in his defense. "That's not fair," she says, and Dekala's glare shifts to her. "He is only saying what your uncle will, and how can you respond to that?"

As if on cue, the wind whips around Ruti, yanking her curls back from her face and pulling at her torso as though to hurl her away, but she doesn't budge, watching Dekala as she grits her teeth and only manages to intensify the biting breeze. Orrin mumbles something about firewood and lumbers off into the forest, and Ruti runs an absent hand through the coils of Kimya's hair and refuses to flee.

It's only once the wind settles that Dekala speaks, calm again. "I know," she says, and her shoulders drop. "I know what my uncle will say." She flicks her palm over to stare at the smoky brushstrokes of her unfinished mark. "I don't need anyone else to tell me that."

Ruti is still feeling belligerent. "And how do your people know that your sewa won't tear down their houses and destroy their crops?" she challenges, and Dekala gives her a sharp glare.

It can't conceal the troubled look beneath it, the understanding of the inevitable danger that Dekala will pose to her people, and Ruti finds herself struggling too, for an answer that she doesn't have.

"If I can fight nature itself once," Dekala says, and presses two fingers to her palm, "then I shall do it again." Her eyes flick to Ruti's cloak. "You collected two vials from the lake, did you not?"

Ruti has no idea how to seal Dekala's sewa–if it would take only a vial, or something far more potent than even that. Sealing a mark is superficial, like erecting an invisible barrier and keeping it there forever. Sealing something innate to Dekala's soul is out of her grasp.

But still, she thinks of it for most of the night as Kimya sleeps beside her. Dekala lies only a few feet away, and

Ruti can see her chest rise and fall in irregular, sleepless breaths.

As they walk the next morning, a city seems to rise in front of them, bit by bit. It gets larger and larger as the forests begin to recede again, sprawling across the south of the peninsula and alive with sailors and merchants. They pawn the ring away at the first shop they find, returning with a bag of coin much larger than the one Ruti had gotten for it in the Merchants' Circle.

With the coin they purchase sandals for Dekala and new, less worn clothing, and they have a meal of cheese and fruit like none they've had since they left Somanchi. Dekala buys a clove oil that protects sun-baked skin at sea and also spends a whole golden coin on an enormous piece of chocolate that she slips to Kimya, who kisses Dekala on her cheek in thanks.

Guder's merchant city is built for the raging winds of the sea. The buildings are smaller than the ones of Somanchi, squat and immovable, and the horizon is wider than any Ruti's seen. The people of Guder are varied and busy–they come in all shades of brown and Ruti even glimpses some merchants so pale that they are nearly white. They dress in Zidesh's fine fabrics and Rurana's gold finery and in strange styles with oddly shaped buttons and laced dresses. The languages they speak are just garbled noise to Ruti, but she knows the tenor of haggling and arguments, as familiar to her here as anywhere else. The shops teem with people inside and out, brushing past their party and paying them little notice.

In a city this large, no one pays them any attention. Dekala moves between the people with her hood down and no one recognizes her as the missing princess, and there is little discussion or gossip about anything but the weather and the sea. They negotiate with the captain of a small ship, unobtrusive and carrying only a few goods out to Niyaru. "I can't guarantee that we'll be stopping at Somanchi," the captain says, accepting the coin that Dekala offers him. "But we will be close enough to the River Somanchi that you can find a ride there. Are you Zideshi?" He looks dubiously at their Ruranan robes and adornments.

"My sister's soulbond is Zideshi," Dekala says easily. "She has told us of Zidesh's prosperity. We go to the capital city to learn a trade."

"Hm." The captain peers out into the water, where Ruranan border guards patrol the sea. "Rurana's been doing well for itself, too. There are more ships out now than there have been since the civil war. And they look newer than any ships I've ever seen in the Southern Sea. They say that Prince Torhvin has been swimming in coin lately, and enough of it goes to the army to keep them happy."

Dekala speaks for all of them, Ruti hanging back to escape any scrutiny. In Somanchi, she can insist that her gloved hands and ill manners are a product of Kaguruk. Here, there are too many ships' captains who might have been there before. "Is the army in control, or is Prince Torhvin?"

"Prince Torhvin keeps a tight leash on the generals, I hear," the captain says, leading them aboard his vessel. "Rurana loves their new prince. But I don't need to tell you that, I'm sure."

"Oh, hardly," Dekala agrees, a dim rumble of thunder sounding above them. "We are all great admirers of Prince Torhvin." Orrin looks displeased at that statement, which makes Ruti smile broadly.

The captain bobs his head, already distracted by new arrivals. "The trip will take four days," he says. "I can offer you three small cabins until the River Somanchi. If you choose to stay on, it'll be more coin." He drifts off, leaving them to board the ship alone.

It takes only two hours on the ship before Ruti is vomiting off the side, dizzy and nauseated by the rocking of the boat. She's never been on one before, and she hadn't been prepared for the constant motion that has her stomach churning. Kimya climbs onto the rail to vomit alongside her. Even Dekala looks a little green.

"I haven't traveled much since my parents died," she admits. "My uncle has kept me like a precious gem, locked away in the palace. I didn't remember it being this. . . ." She clutches the rail for a moment, taking deep breaths as the air whips around her. "I am ill suited for water," she says at last.

Ruti groans and vomits off the side again. By nightfall she is less sick, and she manages to keep down the meal they eat in the galley. The ship is small, but there are a few other passengers aboard, most headed to Niyaru. One or two of them squint suspiciously at Dekala. "Your father's face is on Zideshi coin," Ruti mutters to her. "Think you look familiar to them?"

Dekala scoffs. "It's a butchered version of him. Our metalsmiths are an embarrassment. Nothing like the women we met in the woods." Still, they stay below deck for the duration of the next day, careful to avoid any more glances. Orrin prowls beneath the low ceiling and cramped little square of floor in Dekala's cabin like a caged beast, impatient and irritable, and Kimya sleeps through most of the day and into the night. Ruti sits on Dekala's bed, eyes closed, singing a song she's finally managed to compose to wash away her seasickness.

"Can you really sing anything?" Dekala asks her, fascinated.

"Aside from the obvious," Ruti says, "I don't know. The spirits are fond enough that they favor me with this. I just . . . open my mouth, and the song comes to me." She shrugs, self-conscious. "It was how I survived as a Markless in the slums. I don't know if I'd be nearly as good at it if I'd grown up with a family and no need for it."

"It's a powerful skill," Dekala says. Her eyes glow, and there is an interest in them that is almost envious. "Bonded don't get to choose what they can do. Without training, most won't even reach their full potential at what ability they do have. You can do everything they can and more."

Ruti feels warmth in her cheeks, Dekala's gaze setting her off-balance. It would be so easy now to ignore Orrin thundering up and down the passageway outside the room, to reach over to stroke Dekala's hair and trace the curve of her jawline. It would be so easy to lean in close, waiting for a glimmer of interest in Dekala's eyes, and see if she might forget Orrin for a moment.

Have you forgotten what this journey is about? Orrin's taunt sounds in her mind, and Ruti jolts. They've spent over a week on a quest to bottle an offering to the spirits, and she's been so caught up in getting to know Dekala that she's altogether ignored the reason why they're doing this. Dekala *loves* Orrin, cares deeply enough about him to travel across an entire kingdom to keep him, and what is Ruti doing? What is Ruti if not a Markless girl who is here because she is useful to Dekala?

Pesky, lingering feelings lurch in her chest, refusing to be denied. She's spent too much time with Dekala, has allowed herself to fall in a little too deep, and now she's paying the price. Dekala hasn't invited any of this from her. Dekala has always been upfront about her relationship with Orrin. Ruti has gone soft for a woman with shining eyes and dark brown skin, for a rare smile and the countenance of a queen.

Spirits alive, she's become a *dreamer.*

She shudders at her own thoughts. There's a thump against the boat, enough that the ship shudders with her and she bumps shoulders with Dekala. "Was that your wind?"

Dekala shrugs, suddenly unhappy. "I don't know. I have no control over it. Sometimes it feels as though I can't walk five steps without ominous thunder sounding." She lets out a little huff. "I did once know a man who claimed his sewa would make him float whenever he was angry. He'd make for a sight, flailing and raging and trapped in midair. So I suppose it could be worse."

There's a note in her voice that has Ruti shifting, a steadying hand on Kimya's sleeping figure as she turns to look at Dekala. "You once knew a man. . . ."

It isn't a question and it is, and Dekala says, "My father." She stares out into the passageway. Orrin is still pacing, glancing into the room from time to time to give Dekala an adoring look and Ruti an ugly one. "My mother had sewa too, and they could wield the wind itself and harness it in ways beyond my imagination. They always said it was why my sewa was so strong. It is the Winged One blessing our bloodline."

As if in response to that statement, the boat rocks again, the wind and the waves jolting it to one side. Ruti hears loud shouts above deck as the sailors correct for the wind, and she braces herself against the bulkhead. "Were you close to your parents?"

There's a flicker of hesitation on Dekala's face, an unwillingness to talk about them, but she says, "I was pampered and adored. They made sure I never lacked for anything."

It isn't an *answer*, and Ruti's about to say so when the shouts above them stop abruptly. Ruti glances up at the overhead, suddenly no longer certain that Dekala's wind is what has put the ship in turmoil. "I'm going to. . . ." She gestures at the door, and Dekala nods wordlessly.

Orrin is still in the passageway, but he's also staring up, his big brow furrowed in confusion. Ruti elbows him as she walks past. "Stand guard over Dekala and Kimya," she says. "I'm going up."

"Don't tell me what to do, Markless," Orrin grunts, but he shuffles down the passageway, his shoulders bumping against the bulkhead as he retreats. Ruti creeps forward. There are passengers in a few other cabins, huddled inside and talking worriedly, and none of them seem to know what's going on. Only the sailors on deck will.

Carefully, she eases the hatch open, taking the ladder up toward the deck. She hears an unfamiliar voice and stops, listening before she moves any higher up the ladder. "Our men will collect your cargo," the voice says. "Are there passengers aboard?" There's an accent to it like nothing Ruti's heard before, and she creeps up the ladder, determined to see more.

In the dark, she can make out only a little bit. The sailors are backed against the starboard rail, a few with knives that they no longer brandish. There is defeat on their faces, and the captain says, "We are not a luxury vessel. Our passengers have little with them."

"Nevertheless," the voice says. Ruti can see the speaker now, a Bonded who holds a torch that burns flickering light. His skin is light, tanned only from the sun, and he has a group of others with him with similar coloring and a few who hold torches. The torches are odd, but Ruti can't place a finger on why. "We will search the cabins," the man declares. "All your valuables are ours now."

Diri, Ruti finally realizes. They've been boarded by pirates.

She twists around, racing back down the ladder and through the passageway. "Diri," she says breathlessly. "We've been boarded. They're coming down to the cabins."

Dekala springs from the bed. "What?"

"We need to hide you," Orrin says at once, taking Dekala's hands. "If the Diri find out who you are—the ransom they'd demand—" He wheels around, raising his hands so they spark energy. "I'll protect you."

Dekala shakes her head, her fingers wrapping around his wrist. "*No*," she says. "You need to take care of Kimya."

"Kimya?" Orrin and Ruti say it together, both equally alarmed.

"He is *not* looking after Kimya," Ruti says, eyeing Orrin distrustfully.

"He has to." Dekala is calm again, a veneer of ice cooling over her expression for the first time in a long time. "If the

Diri find me here with a Bonded built like a royal bodyguard, there's a chance they might remember the news from Zidesh and put two and two together. But if they find Orrin with a little girl and us two sisters on a voyage together, we'll go undetected." She turns to Orrin. "I am trusting you to protect her," she says, and her voice is fierce. "With all you have. That's a royal command."

Orrin says, "I won't be parted from you."

"You must," Dekala says firmly. "It's the safest way for all of us. And if we are separated, you will bring Kimya home, do you understand? She will have a place in the palace." Kimya is awake now, seated on the bed and watching them with quiet fear on her face. Dekala meets her gaze and says in a voice that invites no argument, "Be strong, Kimya."

Kimya bobs her head, sitting back. Ruti feels sick at the thought of it, of trusting Orrin with Kimya. But Orrin will obey Dekala, and Ruti can't leave Dekala helpless, either. "I don't like the idea of splitting up," she says, and turns to Kimya, signs to her in question.

"It's the only way," Dekala says, her voice commanding. Feet pound above them, nearing the ladder above deck. They don't have much time.

Kimya's fingers move, her hands slicing up and down in a sharp motion. *Go now*, she signs, and she presses a tight fist to her heart for a moment and pulls it away to spread her hand. Ruti makes the same motion, her heart thumping against her fist.

She flees with Dekala, slamming the door behind them and heading to the compartment two down that has been Ruti and Kimya's. "I don't like this," she says in a low voice.

Dekala is silent for a moment, and when she speaks again, her voice is tight. "Ruti," she says. "What do you think a group of Diri men will do to two girls they find on a captive ship?" Ruti stares at her, eyes widening in horrified realization.

Dekala, who travels with a trusted bodyguard at all times, is aware of it in a way that Ruti never has been. "Orrin will care for Kimya," she says now. "He might not like the Markless, but he will do my bidding." She exhales, her face unreadable and icy with determination. "And the two of us . . . we need to hide."

18

There's a storage compartment beneath the bed that they nearly miss. It's long and shallow, only visible once they pry up one of the rubbery floor mats under the bed. Together they manage to squeeze into the compartment and cover it back up just as the Diri begin searching their passageway.

The compartment is small and Ruti is squashed against Dekala, the two of them pressed together in silence as doors slam open and Diri shout out orders. Someone in the next room gets belligerent, and Ruti hears a cry and the thump of a body hitting the ground. She shuts her eyes, her arms shifting where they're pressed to her sides.

"Can I . . . ?" she whispers, shifting again uncomfortably. They're lying side by side in the compartment, shoulders pressed together and arms at their sides, and there's more space between them and the mat than there is on either side of them. She turns, exhaling as though she hasn't had space to breathe until now, and Dekala follows her lead. Their breaths mingle, the scent of sea-salt air as strong as mustiness in this cramped space, and Ruti's pulse echoes like a drumbeat in her ears.

Ruti squirms in place. "Stop moving," Dekala breathes, her fingers digging into Ruti's waist. "They'll hear us." Their foreheads press together, their legs intertwined, and Ruti slips her arms around Dekala to give them more space. There is a heady scent in the air now, a hint of the clove oil that Dekala purchased in Guder. They're even closer now than they'd been when Ruti had awakened in the guest house in Rurana, and they're awake this time. Ruti feels Dekala's nearness like heat in her belly, coupled with the adrenaline that comes with the terror of being found.

The door to the compartment opens, and a rough, accented voice calls out, "No one in here."

"Someone was staying here," another man responds. Dekala stiffens and Ruti shuts her eyes, unwilling to dare a whispered song. "Cloaks, a bag under the bed. . . ." The voice is closer now, and Ruti feels the vibrations of footsteps against the floor and hears only their mingled ragged breaths. Dekala's fingers are tight against Ruti's skin, Ruti holding Dekala close. "They must have run elsewhere when they heard us board," the man concludes.

"Wait," the other says slowly, and Ruti hears it: the high-pitched sound of wind as it whips around the cabin. *No.*

Dekala squeezes her eyes shut, straining with all her might, but the wind only grows louder. "An Unbonded is in here," the man says with certainty, and Ruti hears shuffling around and the inevitable scraping noise of the bed being moved.

Within moments the mat is yanked up and the two of them are exposed, curled around each other in the ground. The men who stare down at them are unpleasant looking, lips curled into sneers and knives in hand, one knife glittering red as though it's still hot from the forge. A fire Bonded. "Look at that," the red-knifed man says, his eyes narrowing. "Little girls."

Dekala shifts even closer to Ruti, her lips grazing her cheeks as she breathes, "Don't sing." She's right, of course. If the Diri realize that Ruti is a witch, she'll be gagged before they have a chance to break free. Instead, she clamps her mouth shut and allows herself to be yanked up from their hiding spot.

Dekala is being pulled up with the same force, and she makes herself limp, like a doll made of cloth and straw. Ruti wrenches herself free of the red-knifed man, glaring up at him. The mark on his palm is unfinished, she notices in sudden surprise, a half circle of majimm that closes around the knife again as he thrusts it at her. "Don't move," he grunts.

The other Diri glances over at her, his arms restraining Dekala as he eyes her. "Why is she wearing those gloves?" he says suspiciously.

Dekala says swiftly, "It's a sacred Kaguruki custom, don't–"

Red Knife laughs caustically. "The Diri are Kaguruki, imbecile." He moves with unexpected speed, pinning Ruti against the bulkhead. She struggles desperately against him, new terror in her heart as he reaches for her gloves, and he lets out a hiss when he yanks them off. *"Markless,"* he spits out, recoiling.

Ruti shoves him again, and Red Knife catches her this time, hurling her against the bulkhead with renewed force. Her back crashes against a piece of metal that sticks out from the wall and she cries out in agony, falling to the floor. The Diri thrusts the knife at her, tracing a line from her neck down into her shirt. The knife burns as it cuts, cauterizing and blistering at once, and she chokes at the sheer pain of it. "Do you know what we do to Markless in Kaguruk?" Red Knife says darkly, and Ruti can only feel the burn of the knife, the wind whistling through the room and blowing the sliced top of her shirt open.

"Stop!" It's Dekala who speaks, her voice commanding. Gone is the limp, dull-eyed girl who'd been dragged out of their compartment. Instead, she stands in captivity like a queen, her voice unwavering. "Don't touch her. She is mine."

The Diri look unimpressed. "And you are . . . ?" the red-knifed man demands, his knife still burning against Ruti's skin.

Ruti croaks, "No," but Dekala has already begun to speak.

"Princess Dekala of Zidesh," she says, her voice clear, and reaches into her shirt to remove a royal signet ring from where it hangs on a chain around her neck. "If you leave us untouched and unharmed, the ransom you receive will be beyond your comprehension."

The Diri scuttle back, knives still out and eyes on Dekala, and Ruti slumps on the floor and watches Dekala with dismay. Identifying herself means they'll be brought back to the palace for a ransom, and they might make it out of here alive. Unless, that is, the pirates decide that they'd rather take their chances.

The Diri have a hushed conversation, and then Red Knife roughly seizes Dekala's arm. "We'll take you to the captain," he grunts. "Get the Markless." His sharp eyes move from Ruti to Dekala, and he says, "We'll need it to keep the lady in check."

"It?" Ruti repeats, her eyes narrowed, but she is dragged all the same, and she doesn't dare whisper the magic that will heal her chest. As they're pulled down the passageway, she notes with relief that two Diri are exiting the room where Orrin is guarding Kimya, both of them empty-handed.

Now, she only has to trust Orrin.

They're dragged up the ladder and to the deck, where a plank connects the two ships. "We're taking these," Red Knife barks, yanking Dekala along. She elbows him in the side, hard enough that Ruti seethes with satisfaction as he winces. Still, he doesn't let go of her, and Ruti is pulled along with far less gentleness across the plank and onto the Diri ship.

It's around the same size as the transport ship, but more worn and angular, the prow curved to a sharp, high point. There are words that Ruti can't read along the sides of the ship, stained by rust and storm, and the Diri move in the dark through the ship with the swift, subtle movements of ghosts.

"Zahara! Captain!" Red Knife calls, and one of the figures standing at starboard turns. "This girl claims to be royalty of Zidesh."

The captain strides toward them, and Ruti realizes with surprise that Captain Zahara is a steely-eyed woman. The Diri around her incline their heads, looking up at her with respect. She has the same lightly tanned skin as the other Diri, but her eyes are an unnatural shade of blue-purple, her white hair divided into a dozen braids that whip in the wind. "Royalty," she echoes in a hard voice, and puts a finger on Dekala's chin, tipping it up to glare at her with suspicious eyes.

Dekala doesn't move. Against her better judgment, on the verge of doing something uncharacteristically rash, Ruti says, "Don't *touch* her."

Zahara's eyes flicker to Ruti, peering at her. "What about this one?"

Red Knife scoffs. "Markless."

"Markless," Zahara repeats, and her hand flashes out, quick as a wink, and slaps Red Knife hard across his cheek. "A Markless topside on *my ship*?" she demands. "Do you *wish* for the spirits to strike us down?"

Red Knife sputters. Dekala says, "If you wish a generous ransom for me, then both my companion and I must be–"

Zahara laughs, loud and raucous, and the other Diri laugh with her. "You are a captive of the *Djevehav*," she says. "A crown jewel of the Diri, devil of the Western Seas. You don't give *us* orders, Princess. And your uncle will pay for your life, regardless of your condition or the condition of a Markless." She raises a hand. "Take them below," she orders. "I want the Markless out of my sight."

They're dragged below unceremoniously as the ship departs, Dekala shoved with nearly as much vigor as Ruti is. "Stop it," Ruti snaps at the pirate pulling Dekala along. "*Stop it*. She's going to *have you executed* when she gets home."

"I think not," Red Knife says smugly. "Prince Torhvin of Rurana values the friendship of the *Djevehav*. And Zidesh will only be pathetically grateful to have their sole heir back." He shoves Dekala, and Ruti casts aside the caution that has kept her alive for years and launches herself at him in a fury.

She doesn't have Dekala's grace, but she's spent enough years in the slums to know how to fight. Her fists are everywhere, bruising the Diri as his knife clatters to the floor. Dekala is shouting her name, sounding irritated with her, but Ruti ignores her protests and shoves Red Knife. Her skin burns and she's terrified, tired of seeing Dekala yanked around and treated like anything but the princess she is.

"Ruti!" Red Knife is down, and Dekala is staring past her in alarm. There are more pirates approaching, some with the flaming torches and others sparking lightning or hurling water from their hands. Ruti spins around, fists up and ready to fight, and Dekala says, "Sing, you idiot!"

She snaps a metal pipe from the bulkhead and hurtles at them with the grace of a stick fighter, and Ruti raises her voice and sings to the spirits. Lightning is deflected as soon as it comes, water splashing over the Diri instead of Ruti or Dekala. Ruti calls to the sea itself, to the wind and the weather and all the powers that converge around the *Djevehav*, and she feels them answer, hears the howling of the wind on deck from below.

Dekala handles the pipe deftly, slamming it into heads and dodging blows from the Diri. No matter how much Ruti sings, the torches won't extinguish, but she doesn't have time to ponder that now. Instead, she sings for the sea and she sings for Dekala, calling upon both to attack the Diri with equal strength.

By the time she's done, there are six Diri prone on the floor, and the ship is rocking from side to side. "Let's get out of here," Ruti says, taking a breath before she sings again. They run too far, miscalculating the way to the ladder, and instead Dekala opens a door and they find a dank room like a prison, a heavy lock on its door and open chains attached to the wall. Ruti blinks at it, feeling a heavy trepidation that comes from the spirits to her with the sight of it.

"Other way," Dekala says breathlessly, and they stumble topside together, struggling to make it up the ladder as the ship rocks back and forth.

On the deck, there is chaos. Diri run to and fro, pulling at the sails and struggling to stay afloat. Captain Zahara has her hands outstretched to the sea, the waters calming at her command, but Ruti's magic fights against the Bonded's power. Ruti sings harder, the boat rocking with it, and Zahara turns to stare at them in horror.

"You," she says, water spilling from her hands to the deck. "You're a witch!"

Dekala doesn't move. Ruti sings, watching storm clouds gather above them. "We will be returned to our ship," Dekala says, her voice clear. "Or my witch will kill every pirate on this boat."

"It's long gone," another Diri says, staring back frantically into the dark. Ruti sings a little louder, a little faster, and lightning sparks near the edge of the ship.

"Stop!" Zahara holds up a hand. "Stop your witch! We will give you a boat of your own. You can continue unmolested to Zidesh. Just leave my ship!"

Ruti keeps singing. Dekala considers. "We have an agreement," she says at last, and Ruti lets the music stop.

19

They're outfitted with a tiny canoe, small and hardy, and given two oars to push it along. "This is not a large ship," Zahara tells them as they're lowered into the canoe. True to her word, they are untouched as they leave, treated with a healthy dose of wariness and grudging respect. "We have little more to offer you."

Still, rowing is something neither of them has done before, and they're adrift in the sea for a long time after the *Djevehav* sails away. "I can try to sing the boat home," Ruti suggests, a new melody beginning to form in her mind. "Create a current that will lead us toward the north."

Dekala gives her a curt nod. "Heal yourself first," she says, and her eyes linger for a moment on Ruti's cut shirt, the skin just above her breasts still scorched with welts. "We can wait to go home."

Ruti exhales. She's been in pain for so long that she's managed to tune it out, to accept it as a background noise instead of the only thing she can focus on. Now, though, she's suddenly aware of the burns again. She leans back in the canoe, curling against the side in agony, and sings a choked song of wavering melody–long, sustained notes in a minor key–to heal herself.

It takes some time, quiet and long moments in which Dekala sits in silence and listens to Ruti's song. When it's over, Ruti sings again, a chant she's formed that rises and falls in sharp crescendos and will point the current toward Somanchi. The spirits don't budge at first, and she can feel their interest in her wavering and growing dark. *You ask too much*, she feels, rather than hears. *Have we not given you enough?*

Ruti's chant falters and hesitates as she casts an eye around the boat for something to offer to the Scaled One for speed and the Horned One for direction. Her eyes fall to the ornate Ruranan bands that Dekala still wears around her neck, and she reaches out wordlessly for them.

Dekala sees the question in her eyes and nods, and Ruti carefully slides her fingers along them, finding the latch at the back of each one and releasing it. The tips of her fingers graze the back of Dekala's neck, and Dekala shivers. Ruti swallows, pulling off her own bands as well, and raises them in her palms and chants to the spirits again with her hands outstretched.

This time, a gust of wind throws a wave over her hands, washing the bands into the water, and the current shifts to carry them home. Ruti sings in a melisma that flows like the water, and the current pulls them steadily even when her voice weakens and Dekala murmurs, "Take a break. You need to rest, Ruti."

"We need to–"

"The current is still running," Dekala says, and Ruti curls up again and lets exhaustion wash over her. Her magic drains her when she asks too much of the spirits, but she so rarely is confronted with that truth that it makes her frustrated to acknowledge it. "We are far enough from shore that there will be no Scaled Ones or Toothed Ones. Rest. We've had a long night."

"Then you should rest too," Ruti says weakly, a final protest. Dekala doesn't respond, or if she does, Ruti is asleep before she can hear it.

When she awakens, Dekala is asleep beside her, curled against the opposite side of the canoe. Her striking face glows through the grime of days traveling and at sea, two braids wound over her neck and her hands curled up against her chest. Ruti sits back, struck by her, and her throat closes up as she watches her.

The sun is high in the sky, so it must be midday. Ruti sings for a long time, her voice growing raspy, the canoe moving speedily along and the wind sharp on her face. She swats away large bugs and watches for land. They are deep in the

Western Seas now, Ruti hopes. She can't say for sure. Her throat is hoarse and dry, and she curses her own foolishness at not demanding food or water from the Diri for the trip.

Searching the canoe, she finds a little compartment with flasks of water. She drinks part of one and saves the rest for Dekala.

"It's not much," she says when Dekala awakens at dusk. "But I've survived on less. If we can make it to Somanchi in a day or two, we'll be fine. It's a faster journey by sea than on land."

"We should have commandeered the *Djevehav*," Dekala rasps, swallowing the last of the water. She lifts her eyes to the sky, a rueful smile creeping onto her face. "We would have spent the entire journey looking over our shoulders and fighting off attackers, but at least there would have been food."

"I think they might have accepted us," Ruti says brightly. "Well, maybe not *me*." She flips her blank palm upward for a moment. "But they did have a beautiful lady captain already, so they aren't opposed."

Dekala eyes her, brow creasing. "You thought their captain was beautiful?" Ruti shrugs. Dekala looks irritated at this confirmation. "She's a pirate!"

"I know." Ruti licks her lips, if only because it makes Dekala's eyes narrow even more. "But I'm not *blind*."

"She tried to imprison us. She threatened your life."

Ruti props herself up on the seat of the canoe, elbow resting against the flat bench. Dekala is sitting against one side of the canoe, scowling. "You did both of those things to me, too," she notes, stopping short of calling Dekala beautiful as well. Somehow, she suspects that Dekala will not take kindly to that observation right now.

Dekala glares at her. "You have the *worst* taste," she says huffily, and Ruti has to bite her tongue before she can say what she wants to.

Instead she says, "At least I'm not in love with *Orrin*." It's meant to be light, a tease, but it emerges with a sharpness that Ruti regrets.

Dekala doesn't respond, and Ruti turns away from her, squinting into the distance against the orange hues of the setting sun to search for land again. There is nothing but empty sea ahead of them, but for a few suspicious movements that might be sea predators. Whatever they are, the current carries them away from those movements, and Ruti says, "We shouldn't have more than—"

"I'm not," Dekala says abruptly.

Ruti turns to stare at her, bewildered, and Dekala says again, "I'm not in love with Orrin. I have never claimed to be in love with Orrin." Ruti gapes at her, and Dekala says, her eyes boring into Ruti, "Orrin is in love with me."

It's a revelation from Ruti's dreams, an impossibility, and it makes no sense. "But you—" Ruti blinks, shaking her head.

"You want to *marry* him. I don't understand." Dekala has been very clear about her intentions with Orrin, has laid her head on his shoulder and cradled his cheek in her hand. She has never been overly demonstrative about her affection, but Ruti had ascribed that to Dekala being distant and private, nothing more. "You just ran away from home to fill the flasks in my pocket so you could marry him!"

"I do wish to wed him," Dekala says, Ruti still staring at her in outrage and confusion. "I will not be held hostage to the mark on my palm, and I will never be bonded to another. Orrin is infatuated with me. He is a Bonded already, so there is no risk of him leaving me for someone else. He has little interest in being a king, and he seeks no power or control. He is my perfect king."

Ruti stares at her in dismay. "That's–" Dekala watches her evenly, no sign of discomfort in anything she's revealed, and Ruti sputters again. "That's what you want in a husband? Someone you can control?"

"What else is there?" Dekala's stillness belies the calm she's projecting. She sits too stiffly, her face unreadable, and Ruti is certain that she is lying. She *must* be, to be so sure of something that sounds so dreadful even to a Markless doomed to be alone forever.

"What else is there?" Ruti echoes, disbelieving. "What *else*–what about *love*?" It isn't something that Markless are destined to experience, but Dekala is. . . . "Don't you want to spend the rest of your life with someone you're meant to be with? Don't you want to fall in love?" It's baffling to comprehend, being a princess as Dekala is and rejecting a soulbond for no reason but practicality.

Dekala's eyes glow like hot embers, like a determination so strong that it is unquestioned. "I will never fall in love," she says, her voice low and fierce. "*Never.*"

It stings Ruti in a way that shouldn't matter to her, and she swallows and stares out into the sea. Dekala speaks again, the words abrupt and out of place. "My parents adored me," she says. "I adored them, too. My childhood was only . . . me, sitting on my father's lap on his throne as he judged the people. My mother brushing my hair and telling me stories of distant places. I loved my parents with all I had."

"It sounds nice," Ruti says. It does, like a fairytale of what a family should be.

Dekala nods sharply. "It was. It was my *life*. And then my mother contracted the fever." Her face is stiff, carved from stone. "She bled for a day, then two. We cried to the spirits, but the healers could do nothing for her. She was gone within a week."

"I'm sorry," Ruti murmurs. She's never had a family, of course, but she remembers her one ill-fated attempt to live as an orphan with a painted mark, the moment the family that had taken her in had realized, and the pain that comes with *losing*, deeper than never having at all.

"My *father*," Dekala says, and now she's spitting out the words. Thunder rumbles above them, the wind speeding up the boat. "My father who loved me, who had an entire kingdom to rule, who only had a *seven-year-old child* to inherit the land–my father found it too difficult to bear life without his soulbond," she says, and there is raw fury in her voice, fire instead of ice. "He lay down in the bed he'd shared with my mother–the bed that she had died in, that I slept in beside him–and he drank a mixture of herbs with wine he'd specially commissioned my mother's healers to make. It's a common thing, soulbonds who choose to leave this world together. It's *weak* and it's selfish and I swore when I awoke, alone and abandoned, my father dead beside me, that I would never let someone else have that kind of power over me."

The stories had always been that the king and queen had gotten sick, a shared illness that had taken both from Zidesh too quickly. If the king had gone some other way, the palace had kept it a secret from the people. Ruti stares at Dekala, stunned and discomfited at her revelation. "No, Ruti," Dekala says again, blinking as though she's only just remembered who is with her. "I will *never* fall in love. I will never be bonded. I will never surrender my whole self to someone else, even if the wind betrays me every day for the rest of my life."

"That's. . . . ," Ruti hesitates, lost for a response.

Dekala is glaring at her with eyes that are lost and wild, like a feral beast instead of the distant princess she becomes at her most vulnerable, and she barks out, "What? Will you call me *selfish* again for leaving my soulbond unbonded forever? There are worse things."

"No," Ruti says. "I was only going to say. . . ." She watches Dekala, still without the right words, and whispers, "It seems very lonely to live like that." It's a life that Ruti had imagined for herself, loveless and alone and with nothing but her own survival. For Dekala to be that unhappy by choice is heartbreaking.

Dekala's jaw clenches and she twists to face Ruti, glaring at her with eyes that are suddenly very close. "It will make me a good leader," she says. "It will make me the person my father was too fragile to become. Love is nothing, a feeling passing in the wind. I will cling to real things."

It is strange, slipping into the role of advocate for love when Ruti has spent her life telling off dreamers. Dreamers are the ones who believe in love, who fall for a pretty boy or girl or family and believe they can have what Marked possess. Ruti is not so foolish to think she might ever have love, and yet. . . .

Dekala is captivating, and so very close, her breath near enough to leave its warmth on Ruti's skin. Dekala has been all Ruti has been able to think about for a long time, has consumed her with her presence and left Ruti helpless but to drink her in. And she is made foolish with it, is lost to Dekala's eyes, and all she can think to whisper is, "Is this not real?"

Dekala's eyes glitter and the fire fades, melting ice in its wake. Ruti is frozen in place, is afraid to lift her hands and see what they might do, and Dekala moves for them both. With aching gentleness, she slides her fingers into Ruti's hair, her thumb stroking Ruti's chin. "I will never love," she murmurs again, and Ruti closes her eyes and feels, rather than sees, the brush of Dekala's lips against her. "None of this is. . . ."

"Real," Ruti echoes in a breath, her heart racing, and she slips her arms up to clasp against Dekala's back and pull her closer.

The kiss deepens, grows more desperate and wild, Ruti pulling Dekala nearly atop her as their lips lock and separate and lock again. Ruti is breathless with it, opens her eyes at last and sees Dekala's eyes glowing with untamed desire, pulls her closer and falls back against the wall of the canoe and feels heat and want and something that squeezes at her heart as though it might never let go.

She kisses and kisses Dekala, and wonders for an uninhibited moment if this is how it feels to be marked, to have *someone*, to feel and feel and revel in it with no qualifiers. She has had her dalliances, brief and unremarkable, and not one of them has felt transformative as it is to kiss Dekala, to be wrapped in Dekala until Dekala is all she can think about, *Dekala Dekala Dekala* and her heart thrumming with renewed emotion and *hope*, the most vile emotion of all–

The canoe tilts dangerously to one side, nearly capsizing, and water splashes in from the sea to hit them. Dekala wrenches away from Ruti, her eyes wide and horrified, and Ruti can only think to reach for her again, lost without her touch.

No, the canoe *had* capsized, she realizes woodenly, had turned fully on its side, but they are not underwater. The water is too much, too wild and heavy; and yet, impossibly, they remain safely on board, nearly drowning in the water that leaves them soaking. It's almost as though the water has been manipulated, as though–

"Bonded," Dekala rasps, pulling away from Ruti to stare up behind them. There is a ship there, looming over their little canoe. The ship is large and grand beyond any craft Ruti had seen in the Guder harbor, and water Bonded stand at its bow, their hands outstretched toward Ruti and Dekala's little canoe.

Ruti sucks in an unsteady breath, struggling to regain focus. "We've been . . . rescued?" she says dubiously. "Is this a rescue or a capture?"

"A rescue," Dekala says, and her voice is cool again, distant as though they'd never been entwined moments before, kissing as though it was all they could do. Ruti hurts, even as she knows she should have expected this. "And . . ." She stares at her palm, then up at the ship again. "I understand what my aunt has always said about. . . ."

"What?" Ruti says, feeling small and aching with what Dekala has already moved past.

A light-skinned man with a strong jaw and reddish hair calls from the bow, "Throw a rope down! Now!" He wears Ruranan necklaces and royal robes, and on his head, a circlet of a crown glints in the moonlight. Prince Torhvin. It must be. "We've found her!"

Dekala looks at Ruti. Her eyes are opaque, but her hands are trembling, and there is dread in her voice that she hasn't managed to conceal entirely. "That man is my soulbond," she says, and her fingernails dig crescent-shaped furrows into her marked palm.

Ruti reaches at once for the vials in her cloak, her mind racing as she struggles to think past the last few minutes and find the right song to plead with the spirits. This is her moment, the reason why they've traveled for weeks and risked their lives to make it to this point. And now, finally, Ruti must cast her spell.

She pulls out a vial, her fingers closing around the cork.

A hand lands on hers, staying her movements, and Ruti stares up at Dekala again in confusion. Would she prefer they do this in secret, after dodging Prince Torhvin's overtures and risking a bonding?

But Dekala gives nothing away. Her head is steady now, the dread has faded from her eyes, and Ruti doesn't understand. "No," Dekala says.

20

There is a grand feast to celebrate Dekala's return. The banquet hall is opened with the help of some earth Bonded who reshape the wall of the palace, forming a covered open porch on which visitors can dine and dance. The mood is festive, and the princess–dressed in white and gold and wearing fine golden gloves–is particularly beautiful.

Ruti had tried to avoid the party. She doesn't feel much like celebrating. Orrin and Kimya have yet to return to the palace. To clear Orrin's name, Dekala has artfully reframed her disappearance as an attempted kidnapping by the Diri that left her separated from her bodyguard, but Ruti barely trusts Orrin, and every day without Kimya is another spent pacing in helpless dread.

This is the second day since their return, and Kalere had given her no choice but to attend the feast. Ruti doesn't know why. It isn't as though Dekala *wants* her here. Dekala hasn't spoken more than a few curt words to her since the boat, and only in response to her queries about Kimya. Dekala has returned to the untouchable Heir.

So far, that distance has also been extended to Prince Torhvin, a welcome guest in the Royal Square. Ruti despises every bit of him, from that strong jaw to the too-green eyes to the genial confidence with which he carries himself. The Regent adores him. Dekala hardly speaks to him.

"This stew reminds me of a dish we have in Byale," Torhvin remarks to her at the feast. He is seated between Dekala and the Regent, Ruti on Dekala's other side. "It's quite tasty. The cooks once told me that their secret is to let the meat sit on the heat through the night."

Dekala says, her voice icy, "Do you often consult with your cooks on your dinner?"

"I consult with everyone who works beside me," Torhvin says, smiling as though he hadn't noticed Dekala's tone. "Even the humblest position in my palace is worthy of attention. And as I am a third son, I can never forget my own humble beginnings."

Ruti eyes him resentfully. His words are wise and regal, his posture perfect and without strain, the picture of a great ruler, but there is something that Ruti distrusts about him. Perhaps it is only his mark, majimm prominent on his palm and a match for Dekala's sewa. Perhaps it is that he is so calm and pleasant, so wise and caring, that Ruti—who has seen the worst of so many people in her life—is left with suspicion when presented with their best.

Dekala has a new bodyguard while Orrin is away, another man Ruti's seen training with Tembo. Behind Torhvin is his bodyguard, a woman whom he had introduced to Dekala as Winda. She is tall and imposing, scowling down at anyone who looks at her for too long.

There are others in Torhvin's entourage, guards and soldiers and courtiers who sit along the tables in the banquet hall or stand against the walls. A few of the servants against the walls have caught Ruti's eye. They stand alone, fixed smiles on their faces, and they wear paint along their bare arms that winds around in patterns to their wrists. At their wrists, they wear thick black bracelets made of a rubbery material. The bracelets curve around the backs of their hands and over their palms, and Ruti glances back at them a few times as Dekala speaks, her words acid.

"If you spend this much time on the workings of your kitchens instead of the workings of your farms and cities, it's no wonder your harvests for the past three years have been so paltry."

The room falls silent. Torhvin blinks, taken aback. The Regent hisses Dekala's name in a low tone. Ruti smiles into her food.

After an awkward pause, Torhvin lets out a loud guffaw, rich with humor. "What a tongue!" he cries out. "Oh, I can tell this woman is one who will never let me rest." The courtiers laugh with him, the tension in the room fading away, and Dekala sits placidly, thunder rumbling in the distance. "I have wondered for many years when I might find a worthy soulbond," Torhvin murmurs, and he reaches out to touch Dekala's hand. "Then I set my eyes on you, and I knew."

"There are many who have claimed to know that I was theirs," Dekala says coolly.

"And did you don golden gloves around each of them?" Torhvin retorts. Dekala stiffens. Ruti slumps. There is no other justification for the gloves, which Dekala had put on the moment they'd returned to the Royal Square. She hasn't asked Ruti to do her magic this time. Possibly because Ruti is the only person in Somanchi whom Dekala wishes to be around less than Torhvin.

Ruti's lips still tingle when she remembers their kisses, a stolen moment cut short by Dekala's soulbond. *I will never fall in love*, Dekala had declared, and the horror on her face at their kiss had only confirmed that for Ruti. Ruti is a ridiculous sap to crave more, to still touch her lips and remember the feel of Dekala's hands on her skin, to linger in a palace where she is surely no longer wanted.

She shudders now with what feels suspiciously like heartbreak. Absurd, that Ruti has become a dreamer. Absurd, that she had spent so long with Dekala outside of her element that she'd believed they might have mattered.

Still, she remembers Dekala rushing to her in the quicksand, remembers lying in bed with their eyes locked over Kimya's head, and she can't quite dispel the dream altogether.

"I will not be bonded," Dekala says, turning to the Regent and dismissing Torhvin entirely. "I am the heir to the throne, and I will not be bullied into a marriage and a soulbinding by a pair of third sons." Her words are biting, her tone high with disdain.

Torhvin is unbothered by it. "I do understand your hesitation," he says patiently. "I didn't choose this destiny, either. I hoped to be a general in the Ruranan army one day, fighting for my brother, King Jaquil. But events unfolded in a way that left me no choice but to shepherd my kingdom. The one beautifully unexpected element to all this, of course, is you, and I confess that I can think of little else now." His words are pretty as his gleaming emerald gaze, and courtiers at the table swoon over them. The Regent is beaming, his wife's eyes wet and shining, and Ruti violently stabs a fork into her stew and splashes gravy all over the table.

Dekala glances at her plate for a moment, distracted by the minor explosion of Ruti's stew, and Ruti thinks, for an instant, there is humor glimmering in her gaze. It is iced over a moment later, and Ruti watches for a moment too long.

At the Regent's behest, there is a couples' dance next for Torhvin and an iron-eyed Dekala. Dekala's movements are fluid and almost magical, as free and flowing as the wind, and Torhvin moves well to complement her. Ruti watches Dekala, her heart aching. There is no one in the universe who can contain Dekala, no one who will ever be able to match her. She is a vision, so far above Ruti that Ruti doesn't know what she'd been *thinking* in that boat, leaning in, kissing Dekala as though they'd had no tomorrow—or perhaps a tomorrow *together.* And now. . . .

Dekala might not bond with Torhvin, but the possibility of him will remain forever, hanging over her destiny and tempting her on an easy path toward queenship. The Regent will not bend now, especially with a prospect as likable and convenient as a Ruranan monarch. Dekala's only chance is in the two stone vials in Ruti's pockets.

And Dekala wants so little to do with Ruti that she would continue this endless farce instead of letting Ruti work her magic.

The dance ends, and Torhvin says, "I have brought with me three witches." He nods to them now. They are seated at one of the smaller tables, two young men and an older woman, and Ruti turns to watch them, her eyes narrowing. Three witches is more than anyone might need, a show of power that rubs her the wrong way. "Might they perform something for you?"

Dekala doesn't respond, but she doesn't refuse, either. Her gaze flickers over the witches, and Ruti likes to think that Dekala is making the same calculation Ruti just had. Torhvin takes it as acquiescence. "Go," he orders his witches.

They sing, their voices joining in perfect harmony. A weather Bonded stands behind them, and Ruti doesn't miss the significance of that choice. If Torhvin and Dekala are bonded, they'll be majimm and sewa, with mastery over the weather.

The skies open as the Bonded raises her hands, and the witches sing the clouds close, dip them down in magnificent patterns against the sun. They glow orange, rising and falling in what looks nearly like hills in the sky, and Ruti gasps with the crowd, awed at the sight of them.

The hills break, racing through the sky in what is nearly a dance to the witches' song, and then streak downward, joining together in a massive cloud in the distance. Abruptly, the woman witch's voice goes high while the men go low, and the cloud splits, the center soaring back above them while the rest circles into a ring around the Royal Square. At the finale of the song, the center cloud scatters, pouring a burst of rain upon the dancers, and a rainbow glows high and bright across the sky.

Dekala is soaked, Torhvin just as wet beside her, and she blinks, looking a little dazed at the display. "Amazing!" Torhvin shouts, applauding, and the crowd breaks out in cheers. Ruti wonders if she could do the same kind of magic, her own mouth hanging open as the witches bow and her eyes drift back to Dekala.

Dekala is looking back at her now, and Ruti wonders if she's thinking the same thing. For a moment their gazes catch, and Ruti bites her lip and feels all the emotions from the boat return, her heart thumping with new longing in her chest. Dekala's lips part and it looks as though she might speak–

Torhvin seizes her hands. "I have a gift for you," he says, his green eyes glowing. He is handsome, his hair long and pulled back with a band, and they make an attractive couple. The Regentess is whispering about it now to her companions, her hands pressed to her heart as she watches them, and Ruti swallows and looks away from Dekala's gaze.

A servant from the wall comes forward, carrying an ornately decorated silver box, and Torhvin holds it out to Dekala. She opens the box and removes a tear-shaped decoration made entirely from glass. In the center of it, a flame burns, flickering in place. It doesn't grow, but it doesn't go out, either. "It's a warming lamp," Torhvin murmurs as Dekala holds the glass in her hands. "One of our most exquisite. The flame within it will never go out. It is one of our greatest secrets."

"Kuduwaí," Dekala says, her eyes on the flame, and Torhvin nods gravely. "It is . . . it's beautiful," she says at last. The Regentess lets out a little squeak of excitement. Torhvin smiles at Dekala, and Ruti can't bear to watch anymore.

She stands up. The table's attention is fixed on Dekala, and no one pays Ruti any mind when she slips away from the table and into the palace, walking swiftly through the main hall and past the stairs. She wanders aimlessly through the gardens for a long time, Dekala's face when Torhvin presented her with the warming lamp still swimming through her mind.

Dekala is lost to her, though she'd never had her in the first place. Still, Ruti has memorized the feel of Dekala's lips on hers, of secret smiles and quiet conversations and their hands brushing together. She shouldn't, and yet . . . she can't seem to stop.

She cuts through a pathway that will take her back into the palace when she encounters the subject of her brooding. "Dekala," she says, taken aback. It's dark out now, the drums long gone from the front courtyards, and Dekala is alone. Her bodyguard is a few turns back, lurking on the path a polite distance away.

"Ruti," Dekala says, and she looks startled, then expressionless. They stand in silence for a few moments, Ruti drinking in Dekala's face with a hunger she can't sate. "You shouldn't be wandering out here. There are too many strangers in the court tonight."

Ruti bites her lip. "I can handle myself."

There is another silence, this one more protracted than the last. Dekala stares at Ruti, and Ruti can't read her expression anymore. Ruti says, her heart thrumming again, "So Torhvin has three witches. I guess that's better than one you won't talk to, isn't it?"

Dekala's eyes narrow. "I will talk to whomever I please," she says sharply. "I have more important matters on my mind than a . . . a Markless witch who won't let me *be*."

Ruti swallows, a lump in her throat. Dekala hasn't called her *Markless* like that since before Ruti tried to run away weeks ago. "I was here first," she retorts. "I've been here since you were staring doe-eyed at Torhvin's *gift* to you as though you might marry him on the spot."

Dekala sneers at her. "It was lovely. I like lovely things." Her eyes unexpectedly sweep over Ruti. Ruti shivers, feeling Dekala's gaze like a tangible thing. She lifts her head to meet Dekala's gaze boldly, capturing the embers within and holding them.

Her fists tighten, her heart clenching with the same force as her fingers. "Is that what I was to you?"

Dekala's eyes are icy. "Did you think you were anything more than that? Did you think I might fall in love with you?" she says, her voice cutting, and Ruti can only glare back at her. "We were alone on a boat in the middle of nowhere. I take my beautiful distractions where they come."

Ruti laughs, a breath that is somewhere between desperate and furious, and Dekala demands, "What?"

"So you do think I'm beautiful." It's the single most foolish thing she could blurt out right now, short of telling Dekala about *feelings*, but Ruti is made foolish by Dekala's presence, whether it's hurtful or kind.

Dekala's eyes glint, hard but uneven like chipped stone. "I have always thought that you are beautiful," she says, and Ruti hesitates, lost in the wealth that statement brings with it. Dekala reaches out, the tips of her fingers brushing Ruti's skin. She is lost for a moment in her own thoughts, drifting away as Ruti gazes at her and drinks in her touch. When she speaks, it is distant. "And I will never love you."

Dekala's words fall over her like cold water, washing over Ruti to remind her exactly of what this is. "I don't love you, either," Ruti shoots back, and it's instinctive, fighting back as she always does. It's only once she says it that she can feel the lie in the words.

Dekala's eyes narrow, her fingers stiff on Ruti's skin, and Ruti wants to push her, to demand more from her, to press her against a tree and kiss her again. Instead, she takes a step forward, her heart quaking and her skin burning with the need to do *something*, and Dekala doesn't move. She awaits Ruti's approach, and Ruti takes another step forward.

Abruptly, she is hit around the center by a blow that bowls her over. At first she thinks it's Dekala's bodyguard, attentive at last to protect her from Ruti. But the body on her is too small, arms wrapping around her instead of shoving her, and she twists around, Dekala forgotten, and gasps out, "Kimya!"

Kimya beams at her, her skin a deep brown from days spent under the sun, and she begins to sign a flurry of information all at once. Ruti struggles to follow her explanations, her heart settling into warm affection that fills every loss she's been experiencing for days, and she laughs.

Behind her, coming up the path from the back entrance to the Royal Square, is Orrin, looking no worse for the wear, and Ruti can't even muster up the resentment to hate him right now. "Thank you," she says, and a second voice echoes that from behind her.

"Thank you," Dekala repeats, and she smiles at Kimya and Orrin, a warm look for each of them that she had once reserved for Ruti as well. And Ruti, made warm in Kimya's embrace, feels that loss return like a hollowness within her, devouring the joy around it into a miasma of sorrow.

21

With Kimya back, the Royal Square is a little less lonely, and Ruti's restlessness is more muted. Kimya tells her with ever-moving hands the story of an uneventful trip back, Orrin bad-tempered and worried but dutifully paying for passage down the River Somanchi back to Zidesh's capital city. Kimya had been more concerned about them than about herself, and she's exuberant to know that both Dekala and Ruti are safe.

"Prince Torhvin *is* her soulbond," Ruti tells Kimya dully. It's the next day, and they've sneaked down to the kitchens together. Kimya is inhaling everything in sight while the cooks pass her more indulgently. "He's been aggressively courting her since we got back."

Kimya signs a questioning gesture that somehow involves the word *love*. Ruti scoffs. "*Please*," she says, but her stomach wrenches and she can't eat anything else set before her.

Torhvin continues to try to enamor himself to Dekala, who isn't so readily charmed. At dinner that night, he has another of his servants present Dekala with a chain that gleams golden. "To match your sash," he says, and it doesn't escape Ruti that the style is Ruranan, the sort of necklace worn around the neck of the queen of his kingdom.

Dekala accepts it and lets Torhvin put it on. When she turns to grant him access to her neck, her eyes catch Ruti's. They lower immediately, but Ruti first catches a glimpse of Dekala's expression, her gaze hollow.

When she turns back to Torhvin, she's smiling, her lips thin. "Thank you," she says. "It's hardly necessary."

"Oh, I think anything that might win you over is necessary," Torhvin says, flashing her a white-toothed smile. Dekala's thin smile grows a little sharper, Ruti thinks, a little more unhappy.

Ruti looks away from them, her eyes catching on the servant who had brought the gift forward. There is something in the way she stands, in the way that all of Torhvin's servants clasp their hands together and smile at the crowd. They look *afraid*, she realizes at last. But what is there to fear here, when Rurana and Zidesh are at peace?

Orrin glowers at Torhvin from behind Dekala's chair, and for the first time ever, Ruti shares a glance with him and feels as though they might be in perfect alignment. There is odd suspicion in his eyes too, as they flicker back to the attendants, Torhvin's female bodyguard standing with them.

At the end of dinner, Dekala retires to her rooms and Ruti follows her. There are no conversations in the hall anymore, not even between Orrin and Dekala. Dekala has distanced herself from everyone, and they can only follow.

Still, Orrin lays a hand on Ruti's shoulder before she can follow Dekala into her quarters. "Wait," he grunts, and Ruti turns, letting the door slip closed behind Dekala.

"I'm not going to advocate to her for *you* over Torhvin," Ruti says at once. "I don't think you're any better than he is."

"And I don't think she values your opinion at all," Orrin counters, glaring at her. It stings, even from Orrin. "I don't want your help with that."

Ruti's eyes narrow and she remembers their shared glances at Torhvin's servants. "What, then?"

"There's something about Torhvin's attendant," Orrin says. "The woman. There is a sense of. . . ." His brow furrows. "I don't like it," he says finally. "Did you sense it, too?"

She hadn't noticed the attendant as much as the servants, who still give her the oddest sense that there's something awry. But she can work with this. With *Orrin*, who is still unbearable but is the lesser of two evils here. A foolish man will always be less dangerous than a clever one. "I want to talk to the servants," she says. "I think they can give us answers. But they haven't been around except at dinner. Torhvin wanders the palace with the Regent and his bodyguards but never them."

Orrin jerks his head. "I will find out where they are staying," he says. "I agree you should speak to them. They'll . . . they're more likely to trust you than me."

Ruti barks out a laugh. "Because I'm such a proper, unassuming lady?"

Orrin gives her an odd look. "Because they're Markless," he says, and Ruti falls silent, staring at him. "Haven't you noticed?"

She hadn't, but now she knows what has been niggling at her for all this time. Of course. The elaborate paint and thick bracelets that cover their nonexistent marks have been designed to hide the fact that Torhvin has brought Markless into the Royal Square, an action that might be taken as an offense to Zidesh if exposed. "I'll find them for you," Orrin says. "You speak to them." He gives her a dark look that she shares, the two of them united for once. "I don't trust Prince Torhvin, and Dekala should know everything before she. . . ."

His voice trails off and Ruti whispers, "I know." She really does hate Orrin, but tonight, just as heartbroken as he is, she can't muster up any resentment for his grief.

Ruti still accompanies Dekala through her daily routine as a supportive companion, a now-agonizing ritual that involves following Dekala through the Royal Square in silence, hanging back beside Orrin and watching Torhvin as he appears in Tembo's training room. "I have heard stories of your skill as a fighter," Torhvin says. He has taken off his shirt, revealing lean muscle and toned arms, and Dekala's eyes flicker over them for a moment.

"I have heard little of yours," she says, and moves in a blur, stick in hand before Ruti can blink. But Torhvin is *good*, nearly as good as Dekala, and Ruti watches them with a sick feeling in her stomach.

This is what a soulbond is, someone matched to you in all ways. Torhvin moves fluidly opposite Dekala, wields his stick with skill and looks just as exhilarated as she does as he fights. Torhvin is Dekala's perfect equal, and a Markless witch is worlds apart from that.

As is a bodyguard bonded to some long-gone woman, and Ruti sees the dread on Orrin's face as he watches the prince and princess spar. She elbows him. "Torhvin's servants," she mutters, capturing his attention for a moment. "Where are they?"

"Oh." Orrin looks startled. "Uh. . . ." He shakes his head, looking at Ruti with glazed eyes. "Torhvin is being hosted in a complex of guest quarters near the inner left courtyard. There are underground rooms for servants. The Markless are kept there during the day."

"Kept there?" Ruti echoes, but she's already lost Orrin to the fight once more. He stares at Torhvin and Dekala, both of them with sticks pressed to the other's, their eyes narrowed and faces locked. Ruti swallows, tearing her gaze from them.

Dekala is absorbed in the fight, and her eyes flicker only briefly to Ruti as she slips out the door. Carefully, she makes her way across the main courtyard. The Regent is sitting in judgment of the people, but it's a small crowd today, a few local disputes that hardly draw in any visitors. Ruti slips past them without notice, nodding to a few guards who recognize her from around the palace.

No one questions her as she raps on the door to Torhvin's guest quarters. The bodyguard Orrin hadn't liked–Winda, Ruti recalls–opens the door, eyeing her suspiciously. "Yes?"

She is very tall. Ruti blinks up at her, holding her gloved hand out in greeting. Winda is Bonded, ashto and sewa combined, and she looks at Ruti in distrust. "Prince Torhvin sent me," Ruti lies. "He is sparring with the Heir, and he wishes for one of his servants to attend him."

Winda's eyes narrow. "That's unusual," she says. "Torhvin prefers to spar privately."

"Well, the Heir's form has caught his eye," Ruti says, and she wonders if this bodyguard loves Torhvin as Orrin loves Dekala. "Do you have someone or not?"

Winda glances away from her and sighs. "Very well. Wait here." She disappears into the next room, the door still ajar, and Ruti slips into the room behind her.

After all her time at the palace, Ruti has learned many of its secrets, and she heads to the nearly invisible door in the wall opposite her, finding the latch in the wall and pulling it. A door opens, revealing a staircase leading underground, and she climbs down the stairs, closing the door behind her before Winda can see where she's gone.

The servants' quarters here are dank and quiet, which takes Ruti by surprise. In the rest of the palace, they're brightly decorated and full of chatter, servants glad to be working in the palace instead of in some menial job beyond it. But here the staircase is almost oppressively silent, and the quarters below are hardly lit.

It takes a few minutes for her to gain her bearings, and she chants a spell to enhance her vision in the dark for a while. Slowly, as she blinks and sings, she catches sight of the Markless who stood behind Torhvin the night before. They sit against the walls in a room that had been transformed by Bonded with mastery over form. The Bonded who had done it must be from Torhvin's company, but there is something familiar about the new shape of the room nonetheless. "Hello," she says.

They stare at her, silent and still, their faces sullen. They do not speak. Ruti says, wary and uncertain, "Is this how all servants are kept in Rurana, or just the Markless ones?"

Again, silence. Ruti sighs, whispering another chant. A light rises from her left palm, illuminating the room, and she squints at the servants. Her eyes water up at the sudden light, and it takes a moment for them to adjust to the room.

But when they do, her breath whooshes from her. The Markless servants aren't staying still out of suspicion of her or loyalty to Torhvin. There are chains on their wrists that attach to their bracelets, chains she's seen before. The *Djevehav* had a room just like this one, a place that had looked like it was meant for many prisoners.

Ruti takes a deep breath and raises her gloved right hand to her mouth. She bites down on the material, pulling off the glove with her teeth to reveal her own unmarked palm. Dropping the glove to the floor, she holds her palm up so the Ruranan Markless can see it. "The Heir of Zidesh looks favorably upon Markless," she murmurs. "Tell me, are you servants or . . . or are you slaves?"

One of the Markless speaks at last. A woman, her eyes shadowed over in Ruti's artificial light. "In the catacombs of Byale, the Markless of Rurana built a community," she says hoarsely. "And when Rurana's coffers were empty and its fields bare, the prince found a new use for us."

"We are fortunate to have been kept in Rurana," another says mournfully. "My children . . . I don't know where they've gone. When I journeyed from Lower Byale to find them, I was taken. Prince Torhvin's men have gathered the children and stolen them away. His ships–"

"The Diri," Ruti says with cold suspicion. The Diri, who are wealthy enough from looting the continent's shores to laugh off a treaty with a poor prince. Why would they ever . . . ? "That's his agreement with them. That's why he's been. . . ." She thinks of the eternal flame in the heating glass, of the Diri torches and red-hot knife that had never seemed to cool. "He's been giving them the secrets of kuduwaí, hasn't he?"

The servants are silent again, their eyes flickering away from Ruti furtively. They are terrified even now of Torhvin and his people, of what might be done to them if they share too much with Ruti. When she steps forward, another servant strains against his chains to move in front of his neighbor as though to protect her. Ruti shivers, a ripple of disgust passing through her at their state.

For all of Zidesh's neglect of the Markless, the Markless are still *free*. There is no dynasty that would condone a mass killing of Markless anymore, not even in lands where the Markless are despised. And to enslave the Markless—to *sell* them, as though they are less than human—there are lines that even the worst of the kingdoms would never cross.

Or perhaps they would, if Torhvin has found buyers for his Markless.

She shudders, staring at the frightened Markless faces around her. "I have to go," she says. "I'm sorry. I have to . . . to talk to Princess Dekala about this." Dekala would never tolerate this. Ruti might not know Dekala all that well anymore, but she knows that with grim certainty. Dekala had been horrified just at the slums, and this is so much worse, so much more despicable.

She bends down to retrieve her glove and turns to go. But she can't leave. Her heart is pounding and she can't move her feet to walk up the stairs, to leave these Markless to their fate. In Rurana, Markless can grow old enough to be adults without becoming feral and dangerous, and Prince Torhvin threatens to end that altogether. "I can free you all," she says. "I can sing your chains from your wrists. Will you come with me?"

Not one servant moves. Instead they cower back, eyes wide and terrified, and Ruti knows they have seen too much of Torhvin to believe that they can ever be free. The charming, patient prince who is wooing Dekala is nothing like the creature of the Markless's nightmares, and yet, he must be.

She shudders again. "Please," she says. "I don't want to leave you here."

"Save yourself," the first woman rasps. "Save your princess from the prince. Our people are all but gone. Each rebellion leads to greater punishments. If we leave now, others will suffer." She fixes empty eyes on Ruti. "You are Markless, yet you walk among royalty. There is hope for you." Her eyes sharpen, a hint of fire within them, of dreams that have been stamped out and killed but not yet buried in the ground. "Give us a reason to believe that we might have the same."

Ruti has no response.

22

Kalere is in the room with Winda as Ruti escapes back above ground, though for what reason, Ruti doesn't know. "It is a matter of protocol," Winda says disapprovingly, and Kalere catches sight of Ruti and purses her lips. She says nothing, only clears her throat when Ruti darts past, using the noise to conceal Ruti's escape.

Ruti doesn't think about the meeting. She thinks only of one thing as she heads back to Tembo's training grounds. Dekala has to know. Dekala must be told about Torhvin's Markless. But Dekala is gone, the match with Torhvin long over and the sun high in the sky. It's near lunchtime, and when Ruti hurries back to Dekala's rooms, she is already gone.

She doesn't eat. It feels wrong to eat now, knowing what she does about what lies beneath Torhvin's quarters. Her skin buzzes with the need to *do* something, to say something to

Dekala and find some kind of justice for those Markless. *Enslaved.* It had been her greatest fear when she'd come to the palace, that she'd be jailed at the royals' mercy forever. But even her worst nightmare pales in comparison with the picture that the Ruranan Markless had painted for her.

Rurana had once had a reputation for killing Markless as soon as they'd been clearly identified. The practice had ended when a queen, five generations ago, birthed a Markless son. Besides that, Ruti has never heard much about the Ruranan Markless. *Catacombs*, the woman had said. *A community.* The Markless of Rurana had been safe, hidden away from society, and then Prince Torhvin had taken the throne.

Dekala must know. Ruti paces her room, wary of eavesdroppers and overwhelmed with her newfound knowledge. Helpless and furious, she twists her fingers into broken, disjointed signs to Kimya that only seem to confuse her. She has to speak to Dekala.

Finally, impatient with worry and fear, Ruti departs from her room and wanders through the palace, searching for Dekala. The rooms where she studies with tutors are empty, and Tembo's training room is silent. The gardens are quiet too, and guards look oddly at her when she asks if they've seen Dekala.

"I imagine she's with her suitor," one says at last. "I saw them this morning. They looked cozy."

Ruti resists the urge to scream. Instead, she goes back inside, dragging her feet as she gives the front hall one sullen glance. Dekala is gone, disappeared with an evil prince, and she won't be able to warn her until after dinner.

She sinks down onto the stairs, defeated, when she hears a smooth voice that has her straightening and twisting around. "I do think our borders are too sealed," Prince Torhvin says, and Ruti peers through the rail of the staircase to see him walk through the main entrance of the palace. "I urged my father to reopen them, but he thought we would be safer without intruders. It is such a terrible waste to keep our peoples separated. We have so much to learn from each other."

To her surprise, he isn't walking with Dekala. Instead, he strolls beside the Regent, his eyes intent on the Regent's face. There is something youthful and attentive about his expression when he walks with the Regent, feeding into the older man's ego.

The Regent pats Torhvin's back. "You have wise ideas for someone so young," he remarks. "Rurana could have used your insight after the last blight." They walk to the left, off toward the inner throne room and the war room where the Regent governs with the king's advisors, and Ruti follows them.

She hums a little melody, a call to the spirits to conceal her. She isn't quite invisible, but when she looks for herself in a large mirror on the wall, her own eyes seem to slide over her reflection. Carefully, she steals after the Regent and Torhvin, sliding through the open door of the Regent's war room just moments before he closes it.

He turns, eyes on Torhvin, and says, "But that is hardly relevant any longer. Our peoples have had much friction in the past, and King Jaquil seemed determined to continue the hostilities between us when he prepared to take the throne. Our messengers and well-wishers were rebuffed."

"Jaquil was–is–" Torhvin amends, looking chagrined. "He is a man who cares deeply for his people. But he can be short-sighted as well. Like Father, he had little faith in outsiders. I admit that I have not always been so open-minded, either. Dekala has changed me."

The Regent's smile widens, but his eyes do not smile with him. Ruti sidles over to a closet, aware that her magic is going to fade now that she can no longer sing, and slips into it when Torhvin's and the Regent's backs are turned. Now in a crouch on the floor, she watches the royals from an opening in the door. "Such is her power," says the Regent. "She would be a formidable queen for you."

"If she would only bond with me," Torhvin says with a deep sigh. "I *know* she is my soulbond. I could feel our connection from the moment I saw her. And I know she can feel it, too, or she wouldn't be so afraid of our hands touching. Perhaps if you would speak to her–"

"She is headstrong," the Regent says, sitting down heavily at the table. "And she seeks control more than anything else."

"I would give her power," Torhvin argues, and Ruti narrows her eyes at him, at these two men who plan Dekala's future without consulting her. "I would give her a queenship of Rurana and of Zidesh. And together we would rule my kingdom." He looks at the Regent, a slow smile spreading across his face. "You, of course, would have full command over Zidesh. That is what you want, is it not?"

"I want my niece to have her throne," the Regent deflects, and Ruti mouths *Liar* silently. The Regent has done nothing but foil Dekala's quest for the throne from the start, and he has the *audacity* to claim now that this hasn't been his goal all along. "I will abide by what she wishes." The Regent tilts his head, staring down at Torhvin with sharp eyes not unlike Dekala's. "And if you wish to persuade her to bond with you, then you will be served best by more time with her and less time with me."

His voice is hard now, the same uncompromising tone that has always infuriated Dekala at their dinner arguments. "Win her heart," he says. "Ply her with gifts and promises. Tell her of your plan to join our kingdoms and for her to have dominion over two lands instead of one. She will not fold to your charms, nor will I. You know what it is we want."

Torhvin nods gravely. "Our souls are bonded," he agrees. "There is a space inside each of us that can only be filled by the other. She will see reason." The Regent doesn't respond. Satisfied, Torhvin walks to the door and says, "Zidesh will be yours."

"Yes," the Regent says, and Ruti stares at him, at the traitorous smile that curls onto his face, and despises them both. "It will."

Torhvin exits the room, and the Regent pours himself a drink from a cabinet near Ruti's hiding spot and then sits down. As he sits, he says, "Show yourself, girl."

Ruti startles violently, her head banging against the wall of the closet. The Regent heaves a deep sigh. "Now," he commands. "I know you're in there. Did you think me enchanted by your songs?"

There is no malice in his voice, only irritation, and Ruti dares to venture from the closet, the magic hiding her all but gone. "How did you . . . ?"

"When I discovered that Dekala had brought a Markless witch into the palace, I took the necessary precautions," the Regent says, fixing her with a stern glare. "I would not have a witch singing us all into puppets. I take a draught every morning made to protect myself from witchcraft." He swallows his drink, grimacing at its taste. "A useful habit once Torhvin brought in three more witches."

Ruti stares at him, mouth agape. "You . . . you know who I am?" she finally stutters. The Regent has paid her little attention since her first day in the palace, and he'd never let on that he knew she was the witch he'd once put on trial. "But you never. . . ."

The Regent takes another long drink, swallowing and exhaling. "I have long kept my own spies among the princess's attendants. When they reported the unexpected arrival of a Markless girl just as my guards reported that the only witch in the slums had disappeared. . . ." His lip curls.

"And I have been forced to host a Markless at my table. What a disrespect to the crown."

Ruti recovers quickly, her eyes narrowing. "You're one to talk about disrespect to the crown," she fires back, "while you sell your niece to *Torhvin*. Did you know that he's been kidnapping Markless and selling them as slaves to make coin for his kingdom? He's a *monster*. And you're going to hand Dekala over to *him*?" She whirls around, overcome with fury. "Is this all some grand plot to take her crown? Force Dekala to marry against her will and then seize the throne?"

She has to stop, breathless with outrage, and she glowers at the Regent. To her surprise, he begins to laugh. "Is that what she believes?" he asks, and laughs again. "Has she cast me as a villain to you?"

"Well, what else are you?" Ruti demands. "You've been–"

"I've been trying to find her *humanity*." The Regent shakes his head. "Haven't you seen her?" Ruti stares at him, dislike still creeping through her. "Since the day she woke up beside her dead father, Dekala has been . . . well, you know her as well as anyone by now," he says, and he is no longer laughing. His words are heavy. "It's as though she's lost every bit of her compassion. All she thinks about is power and control and how she can wrest them from others. A piece of her broke when she was seven."

Ruti laughs harshly. "Is that what you think of her? You don't know her at all." She has seen Dekala as compassionate, as caring, as willing to risk her life to save Kimya or Ruti or even Orrin. She remembers Dekala walking through the slums with coin out for the Markless, and she remembers Dekala's fingers tracing her palm by the fire. Dekala is more than the Regent will ever grasp.

"I have spent thirteen years raising that girl," the Regent says, unbothered by Ruti's tone. "And I can tell you that she is broken. *Wrong*, somehow. Nothing like my brother and his wife. And when my own wife suggested–well," he says, and drums his fingers against the table thoughtfully. "A soulbond is meant to heal all those incomplete parts of a person. I feared she never would have that opportunity when she fled Somanchi." He looks, for a moment, pensive with what might be grief. "We hoped that if Dekala found her soulbond, she could become the queen Zidesh needs instead of a. . . ." He shakes his head. "Instead of whatever it is that she's become. Cold. Uncompromising. Broken."

"She is *not* broken," Ruti insists, her voice harsh and gravelly. Her heart is still pounding with anger, straining against her chest. "She doesn't trust you, so you don't see the side of her that I have."

The Regent laughs darkly. "You see what she wants you to see. Are you in love with her?" His eyes are sharp as they assess Ruti and find what they are looking for. Ruti feels suddenly naïve for underestimating the Regent, for seeing him as incompetent instead of as the man who has maintained Zidesh's prosperity and power among the kingdoms for thirteen years. "A Markless witch who has nowhere else to go. Don't you see how it serves her for you to be utterly devoted to her?"

"That's not–"

"Isn't it?" The Regent leans forward. "Now that you've become her loyal servant, how kind has she been to you? How much of this secret side of her have you seen?"

Ruti trembles, furious at his claims, at the possibility they are correct. "You're wrong," she says. He *has* to be wrong. Ruti knows what she's seen, knows that it *can't* be an act. Dekala is smart, but she hasn't been manipulating Ruti. She's been *genuine*, vulnerable, and afraid, and she's only shut Ruti out because of that.

"If I'm wrong," the Regent says, his words silky, "then why is her soulbond–the one person in the universe destined to be her equal–a power-hungry slaver?" He closes his eyes, and when he opens them there is simple humanity within them, emotion beyond the challenge that had been in his gaze. "I can't tell you how much sorrow it brings me to know this about her. I love that girl, and I wanted nothing more than to guide her to the throne." He is genuine in his sadness, which infuriates Ruti too. "I have no children but Dekala, who has rejected me as a parent. I have been clinging for so long to the idea that becoming Bonded would give her the stability and love that she lacks. But destiny is unchanging, I suppose. This is Zidesh's future."

Ruti turns and flees.

She runs to the gardens, to the idyllic solitude that they bring her. The Regent is *wrong*. He has always underestimated Dekala, and he continues to do so now. Dekala had been transformed when away from this repressive palace, from the Regent who sees her as inhuman. She is so much more. . . .

Unless, a voice creeps into her mind to remind her, *it is because she wanted you to believe that.*

Ruti shudders. She has to hear it from Dekala herself. Just a few words with Dekala will dispel every doubt the Regent planted into Ruti's mind. Forget Torhvin. Forget the Regent. Dekala is *good*, and Ruti returns to the palace in a rush of determination. Orrin is standing outside Dekala's quarters, a sign that she is inside, and she bursts past him, ignoring his questions, and makes a mad dash for Dekala's private rooms.

"Dekala!" she calls from outside the door, ignoring the scandalized looks of the attendants. "Dekala, I *must* speak with you. Dekala!"

The doors are thin, only sealed curtains, and Ruti sees a shadow of movement beyond them. "Dekala!"

A hand takes her arm to stop her. It's Kalere, her voice somber. "A moment, please." She turns her back to the rest of the room, deliberately shifting Ruti's attention to her. "Today," she says, loud enough that the other attendants crowd closer to hear her, "Princess Dekala agreed to wed and bond with Prince Torhvin of Rurana. There will be a grand soulbinding ceremony in the Ruranan capital of Byale in three weeks' time."

The attendants erupt in chatter, excitement and questions and delight all at once. Ruti stares at Kalere, wordless with shock, with sheer disbelief. It can't be. It *can't*. Kalere's voice is quiet now, a whisper between them both. "I'm sorry," she murmurs. "But you must have known that this was an inevitability." Ruti shakes her head, still unable to speak, and catches sight of Kimya in a corner, looking just as stunned as she feels. "She wishes to be left alone while she prepares," Kalere says softly. She turns to the big window, hands clasped together, and Ruti is left alone in a crowd of elated, celebrating attendants.

23

"**L**ook at her," Orrin says disgustedly, and Ruti blinks at him.

"Dekala?" She's never heard him refer to her in that tone, the exasperated disdain combined with bewilderment.

Orrin shakes his head. "The attendant," he says, jabbing a finger at Winda. Across the courtyard, Dekala is speaking in low tones with the other woman, a smile fixed on her face as they chat about . . . *wedding plans*, probably. "Dekala asked me to give them some privacy. *Privacy* with the *enemy*."

"She isn't an attendant," Ruti points out. "She's a bodyguard. Maybe Dekala is shopping for one who isn't in love with her."

Orrin freezes. "You think the prince is forcing her to leave me behind?"

"I don't think anyone can force Dekala to do anything she doesn't want to," Ruti says wearily. It's the question she's been grappling with most for the past few days. Kalere has directed her to accompany Dekala throughout the soul-binding preparations in Somanchi, and it has been a quiet exercise in frustration.

Dekala doesn't even look directly at her. She brushes aside Ruti's attempts to speak to her privately, and hardly addresses Ruti or Orrin at all. Instead, she's thrown herself into wedding plans and preparations for her formal introduction to the Ruranan people. There is no hesitation in her energy, no lack of enthusiasm or distance to anyone except her two companions.

Ruti doesn't understand it, except through the creeping, sick worry that she's been wrong about Dekala all along. Perhaps the Regent is right. Dekala shaped herself into something new to win Ruti's loyalty, and something else entirely when she discarded Ruti in favor of her soulbond. Spirits know she's done nothing to disprove the Regent's assumptions.

Still, a stubborn part of Ruti won't give up on her and leave. Maybe it's because of Kimya, still placidly chewing chocolate treats from Dekala at night and speaking of her only with unquestioning trust. Maybe it's the memory of Dekala *caring*, of every bit of humanity belied by her actions until now.

Dekala is otherworldly in the gown she wears today, pale white with ornate golden trim. The seamstresses at the palace have taken to the challenge of royal wedding dresses and courting gowns with gusto, and Dekala almost floats as she strolls through the Royal Square, a vision in white.

Beside her, Winda is businesslike, but she sneaks glances back at Orrin and Ruti, eyes narrowed in suspicion. Orrin narrows his eyes back at her. Ruti watches Dekala, who keeps her gaze aloof and looks only to the sky.

"Imagine if they begin their grand ceremony and press their palms together and nothing happens," Orrin says wistfully. "The sheer waste of resources and alliances. And Dekala will return to herself."

"Aren't Bonded supposed to instantly know when they meet?" Ruti says. "They seem very certain they are soulbonds. Do you remember yours?"

Orrin scoffs. "I was a child. I don't remember anything about her. I chose to serve my princess, and her family chose to flee from their duties to the crown. She is nothing like me." He glowers at his palm for a moment. "Soulbonds are not *destined* to be together. They grant each other power in their unification, but that is no guarantee for their lives together."

Adimu and Yawen, in that guest house outside Rurana, had said something very similar. "I don't know," Ruti says, kicking a stone on the ground. It rolls across the courtyard, banging against Winda's sandal, and Winda glances at it and then returns to her conversation with Dekala. "Seems like Torhvin and Dekala are two of a kind."

When Winda finally departs, Dekala waits until they walk to join her. "I will be selecting a number of courtiers to join us on our trip to Byale, Rurana's capital," she says crisply. "We will have Zidesh represented at this soulbinding. Torhvin is planning to open the gates of Rurana to all visitors for our ceremony." There is no hesitation in her voice, no guilt at addressing Orrin about this without apology. Orrin's face falls, and Ruti feels a twinge of sympathy for him.

She says, belligerent, "I think I'll stay home."

Dekala does not look at her. "All of my attendants will join me, of course," she says, still to Orrin. "I will be no less adorned in Rurana than I am in Zidesh, particularly when I become queen."

"And that's all you've ever wanted, isn't it?" Ruti says, another provocation. Dekala does not respond.

Instead she says, "I will take my leave. Torhvin and I have some private matters to discuss."

"There is something we would like to discuss with you as well." It's Orrin who speaks, sneaking a significant look at Ruti. Suddenly, with the fate of Rurana's Markless as the proof of Torhvin's unsuitability for Dekala, Orrin has become an avid protector of the Markless. "It's a dire situation in Rurana–"

Dekala's voice is cold. "I am sure that my soulbond will inform me best on dire situations in Rurana," she says, turning away from them, and again, firmly, "I take my leave." She departs without a second glance, walking toward Torhvin's quarters across the courtyard. Two Zideshi bodyguards part from the crowd to follow her, throwing Orrin pitying looks as they do.

It isn't the first time that Dekala has replaced Orrin over the past few days. Ruti, who has no replacement in the palace, is summarily dismissed instead. She paces in the courtyard, infuriated and close to losing hope.

It had ached before, falling for Dekala while believing she'd been in love with someone else. This burns like an open wound, and she has only herself to blame. Her heart feels fragile, like rapidly thinning glass, as though one more hostile encounter might shatter it entirely.

But Ruti isn't one to let fragility dictate her actions, and her fists clench against the vulnerability. She will speak to Dekala. She will not allow herself to be ignored and overlooked while Dekala makes the greatest mistake of her life.

Yet that is beginning to feel like an impossible task. Dekala hasn't even come to visit Kimya since the announcement. Kimya has signed her displeasure to Ruti, though she is too stubborn to speak it for what it is. *I haven't gotten chocolate in days*, she signs, and her lower lip wobbles just a bit. Ruti signs back reassurance that she doesn't feel, and Kimya scoffs. *She's never too busy for me. Or for you,* she adds slyly, hands moving in a graceful blur that Ruti struggles to follow. *If you would just talk to her. . . .*

But Torhvin monopolizes his future wife's time gleefully, amused by Ruti's distaste for him. "I do think it's charming that you bring a companion wherever you go," he says one day when he catches her glare. In just a few days, a caravan is scheduled to leave for Byale with half of the palace staff, and Ruti is getting desperate.

She glowers at Torhvin, making no secret of how deeply she despises him, and Torhvin says thoughtfully, "Your bodyguard looks at me the same way." He laughs. "Is *every* one of your staff in love with you?"

Dekala gives him a thin smile. "I am sure Rurana is the same for you. You are quite beloved in your kingdom, from what I've seen."

Torhvin shakes his head mournfully. "The people adore my brother, King Jaquil, but he is tragically out of our reach." Dekala listens, her face unreadable. Torhvin spreads his hands. "My father was brilliant, but unwise with our resources. I have learned from his mistakes. The spirits have not always been kind to Rurana, but in recent years, the Maned One has blessed us with more prosperity than ever before. I am only fortunate to enjoy his favor."

Ruti quakes with fury. *Favor*, as though his prosperity has come from anything more than the sale of vulnerable Markless. And Dekala, nodding along, has no sharp words for him anymore.

They are seated together in the Regent's war room, planning a wedding instead of a war. Orrin and Ruti lean against one wall, Winda against the opposite with one of Torhvin's three witches. Dekala and Torhvin sit side by side, Torhvin's hand resting on Dekala's back when he shifts.

"There is much I can learn from your governing," Dekala says. "But I wonder what role you will have in your kingdom when your brother awakens and is crowned at last."

Torhvin removes his hand from Dekala's back to press his fingers together, bowing his head. "I am afraid," he confides, his tone somber, "Jaquil may never awaken. It is a heartbreaking thing to know, but the healers are less and less confident every day. Still, I will do everything in my power to ensure that the Rurana Jaquil awakens to will be the kingdom he deserves."

"You are a noble caretaker for your land," Dekala allows, and she smiles at Torhvin, a smile that Ruti has never seen before on her face. It is almost shy, the timid smile of a girl who has found love for the first time, and Ruti feels sick at it. It doesn't feel like *Dekala*, like the fierce warrior princess who is always in control of her destiny.

She watches grimly as Torhvin strokes Dekala's cheek tenderly. Orrin averts his gaze, glowering at Winda instead, and the others in the room turn to give the princess and the prince the semblance of privacy.

But Ruti can't tear her eyes away, her body buzzing as though she's been electrified by lightning. Torhvin leans forward, and Dekala doesn't lean in or pull away when Torhvin kisses her, his lips moving against hers for too long. It's sloppy and showy, his wide mouth nearly consuming Dekala's fine lips, but Dekala doesn't push him away. Ruti trembles with rage and heartbreak and despair, and it takes all she has not to leap on Torhvin in a fury.

But as Torhvin pulls away from the kiss, his eyes catch hers. "Your companion is quite the voyeur," he says, slipping an arm around Dekala's shoulders. Dekala leans into it, just a little bit. "I have met quite a few Kaguruki, and I've yet to meet one as brazen as . . . Radi, was it?"

"Ruti," she bites out, unable to remain silent anymore. Had it been so long ago that she'd been lurking in shadows in the slums, rather than provoking princes? "And not hardly as brazen as a prince who kisses like a donkey eats an apple." It's nothing close to what she'd meant to say, and Torhvin's eyes widen in startled outrage. Winda stifles something that might be a laugh, and Orrin looks smug and astounded at her boldness.

Dekala says in a low voice, "Watch yourself, Ruti." It's the most she's said to Ruti in days, and Ruti scowls at her, too.

Torhvin's eyes gleam with malice. "Idiot girl. Did you try to bond with my betrothed?" he says, his voice mocking. "Did you think you could ever have what we have together? *Dog*." He sneers at Ruti and moves, quick as a wink.

He is upon Ruti before she can open her mouth to defend herself, and she shoves him back. "Careful," Winda says, her voice dangerous, and lightning sparks from her fingers as she prepares to protect her prince.

But Torhvin is triumphant. With Ruti's movement, he seizes the glove on her right hand and pulls it, exposing her Markless palm to the room. The witch lets out a hissing noise. Winda's eyebrows rise. "Dog," Torhvin says again. "A Markless bitch in the palace, given free rein by my future wife's kindness. I have no such compunctions."

He lifts a hand and slaps Ruti across the face, hard and stinging. Orrin takes a step toward her. Dekala's eyes narrow, though Ruti doesn't know at whom. "I am kind to those who are worthy of it," Torhvin snaps, his voice silky, and Ruti punches him in the gut.

He doubles over. Winda is across the table in an instant, pinning Ruti against the wall, and Orrin wraps a big hand around Winda's neck. "Leave her," he snarls, and Ruti looks up at him in surprised gratitude. Torhvin laughs in shock, stumbling back against the table, his hands on his stomach and his eyes dark and furious. There is something ugly about them, the sly charm gone and replaced with the glare of a man who would have Markless executed for less, and Ruti would care if she weren't shaking with sheer rage.

She opens her mouth, a song rising to her lips, and Torhvin rears up again, crashing a fist against Ruti's cheek. It is hard enough that she tastes blood and feels the bone shift, and Torhvin hisses, "I will take everything from you for that."

She spits blood. "I have nothing to lose," she sneers, the pain threatening to overwhelm her. Torhvin's lip curls and he lifts his hand again–

"Enough." Dekala's voice cracks through the tension like a whip. "Torhvin," she says, and her voice is calm. "Ruti is my loyal companion. She will be reprimanded and this will not happen again. I beg for your understanding." She does not look at Ruti, shows no sign of care for her bruised face, and Ruti rests the back of her head against the wall, wanting to sob.

Torhvin jerks his head in a nod, his features returning to their unassuming smile. "For you, I will try," he says. "Loyalty like that can be useful, I suppose, even from a worthless Markless." Winda lets Ruti go. Orrin reluctantly removes his hands from Winda's throat, the two bodyguards staring at each other with deep distrust. "I am sure there will be punishment."

"Of course," Dekala says, rising gracefully. "It is late, and I must retire for the night. I will see to my rebellious companion before we depart for Byale."

"Of course," Torhvin echoes, and he moves forward to kiss Dekala again, Ruti watching him with pure loathing that grips her entire body. This kiss is even longer, even more of a performance, and Torhvin keeps his eyes on Ruti for the entire kiss.

Ruti jerks forward, seized with the compulsion to punch him again, and Orrin grabs her arm before she can do anything stupid. Dekala pulls away from Torhvin, a hand brushing over his hair, and turns almost reluctantly to walk from the room.

Ruti hurries behind her. "Dekala," she says, remembering her mission. Tomorrow they all leave for Byale, and Ruti will have no time alone with Dekala again. "Dekala, *wait.*"

Dekala stalks faster and Ruti has to run to keep up, humming a quick call to the spirits to ease the pain in her face. "I need to talk to you!"

"Haven't you spoken enough tonight?" Dekala demands, hurrying up the main staircase. "You're going to ruin everything! Torhvin is–"

"Torhvin is a monster," Ruti says desperately. "What he's done–"

"He is my promised husband," Dekala snaps, and Ruti reels at that. It had never hurt quite so much when she'd talked about Orrin like this. "My *soulbond*. And you will stop provoking him, or I will do away with you before you can interfere any more."

"I am trying to *warn* you about him!"

Dekala spins around just outside the door to her quarters. "I don't need your warnings," she bites out. "I know my future, and I have chosen it with eyes open. But *you*–you need to stay away from Torhvin. Do you know what he thinks of. . . ." She glances around, shoving the door open as she lowers her voice. "Of people like you?"

"Do you?" Ruti counters, and a horrifying thought occurs to her. Dekala might *know*, might already be aware of what Torhvin is hiding about Rurana's Markless. And she might have agreed to the soulbinding regardless.

Who is Dekala, really? Does Ruti know? Can she know better than Dekala's soulbond?

There are only a few attendants in Dekala's main hall when they enter, Ruti on Dekala's heels. Everyone is busy with preparations for the trip to Byale, and Kalere hurries the last few in the main hall from the room when she sees Dekala's and Ruti's faces. "Do you know what Torhvin does to the Markless?" Ruti persists. "Because–"

"I am meant to marry him, Ruti!" Dekala grits out. "And I need you to stop acting like a jealous lover around him." Her voice is low and frustrated, and Ruti recoils. "It is humiliating enough that I ever . . . that we. . . ." She shakes. A storm howls through the room, thunder roaring and the wind slamming into Ruti with enough force to knock her over. It hits her bruised cheek and she cries out in agony, tears forced to her eyes from the pain. She stumbles back, pressing a hand over her cheek, and sinks to the floor as the windstorm howls over her.

Dekala is on top of her in a moment, shielding Ruti from the effects of the wind that her sewa still blasts through the room. "I'm sorry," she whispers, and her eyes are stricken as she stares down at Ruti, her arms stiff as she holds herself over her. "Please sing. Heal it."

Ruti sings, helpless in the face of Dekala's concern. Dekala's sewa calms as she does, and the pain begins to abate. The song is quiet, a call to the spirits that is mournful and lost, and Dekala runs gentle knuckles along Ruti's jawbone, eyes fixed to hers.

When she finishes her song she's angry again, and more confused than she'd meant to be. Dekala touches Ruti and her mind goes blank, every doubt gone and compounded at once. Dekala whispers, "Stay away from Torhvin," again, then climbs to her feet and walks toward her room.

Ruti says, "For his sake or mine?"

Dekala pauses right in front of her room and smiles. It is thin and cold, the smile of the Heir instead of the girl whom Ruti has learned to know, and her voice is distant. "Wouldn't we all like to know that."

She turns toward her door then hesitates, turning around again to Ruti. Ruti is close. She doesn't remember how she got here, exactly, except that she is standing right behind Dekala, dangerously close, and all she can think about is her. Dekala is close, and Ruti doesn't know which of them moves first.

All she knows is that they move.

They're on each other at once, kissing desperately as Dekala grabs at her door to yank the curtain open. In an instant they are against a wall, then another, moving from one side of the room and then pushing the other to the opposite side. They scrabble at each other with hands that crave only to know each other, with lips that only seek the other's skin, and Ruti thinks of little but Dekala's touch and the rising ecstasy and warmth that comes with knowing her.

They are tangled limbs and breathless whispers and lips and hands and glowing eyes, and Ruti's skin hums with euphoria, with relief that she knows is fleeting. This can't last, and she knows it with every kiss, with every movement. This can't last, and still, she surrenders to it entirely for a night, to Dekala's eyes and hands and the whisper of her voice.

Much later that night, Ruti lies next to a sleeping Dekala and knows that she will have to leave her. Dekala will not want her here in the morning. Dekala had been very clear, in the quiet conversation between their kisses last night, exactly what this means. *Don't bond with him*, Ruti had whispered. *You don't know what it will do to you.* She fears that Dekala will be lost for good with a touch of her palm to Torhvin's. But Dekala had remained stubbornly firm, certain of what she had to do.

Ruti will not sleep beside Dekala, will not commit to new arguments in the morning. Instead she rolls quietly out of bed, gathering her clothes and pulling them on again. She hesitates for a moment over Dekala's slumbering torso, and cannot stop herself from pressing a kiss to the princess's forehead.

Not princess for long, she knows, and a pang of dread hits with that reminder.

She steals out of Dekala's room, exhausted and sick with tension, but stops short when she sees Kalere sitting at the table in the main hall of Dekala's quarters. "I sent Kimya to bed," Kalere says calmly. "I told her you would be out late tonight."

Ruti swallows. "I didn't–this isn't–" she stammers, and she wraps her arms around herself, afraid of what she's exposed of Dekala and of herself.

Kalere tilts her head. "We are Princess Dekala's attendants," she says, her voice gentle. "We will be discreet. Now and for any other nights that you might. . . ."

"No," Ruti says hastily, and her heart aches at that impossibility. "No, Dekala is . . . she is bonding with Prince Torhvin," she says dully, and the truth of that has never settled into her heart before as it does now.

Ruti walks toward her room, conscious of Kalere's eyes on her back. She swallows, feeling very close to sobs as she takes step after step toward her door.

She pushes the door open, changes mechanically into a nightgown, and climbs into bed. Whatever happens next, she won't regret tonight. She *can't*, no matter how much it might hurt in the coming days as the rest of Dekala's plans unfold. She stretches her legs across the bed and closes her eyes.

They snap open a moment later. Her arms are flung across the bed to the window, but they haven't touched the curled-up girl she is accustomed to sharing her bed with. "Kimya?" Ruti whispers as she squints into the dark, her heart thumping. Kalere said she'd sent Kimya to bed. But Kimya isn't. . . .

Kimya isn't in the room, not in Ruti's bed or the other one. "Kimya?" Ruti repeats, her voice harsh with fear, but there is no response, no movements in the dark or signs that might be Kimya teasing her for her late arrival. "*Kimya*," Ruti says insistently.

Nothing.

Unbidden, Torhvin's cool threat from earlier in the night returns to her. *I will take everything from you for that*, he had said, the promise of a man who knows what there is to take, and Ruti's blood runs cold.

24

Byale is beautiful, full of ornate buildings that rise above the royal carriages in shades of gold and pearly white. The roads are paved and clean, even in the Merchants' Circle, where shopkeepers aren't permitted to bring their wares out into stands in the road. Ruti sees no sign of poverty in Byale as they ride through it. Only the farmland on the outskirts of the city is less than picturesque, with withered plants and brown grass that hint at Byale's recent lack of rainfall.

The lack of crops has no apparent impact on the rest of the city. The palace is enormous, adorned in gold and steel with towers that rise high above the buildings of Byale. There are statues everywhere of King Jaquil, Prince Torhvin knelt beside him, and the sign of King Jaquil–a trident with the pattern of ashto and majimm superimposed upon it–dots almost every building, both public and residential. Ruti notices, though, that the houses and private buildings they pass are far less elaborate than the public property of the city.

She doesn't notice much else, distracted as she is by Kimya's disappearance. No one has given her answers. Kalere was adamant that Kimya had gone to her room and there were no intruders. "She's young and curious," Mikuyi had said gently. "She might have gone out wandering. I'm sure she'll be back."

But there had been something about Torhvin's face as he led Dekala into his carriage that Ruti hadn't trusted. Torhvin has Kimya, and he knows Ruti knows it. He'd had the audacity to invite her into his carriage as well, his eyes glittering with amusement, and Dekala had been the one to say pointedly, "There is a carriage for my attendants."

Torhvin's face had shone with victory. Dekala had leaned against his arm and said nothing more, her eyes burning into Ruti.

As expected, they will not be talking about that night again. They hadn't known about Kimya then. Her disappearance hadn't been a factor. Ruti's skin prickles when she thinks about it, and she is seized on occasion by the compulsion to cry at the thought of the little they'd discussed. She doesn't know if it's for Kimya or for Dekala, for the Markless who suffer under Torhvin's rule or for what she has to do now.

She will pretend, with Dekala beside her, in this unfamiliar city of strangers.

"You can't tell me you believe that Kimya would just *disappear*," she hisses to Dekala in a hall emblazoned with King Jaquil's sign. They had left for Byale just after sunrise, taking a direct route that brought them to the city by midafternoon. Winda has been assigned to their personal security in Byale, and Orrin trails beside her, alternating between glowering at her and looking at Dekala with puppy-sad eyes. Dekala must have spoken to him before they left, because he no longer lingers as though he expects her to change her mind. Instead, he only looks stricken. For a moment Ruti wonders if he, too, is pretending. But no. Orrin has only gotten the bare bones of what will happen next.

Ruti, for better or worse, has gotten the entire feast.

Right now Orrin and Winda are at the end of the hall, keeping a careful distance from Ruti and Dekala as they argue. Other Ruranans scamper down the hall and slow when they pass them, eavesdropping easily on their whispered argument. Dekala's eyes flicker to them and Ruti raises her voice, adds an outrage that isn't hard to find right now. "She loves the palace. She loves *you*. Don't you care about her at all?"

Dekala lifts her chin, resolute. "Kimya is a sweet child and she deserves better than you using her like this to try to disrupt my soulbinding."

Ruti sputters loud enough for their eavesdroppers to hear. "I'm not–I'm trying to *save* you. You can't possibly *want* to marry Torhvin."

"I find," Dekala says, her eyes icy, "that I tire of being told what it is that I want."

"This is a mistake," Ruti says, and she modulates her voice to sound worn and exhausted at this battle, at trying again and again to save Dekala from herself. Sometimes it is so easy to be genuine when she puts on this act. "This isn't you."

Dekala scoffs. "Because you believe you know me," she says. The people around them must see the chasm between them, impassable and filled with ice. "So does Orrin. So does my uncle. I am whatever you need me to be, regardless of what it is that I want to be."

That stings more than it should. "And what you want to be is queen," she says dully.

Dekala doesn't answer, but a wind caresses Ruti's face, an acknowledgement she doesn't need. Ruti stares at Dekala, eyes burning as she clenches her fists and refuses to look at the Ruranans who pass by.

They're interrupted by a man who makes a mad dash around the corner, breathing a loud sigh of relief when he catches sight of them. "Princess Dekala!" he says, pressing his hands together. "I don't know how we were separated again!" Kieran is their guide through the Ruranan palace, a hapless man who is easily lost when they need him to be.

Dekala straightens, turning away from Ruti. "No worries," she says calmly, a picture of grace and elegance now. There is no sign that she'd been arguing moments before, except for the entourage casting worried glances their way. "My guards kept up with me. I know my stride can be a bit much."

"Oh, certainly not," Kieran says fervently. "It is my own fault for falling behind." He blinks down the hall, bobbing his head with relief when he catches sight of Winda. "You've been well protected while I've been searching for you?"

Winda inclines her head. "It is under control."

Kieran swallows, beaming up at Dekala. "Well then, let's get on with it," he says, clapping his hands together. "There is an exquisite tapestry in this hall." He gestures to a woven cloth that covers nearly the entire wall behind Orrin and Winda. "It is a gift from the court weavers to our great King Jaquil, who slumbers still in a room just down this way."

"Fascinating," Dekala says, sounding genuinely interested. Ruti gives her a dark look that doesn't go unnoticed by Kieran. "It must have taken a very long time to create."

"Oh, yes," Kieran says, bobbing his head. "We have been bereft of our king for so long. Torhvin leads handily, of course, but Rurana's soul yearns for Jaquil." A servant hurries to him, motioning at King Jaquil's room and speaking in a hushed voice. Kieran's brow furrows as he listens, and Ruti arranges her face into another glare at Dekala, shifting away from her so she can listen.

The servant is only reporting a strange light spotted from the king's window, and Ruti dismisses it. Kieran turns back to them, a wide smile on his face. "We don't want to disturb his dreams," he says. "Come, let me show you our grand gallery."

Kimya would have happily stolen a dozen of the trophies Kieran shows them next, Ruti thinks as she fingers a priceless jewel that once sat on the crown of every Ruranan king of the Tabia dynasty. Kimya should be here.

None of them should be here, she reminds herself. She snatches her hand away, finding Winda's eyes hard on hers. Dekala hisses audibly from beside her, "I am growing very tired of your provocations."

Ruti's eyes narrow. "You didn't mind them a few nights ago."

Dekala doesn't move, doesn't startle from Ruti's bold statement. But her eyes grow colder still; it reads as an abyss that might consume all who see it and Ruti with them, and she hisses again cruelly, "That was a mistake. A final indulgence before I move on to my future. Stop overestimating your worth to me. You humiliate yourself."

Kieran watches them, inquisitive, and Ruti glares at him until he averts his eyes. To Dekala she says, "You're right. It was a mistake."

She knows they're all watching her, and she keeps her head high. There are secrets she still holds, ones she doesn't dare reveal with even a glance in the wrong direction. And she is determined not to break in front of any of these strangers.

A hand brushes against her own–quick and subtle, just gentle fingers against her skin in a silent moment–and Ruti firms her mouth and walks on.

They do not speak inside their lavish chambers, where every servant might carry their whispers elsewhere. Instead, Dekala slips out onto her balcony and Ruti onto a neighboring one. She climbs over the railing and waits silently.

"So." Dekala speaks with no inflection at the end, no uncertainty in her words. At times, Ruti fears that surety, that confidence in a plan that lies in Ruti's hands. "Is all in place for tomorrow?"

Here in the dark, they can be honest, but Ruti still feels as though she's pretending when she nods her head. "I am ready." She feels ill when she considers what comes next, the places where she might fail. But it's Dekala's part of this that brings her to the point of nausea.

"Good." Dekala is immobile, nearly a queen and already a force that can never be swayed. She made it clear on their single night together that this is how it must be. But Ruti spots, for a moment, a flicker of a girl beneath the queen, an instant of hesitation. Dekala's hand rises to Ruti's face, her knuckles brushing the stiff curve of her jaw, and Ruti exhales with the movement.

Emboldened, she whispers, "Don't bond with Torhvin." A plea she's expressed before. She imagines the moment of bonding far too often, sees the glow of it shine between them and envisions Dekala's eyes softening with love for the prince. Magic is a tricky thing, and soulbonds are never a mistake. Dekala may be ruined in that moment. Dekala may be lost in it.

Dekala's hand stops moving and she turns away from Ruti, staring out at the starlit night. "Would you have me discard my destiny so carelessly?"

"You didn't think you needed it before," Ruti reminds her, digging in her pocket to find the single vial she still holds. "We journeyed a long time for this and the other. If you would just–"

"I am *not* surrendering now," Dekala says stubbornly. For all her positive qualities, Ruti notes with the wisdom of one who shares a deficiency in this area, Dekala still quails at being questioned. "If you're having second thoughts about following me in this, then go. I can find another to–"

Ruti holds up a hand, twisting away from Dekala to stare out into the dark of the palace night. "I'm not Orrin," she says tightly. "I won't keel over and bow because you're offended." She glances back, sees Dekala's face falter with regret at her words, and is emboldened again. "This will not end well. There are too many unpredictable elements. And the worst of them is–"

"I *will* be Bonded," Dekala says quietly, and the certainty in her voice is unchanged even as she reaches out to link her fingers with Ruti's. "I will not bend."

Ruti grits her teeth in frustration. "Then we have nothing to discuss." She thinks of that moment again, imagines Dekala's rare gentleness for Torhvin instead of . . . instead of anyone else. "I don't–"

Dekala's balcony door slides open and Ruti shrinks back at once, slipping into the shadows. Winda stands there, her eyes on Dekala. "Your Highness expressed some interest in the tapestry on the third floor before we were pulled away. I would be honored to escort you there to inspect the detail."

Dekala inclines her head. "A lovely offer," she says. "It would be a pleasure."

She doesn't glance back at Ruti as she departs the balcony.

The Ruranan Markless that Torhvin keeps as slaves are no help to Ruti. When she slips past Winda to demand answers from them, they reveal nothing about Kimya. "She's just a child," Ruti begs, and she searches for a song that might force them to speak the truth. But nothing comes to her, and even brandishing her vial of water from the Lake of the Carved Thousand does little to frighten them.

She doesn't use it. She will not impose more cruelties on people who have been so mistreated. With her wealthy palace gowns and clean skin and full belly, she feels a world apart from her people, a people to whom she'd never felt all that much allegiance before.

But not *no* allegiance, and she thinks with a quavering heart of the little ones. Of Kimya, who trusts her without flinching, who might be afraid and alone instead of safe in Ruti's quarters. If Kimya has suffered while Torhvin has been holding her, Ruti knows she will never be the same.

It is easier than before to dig around in Torhvin's entourage, though that entourage has grown in his palace. The people are distracted, preparing for the grand soulbinding that will end in marriage, and no one pays much mind to Dekala's attendants. Ruti is able to slip past the bulk of them, wandering into sections of the palace that have been opened for courtiers and nobles and Zideshi guests.

In three days' time the soulbinding ceremony will begin, and Ruti squeezes her eyes shut and forbids herself to dwell on that future. Dekala is surrounded by eager attendants now, preparing her for each grand unveiling to come, and she affords little time or energy toward arguing with Ruti. Instead she keeps a careful distance. There is no time for quiet meetings on the balcony again, and the argument from that night remains unresolved.

Today the palace is full, a reality that Ruti wouldn't have thought possible. The Ruranan army, fiercely loyal to their prince, has arrived to pay their respects to their future queen. Dekala is decked out in white with golden Ruranan coils wrapping around her neck, and her hair has been taken from its braids and pulled almost straight so it falls in long, lovely waves down her back.

Ruti watches her, her mouth dry. Dekala says to Kalere, "Will I be expected to speak at this event, or am I only meant to stand on Torhvin's arm and smile demurely?" Her voice is dry, still enough of the Dekala Ruti knows that it washes over her in strange familiarity.

Kalere scoffs. "Well, I hope you won't be stick fighting with the work we've put into your hair." She tugs a few locks of it, wrinkling her nose disapprovingly. "Rurana has no need for a warrior queen. Their army is plenty without you."

"You look beautiful," Mikuyi offers, her eyes shining.

Dekala's lip curls in disgust. "I look weak and artificial," she says, and in that distaste, Ruti finds a thread of comfort.

The ceremony today is a grand feast in honor of the Maned One and Rurana's fighters, with enough food to feed a small city piled in one of the palace's banquet halls. The army is loud and raucous and enthusiastic at the start of the party, and Ruti slips into the banquet hall, lurking near two of the men with the most elaborate headdresses in hopes of hearing something useful. They are generals, a dozen soldiers with spears and scowls surrounding them, and they say nothing of the Markless living in Byale or of one Markless girl in particular.

There is a pool of pure chocolate at a table near the altar to the Maned One, rich and thick and warm, and strawberries line its sides. Ruti takes one, savors the decadence of the chocolate, and misses Kimya even more. She is going to find her. She's going to find her, and they're going to persuade the kitchens at home to create a chocolate pool of their own.

She stands, fists clenched in that vow, and shifts to a corner of the room as Prince Torhvin emerges onto the dais above the hall. "Welcome!" he calls, and the room falls into respectful silence. The soldiers are strong and rowdy but they respect their prince, are utterly devoted to him. "In the name of the Maned One, patron spirit of Rurana, and in the name of my brother the king, we thank you all for joining us for this momentous occasion," he says, beaming down at them.

He looks happy, a boy-turned-man who has gotten everything he's ever wanted, and Ruti feels pure hatred rising in her throat. "I have long searched the land for a woman who might be my perfect match–my soulbond, who would stop me from accidentally overturning your ships in the sea." He lifts his palm, displaying the majimm on it, and a titter runs through the crowd. "And I couldn't be happier to introduce her now. She is the Zideshi queen-to-be, a formidable woman with the beauty and wit that will make her a Ruranan jewel as well. Princess Dekala," he calls, and the crowd erupts in cheers.

Ruti watches the dais, then the door that slides open near the stairs that lead up to it. Dekala is brought through with Winda and Kalere at her sides, and she is resplendent in white and gold. She smiles at the soldiers, her eyes glowing as though this is truly the place she wants to be, and Ruti knows this time that it is a lie.

The anger surges in her again, and she feels her fists tightening, eyes narrowing as she watches Torhvin take Dekala's hands in his own. They both wear gleaming golden gloves now, careful as the soulbinding draws near, and Dekala gazes at Torhvin as though she might love him.

The crowd roars, hoots, cheers for their future queen, and Torhvin smiles broadly at them all. His eyes move across the throng of soldiers, and Ruti sees the instant his smile sharpens and grows like a Fanged One's mouth. He has caught sight of Ruti, and he knows that he has taken everything from her.

Kimya, Ruti thinks, and she moves without a second thought, fury thrumming in her veins as she watches Torhvin begin to speak again. "With this soulbinding, I will usher a new era of peace and prosperity upon–"

She is accustomed to quiet, to shrinking back and avoiding querying stares. She has spent a lifetime hiding in shadows, and only since the palace has she begun to emerge. But today requires her voice, if all is to be as planned. And consumed with disgust for Torhvin and what he's done to Kimya and so many other Markless, she finds the strength to speak.

"Liar!" Ruti snarls, and there is no time to reveal secrets subtly. There is an enormous crowd in front of her, every last one of them armed, but they're so startled by her that no one thinks to stop her ascent to the dais. Kalere looks alarmed, Winda wary and unsurprised, but neither stop her. "You haven't ushered any peace or prosperity!" she bites out, loud enough for everyone around her to hear it. "You've been selling Markless children to fund your extravagances!"

Torhvin looks taken aback. "Who are you? What nonsense are you spreading?" he says, sounding bewildered, but his eyes glint with something cruel and ugly.

Ruti doesn't budge. "Rurana's Markless have been rounded up and sold into slavery," she calls desperately to Dekala. Dekala's gaze is expressionless. "I've been trying to tell you for *days*, but you never–" She clears her throat, speaks so a horde of soldiers can hear her voice. "Torhvin has been sending them off with the Diri. That's why the Diri stopped attacking Ruranan ships. Torhvin has been giving them the secrets of kuduwaí for their silence. He's selling Markless right under your noses!"

Torhvin laughs. "She is mad," he says, shrugging her off.

"I'm telling the truth!" Ruti cries out, turning away from Dekala to the crowd of bewildered soldiers beneath them. Her heart stops at the sheer mass of them, at the hostile, sneering crowd, and she struggles to find the words to get through to them. "This is your prince. He would sell you all into slavery if it meant he could pretend that Rurana is prosperous. Doesn't that horrify you?"

"You know nothing of us," Torhvin snarls. "None of these fine soldiers are *Markless*, nor do they give a damn about them. We take what resources we have and use them. Wheat, sheep, Markless. What difference is there between each?" The soldiers bellow laughter as Ruti's eyes flicker around the room, searching for faces that show some hesitation. She sees none, her moment all but wasted.

All but. Near the front, several of the generals are murmuring to each other with grave scowls on their faces, and Ruti's heart leaps with hope. Maybe–

But it's too late for her. "Seize the girl," Torhvin orders. "I've had enough."

Soldiers are upon her in an instant, leaping onto the dais and yanking her back from Torhvin before she can attack him. She spits out curses, struggling against them, and turns her desperate gaze to Dekala. "You can't be okay with this. You love Kimya. I know you care about–how can you stand by and let Torhvin do this to my people?" she says loudly enough for Torhvin to hear, and she feels furious tears at the corners of her eyes, brought forth by her anguish and threatening to fall.

Dekala watches her, and her eyes flicker with uncertainty and dread. A myriad of emotions passes over her face as her gaze locks with Ruti's and she shakes her head, nearly imperceptibly. Ruti waits, her hands lax against the soldiers as they tighten their grips on her and look to Dekala for her reaction.

"I have tired of your mishaps." Dekala's voice is cold and distant. "You were a fine companion for a long time, but this is my own fault for trusting a Markless." She turns away from Ruti, who sobs tears that appear rage-wild, lurching at her as her fury and grief for Kimya and fear for Dekala meld together into a cacophony of emotion. "Take her to wherever the Markless of Byale go," Dekala says, resting her head against Torhvin's shoulder. "I have no use for this one anymore."

Ruti gapes at her, eyes widening in what any observer would categorize as betrayal and disbelief. "Dekala!" she shouts, scrabbling against the soldiers as they carry her away. "Dekala, please!" Dekala turns away from her, and Ruti catches only one glimpse of apprehension in her eyes as she looks up at Torhvin instead.

One of the soldiers yanks off Ruti's glove to sneer at her palm. "Filthy Markless," he grunts. "I'll show you where you belong."

She is yanked from the banquet hall and outside the palace gates, a chain fitted to her hands and used to drag her along, and she stumbles after them to a pit far behind the palace that stinks of garbage. "There," the soldier says with satisfaction. "The place where all Markless go."

He lets go of the chain, and before Ruti can run or sing, he gives her a hard shove into the pit.

S he lands in garbage, stinking manure, and slop that has her choking at the odor. The slums had smelled, but never quite like this. This is worse than anything she's experienced before, and she gags and tries to move only to discover two dreadful facts. The first, that she's coated in it, and the smell follows her wherever she moves. The second, that the pit is larger and deeper than she'd thought, and there is no escape from the manure.

Still, it's the reason why she hadn't broken her neck. Her extravagant gown is destroyed, her sandals sinking into the manure, and the sky is so far away that she fears she might never see it again. But she is alive, and so she straightens and picks around the disgusting heap of garbage to search for a way out.

It is dark outside. The ceremony had begun at dusk and been lit by lamps, and the stars and moon are too far for her to see anything around her. Wherever she steps there seems to be even more manure, so Ruti holds her breath and picks her way in one direction. If she moves far enough forward, she might be able to find the wall where she'd been thrown into the pit.

But she must be walking in the wrong direction, because no wall comes, nor any relief from the manure. She feels around blindly, gagging at the smell when it grows too strong. The moon still shines above her, barely illuminating the black pit, and Ruti squints toward it and then back ahead.

"You," a voice whispers, and Ruti stumbles back in surprise. "Over here."

Ruti has no other options. "Where?"

"Keep walking. Turn—no, a little less—good. Forward." Before long, she's standing in front of a boy about her age. In the dim moonlight, she can see only the whites of his eyes at first, but he begins to take shape. He is dressed in simple clothing, muted colors and barefoot, but he is clean. "The people like to toss their garbage in here," the boy says. "But we don't use this area except to retrieve our people." Unexpectedly, something washes over Ruti's right hand. Water, from a flask the boy holds.

He takes Ruti's hand and examines it in the moonlight, and she tenses, preparing for a fight when he sees her unmarked palm. Instead, he nods and says, "Come with me."

The boy's name is Kewal, and he takes her to an underwater spring. "I will find you something to wear," he says, averting his eyes as she strips in a rush and climbs in. Ruti blushes, remembering modesty too late. She has had too many baths in the palace.

The pit had led to a long passageway lit by small lamps. Some work with kuduwaí, but others have been freshly lit, the candles slowly melting as Ruti looks around. These are the catacombs that Torhvin's Markless slaves had spoken of, the underground community of Byale. Ruti has found the Markless.

Kewal returns with clothing and an explanation. "This is where the Markless live," he says, gesturing around with bare hands. "You are not from here, are you? Did you come with the Zideshi?" His eyes shine. "Is it true that in Zidesh, the Markless live beneath the sun?"

"It's not as great as it sounds," Ruti mutters, pulling herself from the spring. She is washed now, but she misses soap desperately. "Tell me, have you seen another new arrival recently? A girl who doesn't speak, about seven years old?"

Kewal shakes his head. "Our newcomers are always babies," he says, and Ruti exhales at that confirmation. Kimya is still where Ruti thinks she is, then, for better or worse. "They are left at the northern entrance. They find their way into the catacombs."

Children who never develop the mark on their palms, discarded here as they are in Somanchi. "Of course."

"My mother says that I crawled right into her house and refused to leave," Kewal says, sounding very pleased with himself.

Ruti stares at him, struck by a different piece of that story. "Did you say *mother*? You have . . . you have parents?"

Kewal smiles at her, looking very confused. "Of course. I have a mother and two fathers. In Lower Byale, you must have a family to have a house. And if you have a house, you must raise children within it. How else can Markless children survive?"

As they walk, the landscape changes. The passageways grow wider and there are more lamps with kuduwaí, lighting the passages with their eternal flames. "The First King of the catacombs was the son of a Ruranan king," Kewal says with pride. "The Ruranan King granted his son all he wanted below, and the First King built a city. The rest, the Markless did ourselves." The walls are shaped, doors carved into the stone, and there are more people around as the passageways open into entire caverns. Women and men alike sit on the floors, chattering amongst themselves as they weave with straw and fishbone. Children run in circles, fighting with sticks and playing with dolls and small cave creatures. There is community here, a home like none Ruti has ever seen for Markless, and she stares in startled awe.

The people stare back, curious eyes flickering over Ruti, and Kewal waves to them and keeps walking. "Things have changed over the past year," he says, his voice somber. "Do you see it?"

Ruti glances around, searching for what Kewal is trying to show her. Slowly, she begins to see.

The children run free, but there are reeds hanging around their necks, odd jewelry that she realizes are whistles. And there are dozens of houses in this cavern, an even larger cavern ahead, but she can count only twenty or so children playing in them. They glance over their shoulders a little too often, and the adults are all seated near the entrance and exit to the cavern, watchful even as they appear relaxed.

"The Diri found an entrance to Lower Byale," Kewal says quietly. "No one knows where it is. We've boarded up every exit we know of and guarded the ones where the children enter our city. But they come, and they take children more than anyone else. My own brothers are gone. The Diri came right into our house with flaming torches and subdued my fathers. The people they take are never seen again. We are no match for Diri."

"I see," Ruti murmurs, and she swallows, imagining anew how the Ruranan Markless are suffering. In the slums, people disappear all the time. One harsh guard or a few days without food and that is the end of a Markless. But here in Lower Byale, there are more Markless adults than children.

These Markless have grown up without violence, without the fear that comes with living amongst the Marked. These Markless only know peace and family. And now they are being stolen away from those families by Torhvin's orders, all to fill his treasury with coin. She clears her throat, heart thumping with sadness, and asks, "How do you all live in harmony like this without wars breaking out?"

It is an abrupt change of subject, and Kewal looks startled but answers anyway. "We follow the rules," he says simply. "Everyone does, and we are happy, so there are no wars."

"But who makes the rules?" Ruti prods.

Kewal shrugs. "The Markless Council of Lower Byale," he says as though this is obvious. "Each year, nine elders are chosen. Well, eight right now. We lost Kanika to the Diri several moons ago."

The idea of a council—a leadership made of Markless, living beneath the ground and governing in peace—is something wondrous. Something that has to be preserved, just as this city must be. "Please take me to them," Ruti says. "I have something to tell them."

Ruti has never seen this many Markless elders in her life, men and women with grey hair and bodies wrinkled with years rather than hunger. They look down at her in disapproval from their elevated seats, and Ruti notices the whistles hanging from each of their necks as well. The Diri's arrival has overwhelmed Lower Byale, and the elders look grim.

Still, there is little time to lose. "Have you found a girl here in the past few days? Small, about seven, dark hair and brown skin. She speaks with her hands, not out loud."

One of the elders leans forward to stare at her in disapproval. "You ask for a meeting with us about a missing girl?" she says, scowling at Ruti. "We are all missing our girls. Your child is on a Diri ship somewhere just like the rest of them, and all those we have sent to find them." Ruti's stomach curdles thinking about *that* possibility. No. Torhvin isn't a fool. He will keep Kimya with him because he knows she is a weapon to be used against Ruti. She has been told as much.

But if Ruti is gone from the royal entourage, then what happens to Kimya?

"Kewal said you had information to help us hide from the Diri," another elder says in a creaky voice.

At her look, Kewal shrugs sheepishly. "You said it was important. I didn't think there was anything more important than that."

"Than hiding," Ruti repeats. The elders peer down at her, nodding with Kewal. "What happens when the Diri attack? You run to your houses and hide?"

"Don't be absurd," one elder says reprovingly. "The Diri will find us in our houses. We move into side tunnels."

"The rivers," another offers. "I once made it through an attack with my granddaughters inside the waterfall. We used a tube to the surface to breathe."

"I just run toward the pit," Kewal says. "Even the Diri won't go near that smell."

Ruti stares at them. "So you just . . . run and hide from the Diri? How many come at a time?" She thinks back to the *Djevehav*, which had a crew of perhaps twenty or thirty at best. "There are hundreds of you down here."

"Thousands," an elder corrects her, swelling with pride. "But we are not fighters. We have no weapons."

"Against the Diri, we can only run," Kewal says. "We are a peaceful people. We have no other options." At her disbelief, he spreads his hands. "We are not like you, Ruti, a Markless who lives under the sun. Battle is not our way. We struggle against the Diri when they approach, of course, but they have the powers of the Bonded and weapons like none we've seen before."

"Red-hot knives," Ruti says dully. "Torches that burn eternal. Kuduwaí."

"They can't be kuduwaí," an elder puts in. "Kuduwaí is the tool of the Ruranan generals. No Diri know its secrets."

Ruti doesn't correct that assumption. She had thought, before coming down to Lower Byale, that she might be able to mobilize them to fight back. But she'd also imagined a people like her own, angry and aggressive and scrappy enough to make a dent in the Diri, if united. These people endure because they are not like the Zideshi Markless. In Zidesh, Markless devour each other. Here, they have built a safe place that knows no need for defense.

"Of course not," Ruti says, and lowers her head. "I'm sorry for the interruption. Is there a path that will take me back aboveground?" Dekala might have officially dismissed her, but she isn't done yet. Her stomach churns at the thought of what awaits her in the next few days.

Kewal says, "All of the tunnels are closed off except the children's entrances." He considers her for a moment. "You might be small enough to make it through them. They are narrow and you will have to crawl, but you could get out that way."

The elders murmur to each other, still staring down at Ruti in disapproval. She follows Kewal meekly from the room. "It's not that we don't try," Kewal says as he leads her through the catacombs. "But our boning knives and sticks are nothing compared to the Diri's weapons. We are tunneling deeper into the ground now, making a third level of homes beneath the caves where they might not find us, but that's all we can do. We will thrive again," he says, but he sounds unconvinced. "Lower Byale will be safe once more."

He stops suddenly. "Here," he says, and Ruti sees a crack in the wall, narrow but pronounced. The passageway has been painted by tiny hands in ochre, a bright little tunnel for children to find their way into Lower Byale. "This will take you back aboveground. Are you sure you won't stay?"

he says hopefully. "We have so few children remaining. They're the future of Lower Byale."

"I'm sorry," Ruti says, and she thinks of Kimya, surrounded by other children and the life and joy that comes with it. If not for the Diri, this could be a place where Kimya would thrive.

Ruti might have thrived here once, too. Now her heart is lost in another palace days away, and she doesn't know if she will ever be able to get it back. Even if its ruler is someone unrecognizable when the bonding is complete. "Maybe someday," she whispers, the thought lingering in her mind as she bends down to crawl into the tunnel.

The tunnel is narrower than it had looked, and even the cheerful paints aren't enough to rid Ruti of claustrophobia as she moves through it. The walls close in around her, and it winds enough that she can't see what comes next, only the dimly lit walls ahead. She shuts her eyes, crawling blind, but she still feels the walls bumping in around her in the oppressively tight space.

And then, deep in the tunnel, she hears a piercing sound in the distance. It sounds again, then more and more, and Ruti freezes, something deep within her triggered by the piercing noise. She doesn't know what it is at first, until she hears the shouts and screams that follow it, the noise growing more and more frantic.

The whistles. The Diri have returned to take more Markless, and Ruti is trapped in a tunnel.

She can't turn around in these tight quarters. Instead she crawls backward as quickly as she can, determined not to stand by as more children are taken. The whistles are fewer now, the people fleeing or taken, and Ruti speeds up, squeezes her eyes shut, reaches the tiny crevice at last–

She sings, begins a chant first for her own safety as she emerges from the tunnel and then for the Markless around her. The spirits react at once, granting her requests, and a Diri in the passageway in front of her is blown away by a sudden wind.

Wind, a reminder of Dekala that she doesn't need right now. She squeezes her eyes shut and then opens them, singing louder as she runs down the passageway back to the main caverns.

Inside, there is chaos, Diri with children in their arms and elders barricaded in the council room where Ruti had been questioned. Others have fled, but some of the adults are still fighting the Diri. Ruti spots Kewal in a corner, eyes wide in terror, and he shouts, "Appa!" as one of the Diri seals chains around a man's wrists.

Ruti sings, sings, sings. No one notices her at first–she is small and off to the side, a dark face against a dark wall–but they notice the wind that whips through the cavern, hurtling into them as though they've been struck by fists. "Witch!" a Diri shouts, and Ruti recognizes her. Zahara, the captain of the *Djevehav*. "I am so *tired* of witches," she spits, and Ruti sings harder and faster.

She sings the wind at Zahara with extra vigor, and it throws her off her feet and hurls her into a wall. Zahara slumps to the floor and one of the Diri shouts, "There! The witch is there!" They run at Ruti, abandoning their targets for her, and Ruti changes the pitch of her song.

She goes higher, tries to mimic the urgency of the whistles and temper it with a new song that flows through the room with power and speed. "Get her!" a Diri shouts, and Ruti flinches back but can't run. She's pinned against a wall, Diri descending on her, and her song isn't working as quickly as she needs it to. *Please*, she begs the spirits in song, adding a beseeching note. *Please–*

The closest Diri closes a hand around Ruti's throat, and she chokes, her song stopped with his attack. "This is how you silence a witch," he grunts, and lifts his dagger with his free hand, aiming to plunge it into Ruti's throat.

Instead he staggers in place, eyes widening as he lets out a strangled cry. A boning knife sticks out of his back. Kewal stands behind him, fingers wrapped around the knife, and he looks stunned at his own bravery.

A second Diri grabs Kewal, and a man tears himself from the captives and charges forward. Kewal's father, the chains still wrapped around his wrists, and he can only throw himself at the Diri again and again, slamming his head against the pirate's shoulders. The Diri stumbles, twisting around to raise a knife at Kewal's father. Kewal lets out a cry and shoves him. "Sing," he says desperately. "Sing!"

Ruti sings. The other Markless are emboldened by Kewal and his father, stepping out from their cracks and lingering at the edges of the caves. They don't join the attack, but Kewal keeps fighting, his teeth gritted as more Diri approach him.

A rocky club rolls to a halt in front of Kewal. Ruti blinks, distracted, and sees one of the elders trembling from where she'd thrown it to him, eyes wide in shock. Kewal lifts it, smashing it into the chains that hold his father with little success, and the Diri bear down on him.

And finally, Ruti's song begins to take hold. The chains that the pirates brought for the Markless fly through the air, moving like whips to smack at their heads, and the Diri duck and fall back as Ruti sings off the chains around their wrists and ankles. They cry out in fury, batting them away, but they are no match for Ruti's song. Within a few moments, the Markless are moving forward again, eyes wide as Diri are restrained before their eyes.

More Diri pour into the room, another dozen who see the bedlam they've stepped into and roar in fury, and Kewal cries, "Let her sing! Take the Diri!" The Markless hesitate. Ruti sings, and it's as though she's the one pushing the Markless forward, as though her melody builds their confidence. A Horned One calls from deep within the caverns, a noise that echoes through the darkness. The Diri come forward but the wind sweeps through the cavern again, pinning them all against the wall, and Markless move to bind them in the last chains that had been meant for them.

Soon all of the Diri are incapacitated, and Markless flood into the cavern. Kewal picks up Ruti's chanting as she stops, the Markless transforming her song from witchcraft into jubilant victory. They move between the Diri, staring down at their faces as though they can't quite believe that these are their terrorizers, and Kewal calls out, "Disarm them! Take their weapons!"

Before long, almost every Markless adult is armed. They look at the weapons with trepidation, and an elder says, "We must put them where we can use them for defense."

"Wait," Ruti says, and crouches down beside Zahara. The woman's eyes are flickering open, and they narrow as she realizes she's been chained. "Witch," she snarls. "We were sent to kill you."

"Prince Torhvin wants me gone, then," Ruti says. She isn't surprised, though she hadn't expected this. Trepidation fills her for Kimya and Dekala.

Zahara spits at her. It lands on Ruti's cheek. "I should have done it before you left my ship."

The Markless around Ruti lean in, and an elder repeats, in a trembling voice, "Prince Torhvin?"

"Like I said," Ruti says, her eyes still fixed on Zahara, "I have information for you."

26

The Diri are chained up in a cavern in the catacombs while the Markless debate what to do with them. Ruti comes and goes, watching the Diri with sharp eyes as they pick at the food the Markless bring them.

"Might as well let them starve," she mutters to Kewal. His father is one of a group of men and women who interrogate the Diri on trading paths and routes through the sea, desperately trying to find their missing children. "They aren't going to give you anything."

The Diri treat the Markless with disdain even now, cursing them and spitting in their faces instead of giving them answers. Still, the Markless bring them food and ask them the same questions over and over again, pressing for a response. "We must try," Kewal says simply. "We must do what we can for the children."

Ruti nods grimly. This she understands, even if she can't so much as look at the Diri without imagining a more violent approach. "There was a woman I spoke to from the Markless enslaved to the prince," she says, remembering that dark, oppressive chamber where Torhvin had kept the Markless in Somanchi. "She challenged me to give them a reason to hope."

"We will be that reason," Kewal's father says, and there is determination in his voice, a vow that doesn't waver. "We will not yield to the Diri again."

"Will you be ready when the time comes?" Ruti asks, looking at the faces of the dozens of Markless around her. She has spent time with them, has held each one's hand in her own and sung familiar words as she touched their palms, and she feels a growing obligation to all of them.

Kewal speaks for them all. "We would do anything for you, Ruti of Zidesh," he says gravely. "But this, we do for our people."

"As you should," Ruti agrees as she gathers up her meager possessions. They are all gifts from the elders of Lower Byale: a knife for her side, a gown that is one of their best, a pair of gloves for her hands. There is even a little jar of the remaining inky ash, just in case. None of the clothing is of the quality that comes from Dekala's palace, but she will look passable amongst the throng.

Two days have passed underground, and the soulbinding ceremony is today.

One of the few bits of information they've gotten from the Diri is their entrance route, a path beneath the rocks on the side of the underground river that runs through Lower Byale. Ruti walks carefully inside before she changes into the gown and slides the gloves on.

As she walks, she sees hints of metal between the rocks, holding them in place. This is an artificial entrance built by those who have ashto and endhi on their hands. The First King of Lower Byale's doing, perhaps, a route that would allow him to see the family that had been pressured to forsake him.

The river branches out at the Diri's entrance to the cave, continuing through Lower Byale and running alongside Ruti in this passageway. It moves fluidly here as it feeds into Lower Byale's river, and Ruti is unsurprised when she emerges aboveground on the banks of the River Byale.

She blinks in the rising sunlight, the glare of it striking after days of soft darkness. She peers around, pressing a hand over her eyes. Two unmarked ships are docked in a small harbor–so the Diri can slip in unnoticed to take captives and bring them back to their ships downriver, Ruti guesses.

There is a third ship in the harbor, a grand vessel with the royal seal of Rurana on its side, and Ruti registers where she is at last. This is Torhvin's personal harbor, the guarded inner route that stops just outside the palace. Ruti won't have to break into the palace today–she's already here.

The palace is bustling as Ruti slips through the crowds, unnoticed by attendants and guards alike. There are feasts being prepared, illustrious guests to welcome into their rooms, and a horde of commoners already in the courtyard, crowding in and waiting for a chance to watch the soulbinding. Torhvin's metalworkers have erected a massive stage at the front of the courtyard, his Bonded plant-workers threading vines and flowers around it, and a legion of guards stands around its edges. There are murmurs of discontent among them, an unease that has them on edge, and Ruti listens to their conversation for a brief moment.

They are quiet, and Ruti can barely hear their grumbles. "We must wait on the generals," one says in a low voice. "They will–" The clatter of a cart laden with plates cuts him off.

When the cart is gone, Ruti only hears Prince Torhvin's name and a sullen, "Who are we to question our prince's wisdom?" that makes her lips set in brief, unseen satisfaction.

She continues on, glancing up as her smile fades. The sun has begun its ascent for the day, but there are still a couple of hours before midday, when the ceremony begins.

Ruti swallows back a wave of nausea and finds an unattended food cart near the kitchens. "A morning meal for the princess," she says as she wheels it down the hall. No one stops her, distracted by the flurry of activity around the castle. Ruti walks right past Winda, whose eyes flicker over Ruti as though she hasn't seen her at all.

She remembers the way to Dekala's rooms and swallows back her trepidation as she pushes the cart toward the entrance. Orrin stands guard outside the door, speaking to a grim-faced Kalere, and Ruti wheels the cart over to them, dips her head, and says, "Breakfast for the princess?"

Kalere says absently, "She already–" She stops, her eyes widening. "Ruti?" she says, and Ruti is suddenly in her embrace. "Dear girl," she murmurs into Ruti's ear, and from her there is no hesitation to touch a Markless. "I had hoped to see you today."

When she releases Ruti, it's to shake her head and say, "There is much that needs to be done." She bustles off toward the far side of Dekala's quarters, where the attendants have been entering and leaving in a hurry.

Ruti is left standing in front of Orrin, who watches her silently. Finally, she motions to the door and says, "So . . . ?" expectantly.

Orrin shakes his head, scoffing, and Ruti tenses before she realizes that he's scoffing at himself. "She's inside," he says. "She is ready for the soulbinding." His voice sounds hollow. Something has emptied from him in these last few days, leaving him without his old bravado.

Ruti rolls her eyes. "All prepared to touch her palm to Torhvin's and become his loving wife." It makes her stomach turn to say it, even with wry sarcasm, even with the promise that it isn't how this will end.

"No." Orrin's voice is not resentful, only factual. "She does not love."

"Yes," Ruti murmurs. She knows it now, just as Orrin does. Dekala is governed by ambition, and she sees love as something consuming, something that will make her weak. Dekala fears nothing the way she fears love. "But she cares," she says, another truth. "It's why she won't love."

"She cares for you," Orrin corrects her, and it is matter-of-fact. "She could discard you as yesterday's garbage and she would still care for you. She is a creature of contradictions." He smiles, an expression that looks out of place on his big, glowering face. For a moment, Ruti almost sees a reluctant kindness in his eyes, a hint of why Dekala would have chosen him to marry in the first place. "Go to her," he says quietly. "You will be her salvation."

A look passes between them, an understanding that Ruti doesn't dwell upon, and Orrin silently opens the door to Dekala's quarters. There is no great hall here with its grand window. Instead there is a small room in which to be announced, and Dekala's private room just beyond that. Ruti walks past the attendants, none of whom stop her, and into Dekala's room.

The princess is dressed already, seated in front of a small table covered with all manner of ochre and makeup. Her hair is in thin coils, dozens of them falling back between two elaborate braids. Golden ochre has been threaded into her hair, which glows black and gold, like coin in the depths of the sea.

Her makeup is delicate, sweeping along her cheekbones and adding a dark warmth to her eyes, and her gown is white and sleek, a second gauze of white stretching across her shoulders and arms. She wears a golden headdress like the hair of a Maned One, jewels gleaming at its center, and Ruti drinks her in silently.

Dekala says without turning, "Mikuyi, I am parched, and Kalere tells me I am not permitted to move until she deems me perfect."

Ruti finds a flask of water on a table and pours some into a cup as Dekala goes on, still without turning, "Not as though I can move in this dress in the first place. Ruranan custom seems to believe women should be incapacitated by their gowns." Her voice is dry, but there is tension beneath it, a quiet dread.

Ruti walks to her with the cup, still silent, and tips the water to Dekala's lips. Dekala's eyes flicker upward, and her body goes rigid as she registers who has given her water. "Ruti," she says slowly.

Ruti offers Dekala's reflection a smirk. "You can't get rid of me so easily," she says. It is meant to be challenging, but it only sounds tender to Ruti's ears.

Dekala's voice is only a murmur, muted as Ruti's. Mikuyi walks in, sees their eyes locked through the mirror, and lets out a little squeak before she darts out again.

"I am glad you're here," Dekala says, and she turns, careful not to ruin her hair, and reaches out to touch Ruti's cheek. Old arguments are swept aside in silence, with Ruti's gaze and Dekala's touch. For a stolen moment, they can be honest.

Ruti bears it in silence, aching with every touch, and her heart thumps painfully against her ribs. "I don't suppose I can persuade you to reconsider this?" she tries again, her voice small. She doesn't like being afraid for the future, awaiting further fear and heartbreak. She doesn't like her heart in someone else's hands.

She doesn't have a choice. At least this time, Dekala does not fly into a rage. "I will do what I must," she says. It is simple, quiet, but allows no argument.

Ruti dips her head. "Then I will, too," she whispers. "And you will get what you've always wanted." Dekala has spent a lifetime waiting to be queen, and today she will finally have her wish granted. The Regent has sworn it, has promised a coronation immediately after the soulbinding. Dekala will have all she's fought for.

But there is no excitement in Dekala's eyes as she caresses Ruti's jaw, her hair, running her fingers through the tangled mass that Ruti hasn't cared for properly in days. "My sweet Markless," she says, voice only a hum, and she does not seem to care that Mikuyi is in the room again, rifling through ochres on a back table and pretending not to see them. Ruti shivers under her touch, and Dekala's fingers retreat.

Ruti leans forward, pressing their lips together as her heart swoops in her chest, and Dekala kisses her back, a soft and mournful kiss that could very well be their last. By the end of it, her lips are smudged, the ochre running on her face where Ruti touched it, and her hair is coming free of its braids. She looks like a painting disturbed, perfection ruined by Ruti's unmarked hands.

Dekala's eyes are fixed on her, still as dark and striking as ever. Ruti takes a breath. "May the spirits bless your endeavors, Your Majesty," she says, a formal farewell, and Dekala watches Ruti in silence as she retreats.

Mikuyi hurries over, clucking her tongue as she begins to undo what Ruti has done to Dekala. Ruti's lips still burn as she slips from the room and back into the hallway where Orrin stands guard. She nods to him, hurrying away, and Orrin calls after her, "You have ochre on your lips."

There is a tinge of both amusement and irritation in his voice, and Ruti grimaces and hurries from the hallway. She sneaks back out to the harbor to rinse off her hair and face and attempt to make herself look more passable.

She's surprised to see Torhvin standing at the far end of the harbor with a few of his guards, dissatisfaction on his face as he stares at the unmarked ships still in the harbor. Unable to resist the taunt, she calls over to him, "They won't be back."

Torhvin jolts, twisting around to stare at her in amazed hatred. "You," he grinds out. "You're like a dog that can't be shaken off." His guards flank him, each one Bonded and ready to attack her. But Torhvin laughs. "Winda!" he calls.

Winda emerges from the shadows, and she isn't alone. Kimya is with her, wrists and ankles bound, and she struggles wildly toward Ruti when she sees her. "I thought you might return," Torhvin says smugly. "Call the little brat an insurance of mine, if you will."

Ruti runs to Kimya without thinking, desperately glad to see her. Aside from her bindings, she looks healthy and unharmed, and Ruti wraps her arms around her as Kimya gestures half-formed signs against Ruti's stomach while her wrists are bound. "Kimya," Ruti breathes. "I was so *worried*–"

"Enough," Torhvin orders, and Ruti has the presence of mind in that moment to slip Kimya a quiet weapon: the stone-hard vial of water from the Lake of the Carved Thousand. It might not do her any good, but a knife will be taken from her while a rock will be ignored. *Call it an insurance of mine, if you will*, she thinks snidely.

It drops into Kimya's pocket just as Ruti is blasted with a belated wave of energy, Winda throwing her backward as their eyes lock for a moment. It's a gentle enough burst of lightning that Ruti isn't burned by it. She lands on her rear in front of Torhvin, and he smirks down at her and says, "I suggest you behave during the day to come. Winda is always a little too liberal with her gift."

Kimya gestures again, frantic signs that Ruti reads with ease. Torhvin clears his throat. "I want this one chained up in my dungeons this time–"

Ruti gets up, running at top speed back into the palace before the guards can react. A wave of lightning misses her by a swath and the earth around her begins to shatter. She darts swiftly through the crowds inside, ducking as Torhvin's guards give chase and winding down hallways in a rush of energy.

They still pursue her, undaunted by her speed or the others moving around them, and Ruti charges out the front door of the palace and into the massive, packed courtyard. She shoves through the crowd, ducking where she can and giving the spirits a chant for agility, and soon she is deep in the throng, unfindable. In the distance, she glimpses Torhvin's guards splitting up, heading in opposing directions that both lead away from her.

A horn blows, and the drums sound. The sun is high in the sky, already beginning to dry Ruti's hair. The ceremony is about to begin, and Ruti is deep in the crowd in front of the metal stage, ready to witness Dekala's soulbinding.

27

Whatever signs of unease there had been from Torhvin's strongest supporters earlier, they are not evident in the crowds who throng the courtyard.

The crowd's cheers rise to a roar when Dekala emerges from the palace and ascends the stage, her arm on the Regent's. Ruti can't hear anything, not the words the Regent murmurs to Dekala or how Dekala addresses the crowd. Ruti steals forward, slipping toward the front with a wary eye cast around for the guards, and Dekala's eyes seek her out in the audience.

Dekala smiles, smug confidence in her eyes, and Ruti's fists ball up in new determination. She picks her way through the crowd, making her way to the very front of the stage.

Now, at least she can hear. Dekala still stands in front, flanked by the Regent and a number of guards. A set of altars has been erected in the center of the stage, offerings laid upon them for Zidesh's Spotted One and Rurana's Maned One. Orrin is nowhere to be found, which is unsurprising, considering what is going to happen today. There are several rows of chairs on the stage, wreathed in flowers, with Ruranan and Zideshi generals already sitting in the back. The guards take their seats while the Regent and Dekala remain standing. He speaks to her in a low voice and she smiles at him, her eyes gleaming. He looks taken aback by that.

"I am happy to be here," she says, loud enough for Ruti to hear. "Is that so surprising to you? Soon, I will be a queen."

The Regent nods, looking very ill. "It is what I asked of you," he allows. His gaze flickers around the courtyard as though he'd rather be anywhere else right now. Dekala raises her chin, unbowed, and the crowd roars for her again.

It takes a few minutes of Dekala standing tall for their perusal before there's movement at the back of the stage and Torhvin strides in. His witches and his guards are with him, Winda lurking just off the stage in Ruti's eyeline with a small figure all but hidden behind her. Kimya wears a lengthy servant's gown with long, wide sleeves that conceal her chains, and Ruti looks up at her and yearns to rush to the stage and seize her. This will be no place for a child.

Instead, she waits in silence as the crowd cheers for their prince. In the crowd, she sees soldiers who do not roar for

Torhvin, and others she recognizes from Lower Byale who watch the stage in silence. The Markless in the crowd are numerous now, squinting in the sun, their hands clasped together. Ruti takes a breath and turns away from the audience.

A gong is struck thrice, and the crowd's noise drops to a murmur. The Regent stands behind Dekala and Torhvin, each of them wearing a golden glove over their right hand. "It is a privilege to be here," he says, his voice strained, "as my beloved niece finds love at last. We have searched for a long time, but never could we have imagined that her Bonded would be a man like Prince Torhvin."

He goes on, singing Torhvin's praises and then Dekala's, and Torhvin beams as he looks out at his subjects. The smile falters when Ruti catches his gaze, hard and defiant, and his eyes narrow for an instant before he's beaming at Dekala again.

". . . and it is my greatest pleasure to hold this grand soul-binding for Dekala and Torhvin," the Regent announces, and Ruti watches, her composed expression slipping just a tiny bit. Dekala slides her hand out of her glove and Ruti tenses, her heart burning with denial and despair. She craves suddenly to leap onto the stage, to run between them and seize the vial of water from Kimya to seal away Dekala's soul-bond mark forever. To stop them, to kiss Dekala, to put an end to this before it can begin.

But there is no stopping them anymore. Torhvin holds out his palm and Dekala presses hers to his. For a wild moment of hope, there is nothing, and Ruti stops breathing.

Then their joined hands glow white, and soulbinding magic washes over their hands, climbing up their arms to envelop their entire bodies. Dekala is trembling, eyes wide with awe, and Torhvin smiles in ecstasy as he keeps his hand pressed to Dekala's. The crowd is roaring again, loud and enthusiastic in their approval, and Dekala is Bonded at last.

The gong for silence is sounded again. Ruti squeezes her eyes shut, then opens them, staring at Dekala with hawk-sharp eyes. Is she in love now? Has the soulbond turned her into Torhvin's dutiful wife? Dekala smiles, and her face is gentle, free of the ice that so often coats her expression. "Hello, Bonded," she says to Torhvin, her voice ringing out clear and sure.

"Hello, Bonded," he returns. "My queen."

"Soon," Dekala allows, and Ruti shakes her head, feeling sick at all that might still happen. The wedding ceremony is due to begin now, and a cleric will enter to speak the vows. Sure enough, when she cranes her neck, she can see Orrin guiding a hooded cleric up the stairs behind the stage, help-ing him as he walks with unsteady legs. Orrin looks nearly as heartsick as Ruti feels, and he hardly spares a glare for Winda as he brings the cleric forward. "I wish . . . ," Dekala begins, and then falls silent.

"What is it?" Torhvin asks, solicitous. "Just speak the word, and I will grant you anything."

Dekala smiles at him, her heart in her eyes. "It's only that I have my aunt and uncle with me. I am so sorry that you have no family to accompany you in this moment."

"We are both children of tragedy," Torhvin says gently. "You are all I have." He closes his eyes for a moment, then raises his face to the distant window where King Jaquil's sleeping room is. "I went to see my brother today, of course. I asked him to intercede with the spirits for us."

Dekala touches his arm. "I am sure that he will," she says, her voice ringing out in the silence of the crowd. They move closer, struggling to hear each word. Ruti watches Dekala with narrowed eyes. "Won't you?"

But she is not looking to Jaquil's window. Instead, her eyes are on the stage, on Orrin and the cleric with him. Torhvin looks at her, bewildered, and Dekala offers him a cold, sharp smile. "I have brought you a gift," she says.

The cleric removes his hood, and the people gasp in joyful recognition. There is no withered man beside Orrin, no ancient crone with the wisdom of the spirits in his eyes. Instead, a youthful man stands there, his face handsome and similar to Torhvin's, a circlet resting on his forehead. He is dressed in white and gold, as befits only royalty, and he steps to the front of the stage.

The crowd shouts the same name, over and over again. "Jaquil!" they call, overcome. "Jaquil! Jaquil!"

Ruti moves, tense with what she knows will come next. Torhvin will not rest at this new development. "It is my pleasure," Dekala says thinly, "to grant you and your people the restored health of your king." She reaches out to Jaquil, guiding him to stand beside her, and he gives her a brief nod of acknowledgement. Dekala had been spirited away to Jaquil's room for a conference after her argument with Ruti on the balcony, and perhaps more than once since Ruti's descent into Lower Byale. Now, they stand before the crowd as allies.

"How?" Torhvin demands, his eyes wide and wild. "How did you–"

"It was an unnatural deed, waking up a man cursed into sleep," Dekala agrees solemnly. "It took a vial of water from the Lake of the Carved Thousand, as well as my personal witch." She reaches out to the crowd, to Ruti, and Ruti sings a near-silent chant for strength and leaps to the stage beside her. "But for Rurana, I knew that I must. I awakened the king on our very first day here."

Dekala's hand brushes against Ruti's, a quiet reminder of skin against skin and the night before they'd departed to Byale. They had enjoyed each other thoroughly first, had explored each other's bodies and kissed each exposed bit of them. And then, when they'd been lying together in bed, Dekala had whispered out a detailed, elaborate plan.

They had negotiated different parts of it in heated whispers, Ruti too willing to thrust herself into danger and too unwilling to let Dekala step into it herself. The soulbinding had been the most furious of those arguments, but Dekala had not yielded. *I need this to govern effectively*, she had said, *and I will be queen.*

She'd had no choice but to concede, to agree to a plan that hinged on a hunch about Jaquil and a determination on Dekala's part that she would no longer be uncontrolled and Unbonded. And on Dekala's palm now is a perfect circle, sewa and majimm combined into one as she turns back to Jaquil. "A terrible curse, it was, bestowed upon you by your brother Serrold," she says leadingly.

"Serrold," Jaquil says, his voice loud and authoritative. "Serrold was a perfect innocent!" he bellows, and the crowd roars in acknowledgement. "Serrold was like a child. Easily led, and my youngest brother knew that."

The crowd quiets, sinking into confusion. Torhvin motions at two guards, and Dekala's guards stand to stop them. Torhvin looks trapped, afraid, and Ruti finds that she likes him terrified. "Serrold's betrayal was a tragedy," Torhvin says smoothly. "But hardly enough to turn us against each other. I have done everything for you—"

"Then why was it your three witches who cursed me into slumber?" roars Jaquil, throwing a hand out at the witches still sitting on the stage. "Serrold had ambition, but you—you were the one to pit us against each other and emerge the hero. I have been asleep, yes, but I have never once stopped listening. I lay through your incessant gloating for *years*."

"You are mad," Torhvin says, his face stiff and his fists clenched. "The years asleep have taken their toll on you."

The crowd is murmuring, uncertain, and Torhvin nods again to his guards. This time, it is the generals who stand, moving to flank Jaquil. "Our rightful king," says one, looking to Jaquil in respect.

"Jata," Jaquil says, and he embraces the general like a brother.

"No," Torhvin snaps. "I have done *everything* for our people. I made us rich. I expanded *your* army, Jata!"

"You gave the Diri the secrets of kuduwaí," Jata says scornfully, and Ruti quirks a smile. "You are a traitor to our people."

Torhvin stares at him in dismay, and Ruti can see the moment he pieces together her shouted accusations, all but ignored, and what she had casually revealed before she'd been thrown into the pit. "You would believe the ravings of a Markless witch over me?" he says disbelievingly.

Jata reaches into his robes and emerges with the knife that Ruti had taken from Lower Byale. "I believe what I can see," he says. The knife glows red-hot, eternally aflame. "The army will not stand with a traitor."

Torhvin laughs. It's a wild laugh, furious and on the precipice of madness. "This is obscene. A farce! My men have been turned against me by this . . . these worthless *vipers* from Zidesh!" He gestures at the courtyard, calling attention to himself again. The people speak in angry murmurs as he twists around, his eyes falling on his witches. "But I will not yield. Look at the riches of my kingdom! Look at my people! The spirits have chosen *me*, not my brother. Not this usurper." He throws a hateful glare at Dekala, who stands placidly with Ruti. "The spirits have given me everything, and they will not take kindly to traitors seizing it away from their chosen one."

There is an uncertain murmur in the crowd, a grudging acknowledgement of the splendor that surrounds them. Dekala exchanges a glance with Ruti, a quiet look rife with meaning. Ruti nods, her heart beating fast as she looks over at the three witches behind Torhvin. "Challenge me with your witches, then," Dekala says. "See who it is the spirits choose."

Torhvin needs no further cue. He is upon Dekala in an instant, a spear in his hand with a wickedly pointed edge. He wields it with the same grace as he had the stick, and the three witches begin to chant.

Ruti chants back. She sings Dekala as she has once before, finding a melody in Dekala's movements. Dekala seizes a spear of her own, spinning it around her wrist as the crowd watches avidly, and slices a long slit into her dress and throws Torhvin back. He stumbles, but the witches sing him forward again, and Ruti feels them like an enduring pressure on her song. The spirits respond to her, but they are muted, distracted by three voices tugging them in another direction. It's as though there is something silencing her song, pressing down on it to stamp it out. With no offering, there is nothing to draw their attention.

Torhvin lunges forward and Dekala swivels in a deadly dance, blocking his blow and slicing into his shoulder. Ruti sings, struggling through the murkiness that surrounds the spirits, trying with all her might to shore up Dekala's fighting skills. But Dekala is on her own, Ruti's song all but ineffective. Torhvin's jumps are longer, his movements faster, and even Dekala is slipping up, fighting as hard as she can against an opponent with a boost from the spirits. Ruti's voice cracks, her throat hoarse, and she sings anyway, the melody faltering.

Torhvin moves as swift as an antelope and slams into Dekala, throwing her violently onto the ground, and he rears back with his spear, eyes dark with murder. The witches sing in a madrigal with growing power, and a whirl of energy surrounds them and protects them as they sing. Ruti, her chanting weak, is unprotected at the edge of the stage.

And then, a voice from the captivated crowd, a single cry that Ruti recognizes as Kewal. "Sing with her! Stop the prince!" he shouts. "For Rurana! For Lower Byale!"

Abruptly, Ruti is no longer alone in her song. Chanting is a magic that comes instinctively only to a few, but there is strength in the echoes of her song, in the power that comes with dozens of others thundering out her song with her.

The Markless of Rurana, left alone in their catacombs, must spend much of their time singing. They pick up her melody with ease, lending it the power of many, of voices learning to fight for the first time. And with them comes, to Ruti's surprise, other voices. There are too many singing for it to only be the Markless who have infiltrated the audience–no, others have joined in, whether out of defiance or just because of the sheer energy of the crowd. They do not know that it is a Markless who began the song, because Ruti had painted every palm with ash before she'd left.

Ruti is still one witch singing against three, but she can feel her confidence growing with the song that echoes hers. Torhvin's spear thrusts down toward Dekala and Ruti gives Dekala speed enough to roll away. Ruti still feels the weight of the three witches' song like a heavy cloth surrounding her, pressing her into darkness, and she turns her melody cutting and dissonant instead. It slices through the pressure of the witches' chants, opening up the skies to Ruti again, and she can feel the spirits intimately once more.

Hello again, she says silently, *I need your strength.* She calls for the Spotted One's grace, the Scaled One's speed, the Toothed One's sheer strength, and the Maned One's power. She calls on every spirit she knows, cries to them to right this injustice and gift Dekala the skill to defeat a false, cruel prince.

Torhvin, dodging one of Dekala's blows, slams the blunt back of his spear into Ruti and throws her off balance. Dekala cries out Ruti's name, distracted, and Torhvin bears on her again. Ruti keeps singing, teetering at the edge of the platform.

A strong hand catches her arm and pulls her back. The Regent's grim face meets hers as he steadies Ruti. "How long must we watch this?"

King Jaquil shakes his head. "Until the spirits decide. We can't interfere with their will." Ruti leans back against them both, singing as loudly as she can as the Markless in the audience echo her song. Dekala drops to the ground and sweeps Torhvin's legs out from under him, sending him tumbling, and Torhvin stabs up blindly at her.

Ruti sings to the Toothed One, to the massive creature that can kill a man with only a snap of its jaw. *Help her*, she sings, timbre growing deeper with the chant, and Dekala deflects Torhvin's blow with more force than she's ever swung her stick before. Torhvin's spear flies backward and impales one of the witches. The others stop singing abruptly.

"Well," Dekala says. She is breathing hard, her wedding gown shredded and her hair undone from its elaborate braids, but she is as composed as ever. "I suppose that settles that."

Torhvin snarls at her and charges forward, raising his hands to the sky, and Ruti remembers too late that he has a new weapon at his disposal. The courtyard grows dark, thunderclouds appearing suddenly over them, and a storm begins out of nowhere. People shout, Bonded throwing their own hands up to try to stop the storm, but Torhvin's rage is stronger than their delayed response. Thunder crashes around them, and Torhvin bites out, "I will not go quietly. I will take you all with me!"

The wind begins to whirl violently, twisting into a column that sweeps through the crowd. There are screams as people run for cover, as others are seized up and lifted into the tornado that has taken hold of the courtyard. Dekala's guards charge toward Torhvin, but two of his guards stand between them, stopping their attack. "Winda," Torhvin snarls, and Ruti tenses. Winda is standing with Torhvin, Kimya in her grasp. "Kill the girl."

Winda doesn't budge. Kimya folds her arms around herself, smug with wrists no longer chained. Dekala laughs, her voice as cold as Torhvin's. "Winda has been Zidesh's loyal agent since she was but a girl of three, brought to secret training to become a spy for her people," she says. It has been a point of contention between them in the past few days, Winda supposedly holding Kimya safe in Torhvin's captivity. Dekala had trusted her absolutely. Ruti had been less confident. Now, with Winda standing beside Kimya, Ruti doesn't know why she'd ever doubted her. "You have lost. End this, Torhvin, before we are forced to end you."

Ruti knows what he's going to do before he does it, his wild, vengeful eyes looking only for someone defenseless to hurt. He has lost, and he is desperate only to destroy before he goes. He whirls around, seizing a dagger from his guard's hand, and he is upon Kimya before Winda can stop him, the blade pressed to her throat. "Any last words, muteling?" he says mockingly, and Ruti cries out in horror, no time for song or defense.

Kimya holds up a finger, fear in her eyes but defiance sweeping over her. *One*, she signs in a language Torhvin won't understand. Her hands move outward, a motion that sweeps her fingers away from herself. *Begone.*

In one of her hands, as she moves them outward, is an uncapped stone vial.

When they'd used the first vial to awaken Jaquil on their first day in Byale, as Winda and Orrin stood guard, the spirits had merely taken the offering and left behind an empty vial. They haven't gotten to see what the vial of water can do, bottled up and potent, until Kimya splashes it over Torhvin's face.

He screams. The burns come first, red and blistering, and when he presses his hands to his face, they blister as well. His skin burns and burns until it's blackened, until the water seems to suck all the liquid from his body and leave a husk behind. Brittle stone spreads across his skin, tightening it and turning it into something less than human, and he teeters in place until he collapses under the weight of his own stone body.

In moments, he is gone, the stone shattering across the stage as the sky clears up above them. Dekala raises a hand, calling the sun to dry off the soaked courtyard, and she turns–not to the courtyard, not to Ruti, and not to Kimya, who has rushed past the frozen guards and thrown herself into Ruti's arms.

Dekala turns to the Regent and says expectantly, "I am Bonded now."

The Regent blinks, staring at her in disbelief. "You . . . you have no king," he stammers at last, and his eyes flicker to Jaquil, who is crouched before his brother's shattered stone carcass, his thumb caressing a piece of stone.

Dekala raises her chin. "I saved the Ruranan Markless. I awakened their rightful ruler. I took Torhvin's army from him and his pirates as well." She speaks clearly and precisely, and the people around them listen in quiet awe. "I voyaged across the land to find a magic unnatural enough to make the spirits bow to my will. I defeated Torhvin right here on this stage. And I did it all with only my witch's assistance, while you happily handed me over to a tyrant. I do not need a king."

Her gaze is fierce, uncompromising, and the Regent looks at her as though he is seeing her for the very first time. "So be it," he says.

28

The coronation is scheduled for three months after the soulbinding in Somanchi's Royal Square. The city is flooded with courtiers and dignitaries, with new arrivals who have heard the stories of what happened in Byale. They peer at Ruti with mistrust and curiosity in turn, trying to catch a glimpse of her bare palm.

She has become a celebrity of sorts, a Markless who walks freely within the palace walls. She no longer wears gloves to cover her hands, though Kimya is still under strict orders to keep hers on. Kimya is an unknown, a girl seen often with the princess but with no explanation offered to the courtiers. The court whispers about her. *She speaks with her hands. She is teaching the translators the Niyaru sign language.* The few who know Kimya's identity keep it tightly sealed between them.

Dekala is busy with her tutors, who are now her advisors. Each morning, she sits with them and her uncle, transitioning from his rule to hers. The Regent will remain in the palace for her first year of rule, but after that, he is already speaking about traveling with his wife to her home kingdom of Guder. Dekala will rule alone, as she has always wanted.

In the afternoons, Dekala sits in the main courtyard and judges the people, the Regent silent beside her. The people of Zidesh speak of their warrior queen with admiration and love. There are some who bemoan the fact that they have no king, but they are easily ignored for now. Zidesh has been waiting for its queen for a long time.

Ruti sees little of Dekala during the day. She is no longer her constant companion, nor is Orrin. Orrin has disappeared entirely, and Ruti hasn't had a chance to ask Dekala where he has gone. They don't do very much talking when they're together.

At night, Dekala tugs Ruti into her room and they fall to kisses, to passionate embraces, to relearning each other's touch again and again. It is an unaccountably comfortable thing, being in Dekala's arms, and it is a struggle to tiptoe from Dekala's room each night and back to her own. The attendants gossip, but they are discreet, and the whispers never travel too far from Dekala's quarters.

"What is this to you?" Ruti whispers one night, made bold by Dekala's bright and hungry eyes. "What are we?"

"We are this," Dekala says, and pulls Ruti down to kiss her.

Later, she whispers, "I told you that I will not love. I will not be consumed by someone else. We are not that."

Her eyes are grave, not cold but not hot either, carefully free of the passion that emerges when they are together. Ruti says, "I don't want to be that." There is little else she can say, even when her heart drops and she finds herself craving something she can never ask for.

She loves Dekala, and it stings each time she holds her. She has more of Dekala than anyone else ever has, but she doesn't have all of her. "Good," Dekala says, and she kisses Ruti again, soft and tender and without any of the distance she espouses.

One night, the air is too restrictive when she departs from Dekala's room, and she slips into her room only to make sure that Kimya is there before she steps out again. She longs for the dirt and the wind, for a walk barefoot in the garden, and she slips out of Dekala's quarters.

There are new guards stationed there at night now, a cadre of them who pay her little attention except to recoil when she gets too close. Ruti ignores them and makes her way to the garden.

She's surprised to see that someone is already there. Orrin is seated on a bench near the entrance, staring up at the glow of the full moon. Ruti follows his gaze up, feeling the mighty power of the spirits who reside beneath this sky, and says, "Have you been dismissed?"

"I have been promoted," Orrin says wryly. "Pushed a comfortable distance from Dekala. I am to be a captain of the palace guard. A great honor." He glances at Ruti, his eyes sharp. "I know where you spend your nights. Have you come to gloat?"

Ruti shakes her head. Maybe there had been a time when she might have, before she'd understood Dekala. Now she finds that she has little to boast about. "Dekala doesn't love me."

"She trusts you," Orrin counters. "You were the one she called to make her queen." He is calmer now than he once was, and it isn't exactly resignation in his voice, either. For the first time since Ruti met him, in this quiet night where Dekala is away, Orrin seems comfortable.

Ruti snorts and dares to provoke him a little bit. "She couldn't ask you. Torhvin had the Ruranan army steadfastly loyal to him. If Jaquil had reappeared without our groundwork, Torhvin would have executed a new coup out in the open."

"The army had to know that Torhvin had betrayed them and given the secrets of kuduwaí to the Diri," Orrin agrees. "But I could have shared that with them. I spent all of our time in Byale with them."

"Except that you're as subtle as an angry Maned One," Ruti points out, and she's surprised when Orrin lets out a snort at that.

He spreads his hands, the mark on his right palm bright in the moonlight. "I will not begrudge you her favor."

Ruti wrinkles her brow, dubious. "No?"

Orrin meets her eyes, and in his gaze Ruti sees the fierce loyalty to Dekala that has always guided him. "Dekala will be surrounded by vipers from the moment she takes that crown. There will be many who seek her power or wish to manipulate her for their ends." He broods for a moment, still the same old Orrin, and shakes his head. "She will need those who are loyal to her and not her power."

"Then she will need you as well," Ruti says quietly. It's a peace offering, a recognition that they are on the same team now. "Regardless of where you've been placed in the palace."

Orrin looks hard at her, then sighs. "Please don't tell me we'll have to be *friends*."

Ruti shudders. "What a horrific idea." She smirks, unable to help herself, and turns when she hears movement in the garden.

Winda stands at the edge of the path, her eyes taking them in as she says, "Princess Dekala has sent me to locate you."

Ruti tenses. Dekala had been asleep, or so she'd thought, and she hadn't expected that her departure would have been noticed. "Does she require my presence?" She glances at Orrin, self-conscious, but he's watching Winda instead. His eyes bore into her, his lip curling, and Winda only stares emotionlessly back.

"I do not believe so," Winda says. Ruti chews on her lip, stymied at this order that is not an order. She has been located as a missing possession, ready to be placed back on a shelf for its owner's future needs. She quails at this new categorization, and lingers in the garden.

But before long, the silence outside is as oppressive as Dekala's quarters had felt, and so Ruti turns to go inside. Winda remains in the garden, and Ruti can hear Orrin's voice again as she returns to the castle.

A week before the coronation, Ruti is summoned to Dekala's war room. "Kewal!" she cries out in delight. The table is crowded with advisors, but there is one side of the table that is almost empty. Kewal sits there with one of the elders of Lower Byale, a woman Ruti remembers is named Phailin. Across from them is King Jaquil, who looks uneasily at the Markless at the table and keeps a safe distance.

The only one who sits near them, unbothered by their closeness, is Dekala. She says, "We have reached a consensus on the Markless."

Ruti blinks. She hasn't pressed the issue in the months building up to the coronation, certain that Dekala has other matters to concern herself with than the children of the slums. "Consensus?" she repeats warily.

"We are doing what we can to trace the trade routes of the Diri, but they have been scarce since my brother's death," Jaquil says regretfully. "Only some children have been returned to Lower Byale. But the people of Lower Byale have also expressed an interest in helping Somanchi's Markless children."

"The orphanages must be revitalized in the meantime," Dekala explains. "I would like the slums rebuilt, and the Markless taught trades."

Ruti gapes at Dekala. *The slums rebuilt. The Markless taught trades.* It's a fantasy beyond anything Ruti would have dared to dream, once upon a time. It remains a foreign concept even now. Ruti tries to imagine it and cannot, but the idea leaves warmth surging through her body.

Someone else speaks up. Orrin, whom she hasn't seen again since the garden. He sits with Winda on one side of the table. "The people of Somanchi will not purchase items sold by the Markless," he says. His tone is frank rather than offensive, an unfortunate fact that he states. Ruti glares at him anyway, but she can't deny it. Orrin's voice gentles. "I know you have a different perspective on this than your people, but you can't enact successful change overnight," he says. There is something different in how he addresses Dekala, and Ruti studies him for a moment.

He still looks at her with affection and loyalty, but there is none of the dedicated obeisance that there once had been. Orrin has let go of his infatuation, it seems.

Ruti has been less successful at that.

Dekala scoffs. "I'm aware of that," she says. "But we must give the Markless the tools to endure despite that. For too long, we have ignored Zidesh's Markless problem. I will ignore it no longer."

Phailin says, "We will be happy to take in many of your children. Lower Byale has been quiet for too long." Her eyes move to Ruti. "And we will need an ambassador from Zidesh as well."

Ruti stares, startled. "Me?" she blurts out. Kewal grins at her. "What would I–"

"You would assist in the transport of Somanchi's children," Phailin says. "And you will aid in their adjustment and in any structural issues we encounter as we dig further beneath the ground. Our people are beholden to you, Ruti of Zidesh. We wish to elevate you to a position as a leader in Lower Byale." Kewal is beaming. Orrin looks nonplussed.

"Leader," Ruti echoes, and she looks to Dekala. Dekala's eyes are narrowed, taken aback but giving away nothing. "I would have to leave Zidesh."

Kewal says, "What can you do in Zidesh that could be greater than what you can accomplish in Lower Byale?" Ruti has no answer for him. Here in Somanchi, what is it that keeps Ruti tethered? She hesitates and looks to Dekala again. Dekala says stiffly, "I suppose there's no reason not to send her with you." She doesn't look at Ruti again for the duration of the meeting.

Kimya is livid that Ruti agreed to this before asking her about it. Her hands fly, and Ruti says helplessly, "I *didn't*. Dekala agreed to it and I just–you'll *like* Lower Byale, it's perfect–" But Kimya doesn't want to hear it. She signs again in disbelief, the same question for Ruti over and over: *How can we leave Dekala?*

"Then you can stay," Ruti finally says in a surge of frustration. "I'll go." She rises from her bed and stalks out of the room.

She will leave after the coronation with the first caravan of Markless children. Dekala's soldiers have flat-out refused to accompany the children, so Lower Byale will send caretakers to guide them through the trip. Ruti is meant to supervise the entire thing. Kewal tells her that she's a hero of Lower Byale now, and they are eager to have her with them, but it doesn't seem as though she's needed as anything more than an icon. They will find reasons to use her magic, but they don't require it, just as no one in Somanchi does.

She aches suddenly for the early days in the palace, provoking Dekala and walking beside her each day. It had been simpler before she'd loved Dekala. Still, she can't quite find it inside herself to reject that love altogether. It has left her changed, has transformed her from a bitter child of the slums and left her a soft dreamer. *Too delicate*, the girl she'd once been would say, but she clings to her heart regardless.

She spots a movement ahead, and she knows who it is before she hears her voice. Dekala is walking through the garden alongside Orrin, smiling up at him as she is wont to do more often these days. The smile freezes when she sees Ruti in front of her. "Oh," Ruti says.

She looks at them for a moment, the comfortable way they walk side by side, and wonders with sudden despair if Orrin hasn't moved on at all. Perhaps he has only grown from infatuation to something more profound, to a connection between them that has left him at peace. Perhaps–

Orrin looks between them, his eyes widening at Ruti's expression. "We aren't. . . ." He looks sheepish suddenly. Ruti glares at him, lost and growing increasingly frustrated. "I am not–I have a soulbond!" Orrin blurts out, holding up a hand. "I found my Bonded."

Dekala's lip curls into a smirk. "*I* found your Bonded, you mean," she corrects him, then amends, "Though I wasn't aware of it for a very long time." She shakes her head. "Go," she says, nudging Orrin's arm gently. "King Jaquil will need an escort home. You're going to be late."

Orrin nods to Ruti, disappearing into the garden and leaving them alone. Ruti ducks her head, embarrassed at her own discomfort and frustration. "Winda," Dekala says abruptly, and Ruti looks up.

"What?"

"Winda is Orrin's soulbond," Dekala says, and she smiles suddenly. "As far as we were all told, her family refused to send their daughter to the palace and disappeared. In actuality, she was drafted into an elite unit of Zideshi spies who have infiltrated various other kingdoms. I have been in contact with Winda for a long time, but I never put it together. Orrin didn't recognize her all these years later. He only realized when I told Torhvin that Winda had been mine since she was three."

"Oh," Ruti says, struck by that. "*That's* why he was always so grouchy around her. He kept saying he had a bad feeling about her."

"Trust Orrin not to recognize his own connection with his soulbond," Dekala says lightly, and they catch each other's eyes and smile. Ruti's chest is full and hurting at the same time.

Dekala clears her throat. "So you will be leaving with the Markless?" she says. It's uncertain, particularly from someone who had said it with such certainty earlier.

Ruti shrugs. "I can do good there. I am not needed here."

Dekala's face darkens and her eyes close off from Ruti again. "You have your . . . uses here," she drawls, and it is distant and intimate enough that it makes Ruti's cheeks burn. "As my witch, of course." She leans forward, her eyes inviting, and Ruti cups her cheeks, lets their lips brush together, and knows that she cannot do this anymore. She is drowning in a deluge of her own overpowering love, and she has finally learned what it means to have value.

It is not this. Never this, a consort and a distraction, a girl wanted but unloved. "I think you might destroy me if I stay here any longer," Ruti says, and the admission carries forth all the words she cannot speak. It leaves her drained and empty and so very sad.

Dekala draws back as though she's been slapped. "Then go," she hisses, and Ruti can't read her at all, can't piece together what must be rage and hurt and betrayal. "I warned you. I told you–"

"I know," Ruti says numbly, and she turns away from Dekala and stumbles back toward the palace entrance.

Dekala does not pull Ruti into her bedroom again. They hardly speak in the weeks that follow, and when they do it's only to convey information. There are times when Dekala's eyes follow Ruti through her quarters, when they seem to burn into her and Ruti thinks that Dekala might say something, anything, to have her again.

But Dekala is silent. The coronation is close, and with it comes a ragtag caravan of adult Markless from Lower Byale who look upon the orphanages in quiet horror. "They are . . . very much there," one of the Markless volunteers. It's the kindest thing that can be said about them.

"They are that," Ruti agrees matter-of-factly. The children of the orphanages stare up at them with blank and wary eyes, and they recoil from touch. "Look," Ruti says, holding out her hand to show them her palm. "See? I'm like you."

Their eyes flicker over her royal finery, and then to the Ruranan Markless behind her. "Things are going to change around here," Ruti promises. A part of her still recoils at promising dreams to the children, but it grows more muted every day. The little ones look at her with dawning understanding–with *hope*, once fool's gold in the slums–and she can meet their eyes as someone who refuses to leave them behind.

One boy says in a whispery voice, "Queen Dekala." It's an affirmation and an explanation, and Ruti nods.

"Yes," she says, and smiles, because anything more might hurt too much. "Queen Dekala is going to change everything."

There is much work to do, though Kimya remains stubbornly determined to stay in Somanchi. *I won't leave Dekala,* she signs, and Ruti says in frustration, "So you'll leave me instead?"

You're the one who's leaving, Kimya retorts, but she looks torn and very sad. On the night before the coronation, she abruptly signs to Ruti that she will go to Lower Byale. They are lying in bed, the two of them staring at each other, and Kimya signs an additional comment, a stubborn, *I don't want to.*

I don't want to, either, Ruti signs, and tears spring to her eyes. "But I don't know what else–" And she is crying with terrible heartbreak, with weeks of loss and longing that have come to this. Kimya squirms over in the bed to wrap her little arms around Ruti, and Ruti holds her tightly, cries into her shoulder and hates every instant of it.

When she looks up, there is a shadow at the curtain outside their room. "Come in," she barks out, her voice hoarse.

She doesn't bother wiping away the tears, not when their visitor has certainly already heard her.

It's Dekala, of course, because there is little more humiliating than this. "I . . ." She hesitates, her eyes flickering over them. "I brought something for Kimya," she says finally, holding out a little wrapped chocolate. Kimya climbs off of the bed to take it from her, signing a flurry of information to Dekala. Dekala responds, her hands moving nearly as confidently as Kimya's, and she is so gentle with Kimya that Ruti can't bear to watch them.

She averts her eyes and finds that it's even worse, hearing the whisper of movement without following the motions. She turns back and sees Dekala's eyes on her. "You should sleep," Ruti says flatly. "Your coronation is tomorrow."

"Yes," Dekala murmurs. "And the caravan—"

"We leave immediately after the coronation," Ruti says, and it gnaws at her in terrible agony. "Your advisors have informed me that the city grows restless with so many Markless in the Inner Circle. So . . . I suppose this is goodbye."

Dekala stares at her, and there is something naked in her eyes, stricken. But she does not speak, only nods abruptly and enfolds Kimya in an embrace. Ruti turns away, her heart thudding against her ribs.

Morning comes, and with it, the coronation. Ruti has a place near the front with Kimya, standing beside Orrin and Winda and Kalere as the Regent lowers a crown headdress with the markings of the Spotted One onto Dekala's head and the people roar their approval. Dekala raises a hand to the skies, clearing them for a moment to let the sun shine through, and a rainbow arcs over the Royal Square. "Today," she proclaims, and she smiles, the look of someone who is at peace. "I am your queen."

Ruti applauds with the people, and she drinks in every sight of Dekala, of her long coiled braids and her royal clothing, of the determination in her eyes to serve her people well. This is how it will be best to remember Dekala, a queen who has earned her throne and will use it as it should be. This is Dekala as she loves her, and Dekala as she will never have her again.

She lingers at the coronation feast, unwilling to leave until the caravan is absolutely ready to go. Instead she eats sweets with Kimya and makes awkward conversation with courtiers who see her as a curiosity. Dekala is surrounded by well-wishers. It would be impossible to break through the throng to see her.

Ruti sees Kewal in the crowd a few times, cheerfully fighting past the other diners to reach Ruti, and he motions for the door. It is time, then.

She takes Kimya's hand. "We need to go," she murmurs, and Kimya gazes around with a hollow expression of loss on her face. Together, they depart from the banquet hall, walking through the main courtyard to the outer courtyard where they've hardly ever gone before.

The courtyard is noisy, alive with the sounds of Markless children who have taken seats in carts and chariots and are already squirming with excitement. Their Ruranan guides are fond and alight with energy, soothing some and chattering with others. There is an undercurrent of enthusiasm around the caravan, and Ruti wonders if she might find a place here after all.

"Wait." The voice is quiet, and Ruti thinks for a moment that she's imagined it. But no, Dekala is standing in the shadows of the outer courtyard, her eyes sorrowful and fixed on Ruti. "Ruti," she whispers, and Ruti comes to her, helpless as always when Dekala is around. Kimya stays back, standing with Kewal, their eyes glued on Ruti and Dekala.

"Stay," Dekala says, and Ruti has the presence of mind to be angry.

"Stay?" she repeats, disbelieving. "You sent me away! I won't–I'm not going to stay to put myself through the *agony* that–"

"Stay," Dekala says again, and she looks at Ruti with eyes that are beseeching, with a gaze so nakedly raw that Ruti's anger begins to fade. "I can't bear the thought of being without you." Ruti gapes at her, and Dekala dips her head and kisses Ruti, heedless of the caravan and the numerous guards and guests milling about in the courtyard.

There are eyes on them now, whispers and gossip thrumming through the courtyard, but Ruti can only see Dekala in front of her. "I love you," Ruti whispers. "I do. And I can't–"

Dekala strokes Ruti's cheek, the tips of her fingers running over Ruti's hair. "I . . . , she begins haltingly, then shuts her eyes and tries again. "I want. . . ." She laughs, a choked little sound that might be a sob instead. "I don't know if I can love anyone," she finally says, and her eyes glimmer with quiet misery. "I have wondered for months if I am capable of it. I have spent so long pushing away that part of myself that I think I might have lost it for good."

She cups Ruti's face in her hand, and Ruti can only stare up at her. "But I find that for you, I want to learn to love. I want you here beside me," she says, and she doesn't seem to notice anyone else in the courtyard, any of the eyes that linger on the two of them. "I want my witch, my advisor, my equal," she murmurs, and Ruti reaches up to take her hand and tug it down from her face. Their fingers tangle together and hold. "The soulbond I choose, rather than one chosen for me," Dekala says, and Ruti hears the hammering of her pulse in her ears as Dekala looks at her, uncertain. "Is that not a kind of love, too?"

Ruti's hand closes around Dekala's, their palms locked as firmly as their gazes, and she can't help but smile, an odd peace settling over her. "It's how I feel, too," she whispers, leaning forward to press her forehead to Dekala's. Kimya is signing from the caravans, an insistent demand to *stay!* that has Ruti laughing helplessly, overwhelmed at her own joy in this moment. Dekala laughs with her, shaky little bursts that have them both clutching on to each other.

The winds no longer whip around Dekala, but the skies turn grey and tiny, soft white flakes that Ruti's never seen before flutter from the sky to land around them as they laugh. They dot their hair and eyelashes and Dekala's crown, and Ruti tastes them like little drops of water against Dekala's lips.

Acknowledgements

This book would never have existed if not for the support of my very favorite found family: my fandom readers and friends who have always been my most steadfast fans. There are so many of you that I don't dare to begin naming people for fear that I forget some of the most important ones, but I do want to say, thank you for believing in me! I hope that you've enjoyed the book–it is yours as much as mine.

I am privileged to publish with Levine Querido, who do tremendous work, and it's been a fantastic journey throughout. Arely Guzmán has been so efficient and a wonderful partner in this! Freesia Blizard, Danielle Maldonado, Kerry Taylor, Irene Vázquez, Antonio Gonzalez Cerna: thank you for all that you've put into bringing *Markless* to life. I am also very appreciative to the sensitivity readers who looked at the book and elevated both the quality of the material and the messages that it sends. The gorgeous cover by Matt Roeser is so distinctive and yet captures the tone of the book perfectly, and the interior design, by Maya Tatsukawa, is a wonderful counterpart to it.

Markless took its time coming together, and the finished product still amazes me. I have to thank Tamar Rydzinski, tireless agent, for the months of edits back and forth until we were satisfied, and of course, Arthur A. Levine, who spins straw into gold with every editorial suggestion. I'm so glad that we're in this together.

Some Notes on This Book's Production

The art for the jacket was created digitally by Matt Roeser in Adobe Illustrator and Photoshop. He was inspired by the story's imagery of hands interacting with magic. The text was set in Legitima, a round serif created by Colombian graphic designer, César Puertas. It was composed by Westchester Publishing Services in Danbury, CT. The book was printed on 78 gms FSC-certified paper and bound in China.

Production supervised by Freesia Blizard
Cover art and design by Matt Roeser
Book interior designed by Maya Tatsukawa
Assistant Managing Editor: Danielle Maldonado
Editor: Arthur A. Levine

LEVINE QUERIDO